No Way Out

No Way Out

Fern Michaels

WHEELER PUBLISHING
A part of Gale, a Cengage Company

LIBRARY OF CONGRESS CIP DATA ON FILE.
CATALOGUING IN PUBLICATION FOR THIS BOOK
IS AVAILABLE FROM THE LIBRARY OF CONGRESS.

ISBN-13: 978-1-4328-8664-6 (hardcover alk. paper)

Published in 2021 by arrangement with Kensington Books, an imprint
of Kensington Publishing Corp.

Printed in Mexico
Print Number: 03   Print Year: 2021

No Way Out

CHAPTER ONE

Ellie Bowman knew that there were murmurs from the neighbors and cruel jokes from the kids on the next block, but it didn't matter. It had been two years since the thirty-four-year-old had moved into the cottage at the end of Birchwood Lane. She was happy that it was located where it was — as far away from the rest of the houses on the block as possible. With each house sitting on a full acre, there was a comfortable distance between them. The homes were modest ranch-style houses built in the fifties.

Thank goodness for Hector, her gardener, assistant, and friend. Without him, she would not have been able to look outside her window and see beautiful flowers. Without him, she wouldn't have groceries, either. He knew the rules and respected her wishes. The only access he had to the house was to the rear porch, where he would deliver her packages and pick up her trash.

The other thing she was grateful for was his willingness to clean up after Buddy, the black Labrador retriever she had rescued from the local shelter when she had moved to Hibbing.

The fenced-in yard made it easy for Ellie to let him go out through his doggie doors to do his business and chase the squirrels around. Percy, her cat, couldn't care less about going outdoors, which was a good thing. Ellie wouldn't have let him out even if he wanted to go. Her seclusion was a comfort. It was better than the alternative.

Colleen Haywood lived down the street from Ellie with her eight-year-old son, Jackson. She was excited when she learned another woman was moving onto their street but was disappointed never to have met her. It had been two years, and the woman appeared to be a hermit. A total recluse.

She had tried numerous times to get Ellie to come over for tea. She didn't have Ellie's phone number, so she would leave notes in her mailbox. In turn, Colleen would get a note back in her mailbox politely declining, saying she had a headache or was on a deadline.

One afternoon, Colleen thought a personal invitation might do the trick, so she walked over to Ellie's and rang the doorbell. Colleen was about to leave when she caught a glimpse of Ellie's face as she moved across the living room. From the brief peek, Colleen saw that Ellie was pretty, with big eyes and blond hair in a short, blunt cut. She couldn't tell how tall the woman was, but she looked like she was in pretty good shape for someone who never left the house. At least, no one had ever seen her leave the house.

Colleen was about to give up. Obviously, the woman didn't want to be bothered. Then Colleen jumped as Ellie's disembodied voice came through the speaker on the intercom. They had a brief exchange, but Ellie once again politely declined Colleen's invitation.

Colleen made another attempt, but when Ellie had made another excuse, Colleen gave up trying to be sociable. It was too bad. They were around the same age, and Colleen could use a friend.

Colleen finally accepted the idea that Ellie was very shy and probably a shut-in. It was odd for someone so young to have agoraphobia, but she could not think of any other reason for her behavior. But if she really was agoraphobic, then how did Ellie's notes of regret get into her mailbox? *Maybe she's a vampire and only comes out at night.* Colleen laughed to herself. Even in witness protection, people who assume new identities live a somewhat normal life.

The only interaction between Colleen's household and Ellie's was that Colleen's eight-year-old son, Jackson, would visit Buddy, Ellie's Lab, every afternoon while the dog was in the yard.

Ellie didn't mind Jackson's leaning against the fence across the front yard and talking to Buddy. Jackson was just tall enough that his head was barely above the top of the fence. As long as she didn't have to go outside, it was all right; she figured Buddy could use the company.

Ellie had a job that preserved her anonymity. She was a tech geek in the world of IT. She worked from home, answering questions from frustrated people who could not set up their computers or whose computers had crashed. She also worked with a number of tech companies, testing new software programs. Being a techno whiz, she had no problem hiding her real identity from others, including those who were as savvy as she was with technology. That was the reason she was able to live a quiet, solitary life. It also enabled her to communicate with her mother and best friend, Kara.

Before moving to the small town of Hibbing, Ellie had purchased dozens of burner phones to use to make calls. She also changed her Internet service provider address every couple of days. She didn't want anyone to be able to trace her location. If anyone asked, which was usually only her mother and her friend Kara, she would tell them she was working on a government contract and being sent to various parts of the world and would not be able to return until all the aspects of the project were complete. It was all "very top secret." So far, she had been able to pull off the deception for two years. As much as she missed the two of them, she had no other option.

Ellie also didn't use any of the video-calling technology. No FaceTime, Zoom, Skype, or anything where they could see she had cut her bangs, chopped off her hair, and bleached it blond. That was another thing Ellie missed: going to a salon and getting her hair and nails done professionally. She had learned how to do both by watching YouTube videos. She remained isolated from any direct human contact. *For the moment, there was no way out.*

CHAPTER TWO

Colleen was a second-grade schoolteacher at the local grammar school. Colleen had recently separated from her abusive husband, Mitchel. She and Jackson spent their weekdays at the same school. They would walk to school together until the last few blocks. Jackson didn't want the kids to make fun of him for "walking with his mommy." The routine reversed going home. They would meet up at the same corner every day. Once they got home, Jackson would do his homework, then go outside to play. He was particularly interested in the dog down the street, the one who lived with the strange lady who never went outside. Colleen tried to explain to Jackson that the lady was nice, but she wasn't well. She didn't go into any detail about what the word "well" meant because she didn't really know, but it seemed to satisfy her son's curiosity. And Colleen was grateful that Jackson had a new way of spending his time, playing fetch with Buddy. That was, at least, one thing she got out of her brief conversation with Ellie through the intercom. Colleen recalled the encounter.

"Hello, Ellie. How are you today?"

"I'm OK. How are you?"

"Very well, thank you. Listen, I wanted to see if you'd like to come over for tea?"

"Uh, thank you, but I'm on a deadline," Ellie answered.

"OK. Perhaps another time?" Colleen offered.

"Maybe," Ellie lied.

"I hope you don't mind my son, Jackson, stopping by to say hello to your dog."

"No. Not at all. Buddy can use the company since I'm so busy." Ellie was calm and collected.

"Well, thank you for indulging him. He's been through a rough patch lately. His father and I recently separated, and he's having a bit of a hard time adjusting." Colleen could have stayed there and chatted for an hour, but Ellie cut the conversation short.

"I have to get back to work, but thank you again for your offer. And tell Jackson he can stop by anytime Buddy's in the yard." She smiled and pulled the curtain back in place.

Colleen turned her thoughts back to the job at hand — grading papers — while Jackson finished his homework.

"Mom? Can I go visit Buddy now?"

"Of course. But remember, don't bother Ms. Bowman. She is terribly busy with work."

"Mom?"

"Yes, honey?"

"Why do you think she never comes outside? I mean, like never."

"Honey, I'm not really sure, but I think she may have some health issues and can't go out. But let's not dwell on that, OK? She's totally fine with your tossing the ball over the fence to Buddy."

"Goodie! I really like Buddy. He's one smart dog!" Jackson grabbed his baseball glove and a ball he set aside for playing with Buddy. He pulled on his cap and headed out the door. "Bye, Mom! See ya later, alligator!"

"After a while, crocodile!" Colleen said in return, chuckling.

Once Colleen finished grading the papers, she went into her bedroom to finish sorting out Mitchel's clothes. She had a court date to get the temporary restraining order made permanent. The custody battle was just beginning, and she was anticipating that it would be brutal.

As it stood, Mitchel's visits with Jackson had to be supervised. He could see Jackson one weekend day each week. Had Mitchel not tried to punch her in the face, which had resulted in his fist going through the wall, or had he not trashed the kitchen, perhaps things would have gone differently for him. But the police report told of bruises on her arms and a hole in the Sheetrock. She shivered at the memory of that particular night and recalled the days preceding it. In retrospect, what had happened was inevitable.

Things with Colleen and Mitchel had been escalating, along with his drinking. With each argument, she thought he would strike her, but she had always managed to defuse the situation by agreeing with him or taking the blame for something she didn't do, something he imagined she had done. It was when he grabbed her by the throat and pushed her up against the wall that she knew the end was in sight. But she didn't want it to be the end of her. Just the end of their marriage. She couldn't count the number of times she cried herself to sleep, waiting for him to stumble home. She had tried to shelter Jackson from Mitchel's hostility, but Jackson was a smart kid. He knew when his dad was acting mean.

At first, Jackson thought his dad was mad at him. But then he overheard his father screaming at his mom, using some awfully bad words. Jackson had pulled the pillow over his head to muffle the shouting. The next morning, Jackson noticed that his mom's eyes were really puffy and her nose really red. He knew she had been crying, but she smiled anyway and made breakfast.

Jackson was fiddling with his cereal. "Mom?"

"Yes, honey."

"What were you and Dad fighting about last night?" He looked up sheepishly.

"Oh, just grown-up stuff. You know. Mommy and Daddy stuff." Colleen was trying to smooth over Jackson's fears.

"But I heard Daddy call you some very bad names."

Colleen put her coffee cup down on the table and pulled up a chair. "Daddy and I are trying to work out some problems. You know, like the ones they give you in school?"

"Like a puzzle?"

"Sort of. But I don't want you to worry about any of it, OK?" She took his chin in her hand.

Jackson grimaced. "Well . . . OK. But it scared me."

She gave him a big hug. "I don't want you to ever be afraid because of us." She looked him straight in the eye. She knew that if Mitchel ever tried to do anything to her son, she would kill him. Literally.

"No, I mean I'm scared you and Daddy will break up. Like Judy's mom and dad." Jackson started to sniffle.

"Sweetie, we'll figure it out. Now, let's get ready to go to school, OK?"

He hopped off his chair and got his jacket and backpack. "Ready when you are!" He dashed out the front door. He wanted to be out of the house before his father got out of bed. His dad was often in a nasty mood in the morning, especially if he and his mom had been fighting, which seemed like almost every night. And Jackson especially didn't like the way his father smelled in the morning. It was a stinky beer odor, and his face was scratchy from not shaving for days at a time. Jackson wondered why things had changed. And when. He was deep in thought when his father came roaring out the front door.

"Hey! Jackson!" Mitchel shouted as he stood on the front porch in a stained T-shirt and boxer shorts. "Don't you want to say good morning to your old man?"

Jackson looked around to see if there was

anyone watching. This was the first time his father had put on such an embarrassing display outside the house.

"I said, 'Say good morning!' " Mitchel's eyes were wide with fury. Jackson didn't know what to do and was frozen in place. A minute later, Colleen was out on the front porch.

"Mitchel, please get back in the house," she said in a very mild-mannered voice.

"Don't tell me what to do!" Spittle was coming out of his mouth.

"Mitchel, please. You're making a scene."

"Making a scene?" His voice got louder.

Colleen knew there was no way she was going to convince Mitchel to go back into the house, so she pushed past him, grabbed Jackson's hand, and hurried down the street.

"Yeah! Go ahead! Run, you stupid wretch!" he screamed at the top of his lungs. "And Jackson, you spoiled little creep . . . I'll remember how you treated your daddy."

By the time he choked out the last sentence, Colleen and Jackson were no longer within the sound of his maniacal voice.

Colleen knew Jackson would have a lot of questions and also a lot of anxiety. After they crossed the next block, she stopped.

"Are you OK?"

Jackson tried to remain calm, but the tears

were streaming down his face. Colleen pulled out a tissue and handed it to him.

He was starting to stutter, something he hadn't done since he was five. "MMM . . . Mom . . . I . . . I . . . I'm rr . . . really sccc . . . scared. DD . . . Daddy nnnn . . . never did th . . . that . . . bbb . . . be . . . fffore."

"I know. But listen to me. It's not your fault. Daddy was in a very bad mood this morning."

Jackson had calmed down a bit. "Because of the fight?"

"That's part of it."

"And why is he so stinky in the morning?" Jackson had a lot of questions that Colleen knew she couldn't answer at the time. How do you tell your child that his father has become a raging alcoholic? Perhaps that was a question for Al-Anon. Going for help was something she had been reluctant to do, but clearly it was time for some intervention. If not for Mitchel, then for herself. She had a child to protect.

"I want you to listen to me." Leaning over, she looked him straight in the eye again. "None of this is your fault. Daddy is going through something right now that I can't explain. I just want you to try to do the best you can today. Try not to think about his bad behavior. Remember, the only person who should feel bad is him. Not you. Got it?"

Jackson wiped his nose with the tissue and saluted. "Got it."

"Great. Now, you go catch up with your friends, and I'll see you in a bit. OK?"

"OK!" Jackson gave her his best smile and headed down the street.

Colleen was certain that would not be the last of Mitchel's outbursts. That very evening, he stumbled in around midnight, reeking from booze and cheap perfume. There was the clichéd lipstick on his collar, too. But she didn't care. She suspected he had been having sex with someone, probably another drunk. The trick was to figure out how to extricate herself and her son from this whirlpool of horror. She just didn't think it would be that day.

As he staggered into the bedroom, he blew up at her for the morning's clash on the front porch. "How dare you take my son when I'm trying to talk to him?" He pushed her onto the bed.

"Mitchel, please. I was not trying to take your son anywhere except to school." Colleen was desperately struggling to defuse the situation.

He caught her wrists, held her down, and

pushed his face into hers. She could almost taste the foulness of his breath. "You don't ever try to keep me from my son." He loosened his grip, and she rolled out from under him. He grabbed her shoulder and aimed his fist at her face, but she was quick enough to dodge the punch, causing him to put his hand through the wall. Colleen ran from the bedroom into Jackson's room, locking the door behind her. She pushed his dresser against the door.

Jackson awoke with a start. "Shhhh . . ." She put her finger up to her lips as Mitchel made his way down the hall and into the kitchen.

He began clearing the counters with his arms flailing, breaking dishes and glasses along the way. Thankfully, she had had the presence of mind to grab her cell phone as Mitchel cursed and freed his bleeding hand from the wall. Praying she had service, she dialed 911.

"Nine-one-one. What's your emergency?"

"Domestic dispute at Thirty-two Birchwood Lane. My name is Colleen Haywood. My husband is on a rampage."

"Where are you right now?"

"My son and I are locked in his bedroom. Please hurry."

"Yes, please stay on the line with me."

21

"OK." Colleen made her way to the window, just in case she and Jackson had to climb out. She could hear Mitchel's manic behavior and cursing through the walls. The dispatcher continued to talk to her.

"Are you and your son all right? Do we need to send an ambulance?"

"We're fine right now." Colleen kept the panic out of her voice, clutching Jackson in her arms. She whispered in his ear, "You're being very brave," and kissed him on the top of his head.

Jackson whispered back. "Why is Daddy so mad?"

Colleen gave him the finger-to-her-lips signal again.

"We have a patrol car a block from your house. Please continue to stay on the line."

"Yes. Of course. We're next to the window, and we can climb out, if necessary."

"OK, Colleen. What's your son's name?"

"His name is Jackson."

"How is he doing?"

"He's a bit scared, like me." She winked at him, trying to keep him calm.

After what seemed like an eternity, Colleen finally heard the siren of a police car and could see the flashing lights. A moment later, there was a loud bang on the front door.

"Police! Open up!"

"Go to hell!" Mitchel screamed back.

"Mr. Haywood, if you don't open the door, we are going to have to break it down."

"Screw you!" Mitchel shouted.

Colleen and Jackson heard the rumbling of the front door being bashed open. "Mitchel Haywood?"

"Who wants to know?" he said in a surly manner.

"Officer Pedone. Hibbing Police Department. Put your hands behind your back, sir."

"Put your hands behind *your* back, sir," Mitchel replied mockingly.

"Mr. Haywood, you are under arrest for assault."

"Like hell I am," he slurred back. "I didn't assault anyone."

"Then can you tell me how your hand got so bloody? And how your kitchen got trashed."

There was a knock on the closed bedroom door. "Mrs. Haywood? This is the police. I'm Officer Davis, with Officer Pedone. Are you all right?"

Colleen spoke to the dispatcher and told her that the police had arrived. She pushed the small dresser away from the door and unlocked it. She almost crumbled in relief.

"We have your husband in custody now. It's safe for you to come out."

She peered down the hall and saw Mitchel slouched over on the sofa. "Can you take him outside so my son doesn't have to witness this?"

"Certainly. As long as you are both all right. Do either of you need medical attention?"

"We're OK." She hugged Jackson tightly against her. "No need for an ambulance," she said, reiterating what she had told the dispatcher.

"Wait right here, please," Davis instructed her.

Mitchel was still protesting as Pedone escorted him to the patrol car, guided his head into the vehicle, and locked him in the back seat.

"Jackson, honey, I want you to stay in your room for a little while, OK?" Colleen pulled the words out as soothingly as she could muster. "You can even play with your tablet."

"But, Mommy, what about Daddy? And the policeman?"

"I'll tell you all about it in a little while. First, I have to talk to these nice policemen. Then you and I will have some ice cream."

Jackson wasn't sure how to react to any of

this, but he listened as Officer Davis squatted down to talk to him. "It's going to be OK, son. Do as your mom asks, then ice cream. You got any questions for me?"

Jackson was immediately distracted by the interest the police officer had shown. "Did you ever shoot anybody?"

Davis chuckled. "Do you know how many times people ask me that question?"

Jackson smiled. "A bazillion?"

"Yep. And, no, thankfully I never had to shoot anyone." He tousled Jackson's hair.

"So what's going to happen to my dad? Is he going to jail?" Jackson sat down on his bed, trying to hold back tears.

"That's going to depend on your mom. Like I said, we have to clear up a few things. Now, go do what your mom said. We'll be right down the hall."

"OK." Jackson seemed to be a bit more relieved. And safe.

Colleen's eyes swept across the kitchen. It looked as if someone had thrown a hand grenade. "Do you mind if I pour myself a drink?" She began to shake. It's common knowledge that during times of extreme stress, our fight-or-flight instincts take over. She had fought back, and now what had just happened began to sink in.

"Let me get that for you," Pedone offered.

25

Colleen pointed to the liquor cabinet above the refrigerator. "Scotch, please." She rarely drank any hard liquor, but it seemed like a good idea at the moment. He looked around for something to pour it in.

"There are glasses in the dining-room cabinet," Colleen said.

A few minutes later, Pedone returned with her drink. Her hands were trembling so badly she needed to use both of them to hold the glass.

"Can you tell me what happened this evening?" Pedone pulled out his notebook and began to write as Colleen recalled the events of the evening. It took about a half hour for her to explain everything, starting with Mitchel's behavior that morning.

"Do you want to press charges?" Pedone asked.

Colleen gave it some thought. She knew it was going to be a nightmare going forward, but she also knew that the marriage was over, and she could be putting herself and Jackson in further jeopardy by pretending it hadn't happened. Besides, she just didn't care anymore. Not about Mitchel. Not about the marriage. The only thing she cared about was raising her son in a loving environment. And this certainly wasn't it.

"Yes. What do I have to do?"

"You'll have to come down to the station to file a formal complaint. Is there anyone who can look after your son?"

"I'll call my mother. She lives about fifteen minutes away."

She dialed her mother's phone number, knowing the woman would panic at her phone ringing in the middle of the night.

"Yes! Colleen! Is everything OK?" She could barely catch her breath.

"I'm OK. Jackson is OK." Colleen took in a big inhale. "We have a situation here, and I need you to come by and sit with Jackson for the rest of the night."

"What on earth is going on?" Judith Griffin demanded.

"Mom, I'll explain everything later. Can you come over now? Please?" Colleen knew her mother had never approved of Mitchel, and she wasn't in any sort of mood to be lectured.

"Yes. Of course. I'll be there as soon as I can." She sounded a bit exasperated rather than inconvenienced.

Colleen thought to herself, *If she hadn't been so controlling, maybe I wouldn't have rebelled and married that creep.*

"Thank you. And don't freak out when you see the police car." Colleen cringed, waiting for the interrogation.

27

"What police car? What are you talking about?" Judith was incredulous.

"Mother, please. Just come over. I will tell you everything later. Please!"

CHAPTER THREE

Ellie felt terrible that she couldn't befriend Colleen. She knew that things were bad at the Haywood house. She thought back to the incident that had taken place two weeks before. The entire block couldn't help but notice the commotion coming from the house that night. Ellie had headed to the second-floor loft, with Buddy hot on her heels. She pulled out a pair of binoculars to see if she could figure out what the ruckus was all about. She crouched down and pointed the lens at the Haywoods'. From her angle, she could see someone in the back seat of a police car. His face was obscured by the door frame, but it looked like it could be Mitchel. She wouldn't be surprised if it was. After his rude display that morning, no one would have been shocked. Screaming at his kid while he was in his underwear. She felt sorry for both Jackson and Colleen. She knew very well what it was like to be terrified.

The police car had been sitting in front for almost an hour when she noticed the BMW that Colleen's mother drove turn into their driveway. She saw Colleen's mother exit her car and peer into the police car. Judith Griffin gave the man in the back seat a disgusted look and went into the house. A few minutes later, Colleen and two police officers exited. Colleen got in her own car and followed the police. Ellie assumed they were on their way to the police station and that Mrs. Griffin was looking after Jackson. *That poor kid,* she thought to herself. Ellie liked Jackson, even though they had never interacted, but she could tell a lot about his character by the way he played with Buddy.

Over the next two weeks, there had been no mention of the incident in the local *Patch,* but maybe they were trying to keep it quiet for Colleen and Jackson's sakes. Kids could be horribly cruel.

Ellie imagined that Jackson and Colleen were going through an exceedingly difficult time. Even though there was little she could do to help them, she felt good that Jackson came by every afternoon. He would spend well over an hour just throwing the ball across the yard and giving Buddy a pat on the head when Buddy jumped up on the fence with the ball in his mouth, returning it to Jackson. Ellie would watch from inside, happy that two innocent creatures could give each other so much pleasure with the simple gesture of throwing a ball. How she missed the outdoors.

One afternoon, her doorbell rang, and she gasped with fear. She checked the closed-circuit security camera and noticed a small bouquet of flowers on the doorstep. She thought it could be a trick, so she left them there. She figured Hector would bring them inside the porch later that day.

The next afternoon, she noticed that Jackson didn't come by to play with Buddy. She didn't know if she should call Colleen or not. She didn't want to be a busybody, but Buddy was pacing the yard. She decided to call — something she rarely did. She went up to her office, Googled Colleen Haywood, and found her phone number. Luckily, they had a landline, but that was pretty standard for Hibbing. It was a rural town with not a whole lot of good cell service. She picked up one of her burner phones and dialed.

A hesitant "Hello" came in response. It was Jackson. "Hey, Jackson. This is Buddy's mom. How are you doing?"

Jackson hesitated. He didn't know what to

make of this unfamiliar voice over the phone. "Hhh . . . hello?"

Ellie repeated. "Hey, Jackson. This is Ellie Bowman. You know, the lady who owns Buddy, the dog." She wasn't used to speaking to people she actually knew, except for Kara and her mom. Most of the interaction she had with people was for work, over an Internet connection — one computer talking to another.

"Oh, hi. Let me go get my mom." Jackson quickly put the phone down and yelled for his mother. "Mom! It's that lady down the street. Buddy's owner." He sounded a bit unhinged.

Ellie could hear footsteps moving closer to the phone.

"Yes?" Colleen sounded a bit terse. "What can I do for you?"

"Hi. I was just checking on Jackson. Buddy has been pacing the yard. Is everything OK?"

"Well, to be perfectly honest, Jackson's feelings were hurt when he saw you left the flowers on the front porch. He wrote a note thanking you for letting him play with Buddy. He didn't think he was welcome anymore."

"Oh my gosh! I am so sorry! I had no idea!" Ellie was mortified that she had hurt the little guy's feelings.

"Yes, well, when he was leaving for school this morning, he saw that they were still there on the front porch. He said he rang the bell yesterday when he left them."

"I am so sorry. I was up in my loft on a tech call for several hours and forgot about the doorbell. Ellie was getting particularly good at lying and covering her tracks. In fact, she was almost a genius at it by that point. "That was so sweet and kind of him. May I apologize to him, please?"

Ellie heard Colleen hand the phone over to Jackson, and whisper, "She wants to apologize. Here."

"Hello?" Jackson was still uncertain.

"Jackson. Thank you for the flowers. I apologize for not picking them up. I was working upstairs when the doorbell rang, and I was on the computer with a client for a few hours. By the time I finished the session, I had completely forgotten that the doorbell rang. Can you please forgive me? I know Buddy missed you today."

"Oh, sure, Ms. Bowman. That's OK. I kinda felt a little goofy after I left them."

"Oh, no, you were not at all goofy. That was truly kind." Ellie smiled into the phone.

"So is it OK if I visit with Buddy today? I finished my homework."

"If your mom says it's OK with her, then it's OK with me. I'm sure Buddy will be happy to see you."

"OK. Here's my mom." Jackson handed the phone to his mother.

"Hi, Colleen. I am really sorry for this mix-up. If it's not too late, Jackson is more than welcome to play with Buddy today."

"We're having dinner in about an hour, so I guess it's OK for him to come over."

Ellie hesitated for a moment. "Are you all right?" She then grimaced, feeling as if she had overstepped.

"As good as I can be." Colleen sighed. "We're hanging in there."

A moment of silence fell between the two women. For some reason, each of them seemed to know how the other was feeling.

"Good. Again, I'm sorry about all this. I hope it doesn't deter Jackson from future random acts of kindness."

"Letting him play with Buddy is also kind. Have a good evening."

CHAPTER FOUR

Ellie lived a very routine life in spite of never leaving the house. Each morning, she would get up, make her coffee, let Buddy out, feed Percy, change his litter, let Buddy back in, feed Buddy. Then she would spend twenty minutes on the treadmill in the second bedroom. After her workout, she would take a shower, wrap her hair in a towel, and fix some breakfast. It was usually a toasted English muffin smeared with butter and a piece of melon, if it was in season. Once she finished her light breakfast, she would put on a fresh pair of yoga pants and a hoodie and finish drying her hair. Then it was up to the loft and begin working.

The loft looked like a mini NASA space center, with multiple computers, phone lines, and gaming devices. That's how she had met Hector. Online gaming. Before her seclusion. Her screen name was Firefly, and she was one of the best at Fortnite and

Minecraft, beating some of the most highly skilled players across the globe. When they were not playing, she and Hector would exchange ideas for creating new games. Eventually, they designed a kids' game and, through Ellie's contacts, were able to sell one to Arcadia for a handsome sum. It was enough money for her to be able to buy the cottage she was now holed up in and for Hector to go to any college he wanted, provided he was accepted. Ellie had no doubt MIT would be chomping at the bit for someone with Hector's talent.

Funny thing, though — they had never met through Skype or Zoom until she needed to go into isolation. And Hector owed her big-time. The first big favor was during a serious video match. One of Hector's rivals had hacked into Hector's computers and crashed his system, costing him thousands of dollars in bitcoins and real dollars. Being a super code writer, and a computer aficionado, Ellie was able to trace who the culprit was, and she unleashed a computer virus that tore through his entire gaming collection. She was also able to recover the bitcoins that the perpetrator had scammed from Hector. Hector was forever grateful, and they bonded as geek-friends.

Then there was the game he and Ellie

devised and Ellie had been able to sell. When Ellie reached out for his help, he was more than happy to do whatever he could for her. She knew he was the only person she could trust under the circumstances.

Every morning, Hector would check the small table in Ellie's enclosed rear porch for notes, packages, or instructions. Ellie would leave a note and some cash in an envelope on the table next to the kitchen door for Hector to take to the grocery store, drug-store, or wine shop, where she had house accounts. Every month, she would deposit an amount of money into those accounts to replenish them. She joked to herself that it was like E-ZPass.

Depending on what she needed, the store, especially the wine shop, would deliver the goods she'd ordered to her front porch. But if there weren't too many items, Hector would bring them on his bike at the end of the day.

Three or four times a week, Hector would clean up the yard and remove the trash bags left on the porch. Any mail was pushed through an old-fashioned mail slot in the front door. That's how Colleen had left her notes inviting Ellie to tea. All other outside deliveries would sit there until Hector arrived and took them to the rear porch.

Hector had already made his rounds the day Jackson had left the flowers, so they sat overnight on the front steps. Hector had a late meeting with his guidance counselor and hadn't come by that particular afternoon. Unfortunately, the flowers had wilted and remained there until the next morning. Thankfully, the misunderstanding was over, and Jackson's feelings had been restored.

Ellie thought again about letting Jackson into the yard. She decided to run it past Hector. Even though he was only eighteen years old, Hector had a wise soul. She wrote Hector a note:

Hector:
Jackson seems to be a genuinely nice boy. He loves to play with Buddy, and I know there have been a lot of family issues. What do you think about letting Jackson come into the yard? My only concern is that he might accidentally leave the side gate open. Thoughts? Ring the bell later, and we can talk through the kitchen window. Thanks!
F.F. (Firefly)

Hector read the note and knew exactly what she needed. Later that day, he appeared with a box of gadgets, including a

38

mechanical device that would open and close the gate. There was already a security code needed to open the gate, but now there would be access from inside the house. Once it was installed, Ellie would be able to control it from any of the security panels that were in each room. He also installed a doorbell buzzer next to the lock both inside and outside the gate. The plan was for Jackson to ring the gate buzzer, and Ellie would open the gate from her security panel, then the gate would close automatically.

The front gate was on an automatic hinge that closed, but it also had a motion detector alerting Ellie (and Buddy) with a repeated chime if someone was coming to the front door. She wanted Jackson to use the side gate so people wouldn't feel free to come into her yard, and so that the chime at the front gate wouldn't be going off when it wasn't necessary.

After Hector installed all the necessary items, Ellie left a note for him to deliver to Colleen's mailbox.

Hello, Colleen,

I'd like to invite Jackson to play in the yard with Buddy. I've installed a security system to ensure the side gate is never left open, as I would prefer he enter and exit that way. Jackson simply has to press the buzzer and I will open the gate from inside the house. When he's ready to leave, he can press the button to let me know he's heading out. I'm able to see the yard from my office, so I will always be available. Please let me know if this is workable for you. I know how fond Jackson and Buddy are of each other. Here is a phone number if you need to reach me. 846-555-9091. That number is good for the next five days.

Kind regards,
Ellie

Ellie was a bit concerned that the last sentence regarding the phone number might raise some sort of suspicion, but she would explain that her "high-security job" required her to rotate phones. It didn't really, but she had to be consistent with her story. The truth is much easier to remember because when you tell a lie, you have to keep track of the tales you tell.

Prior to moving in, Ellie had had Hector install a very intricate security system surrounding the property and her house. It relied in part on closed-circuit television surveillance that she could see from any of the security panels in the house. It wasn't enough that she couldn't leave. She had to be certain no one could get in without her knowledge or permission. So far, only Hector had been in her yard. After two years of tight security, she thought it might be time to let a little boy in to play with her dog.

CHAPTER FIVE

While Jackson was getting ready for school, Colleen opened the note, which was written on fine card stock. She read it twice. She was surprised that Ellie had reached out. It was only the second time in the two years that Ellie had lived there that there was any direct communication from her. Colleen wasn't sure if she was comfortable having Jackson play in the backyard of Ellie's house. She was able to see him if he was in the front, but considering that Mitchel was stalking him in his car, it was probably less dangerous for him to be in Ellie's backyard.

The order of protection limited Mitchel's proximity to one hundred yards. That meant that he couldn't be any closer than a football field away. Ellie's property was just outside the boundary from Colleen's house, so theoretically Mitchel could park in Ellie's driveway to be beyond the hundred-yard limit. But from her limited experience with

Ellie, Colleen was sure that Ellie would not allow anyone in her driveway.

The problem was the other end of the block. There was a parking space just outside the boundary, where Mitchel could park his car and watch the house. He also could sit outside the parking lot of the school. To Mitchel's way of thinking, the restraining order was just a piece of paper, and as long as he kept his distance, he could spy on his family all he wanted. That part gave Colleen the creeps. But until he violated the order, there wasn't much she could do about the situation.

She thought about buying a gun, but she didn't want to keep one in the house. Besides, that idea also gave her the creeps. Plus she would have to take lessons. Then she thought about a stun gun. But where would she begin? She spotted Officer Pedone's card on the bulletin board and decided to speak to him about it. She pulled the thumbtack out, pulled the card off the board, and dialed his number. She knew she had only a few minutes before Jackson came into the kitchen, and she didn't want him to hear her conversation.

"Pedone," he answered

"Hello, Officer Pedone. This is Colleen Haywood."

"Hello, Colleen. Everything OK?"

"Well, yes and no." Colleen was hesitant, not wanting to seem like a damsel in distress. But perhaps she was.

"Tell me the no part first." Pedone was warm and kind.

"Mitchel is stalking us."

"Is he disobeying the order?"

"Not exactly. He stays a hundred yards away, but he's always at the end of our street and just outside the parking lot at school. I work at the same school Jackson attends."

"Unfortunately, there isn't anything that can be done about that."

"Yes, I know. I think he's become irrational since the night of the episode. He had a hissy fit in court when the judge only granted him supervised visitation rights, and because of his outburst, the judge only allowed him one day each weekend. He was so angry, I thought the veins were going to pop out of his head."

"Where is he staying now?" Pedone asked.

"At his brother's house, in Manchester." Colleen gave Pedone the address in that town, which was only a few miles away.

Pedone wrote down the information.

"How often is he on your street?"

"Every day."

"Does he have a job?"

44

"No. He lost it after he was arrested. He had already been put on probation, and the two days he spent in jail put his boss over the top."

"Have you settled on child support?"

"Not yet, but according to human resources, it will probably be a hundred and fifty dollars a week, due the first week of each month."

"Has he given you any money in the meantime?"

"No. Nothing." Colleen was surprised at Pedone's concern. "But it will be retroactive."

"OK. You let me know if he is ever late with a payment. Our local judge does not look kindly on deadbeat dads."

"Thank you," Colleen said. "Officer . . ."

He interrupted her. "Please call me Bob."

"Uh. OK, Bob." Colleen smiled for the first time in two weeks.

"Sorry for interrupting. How is Jackson doing with all of this?"

"He's doing as well as one could expect. He asks questions like, 'Is Daddy ever coming back?' 'Why can I only see him once a week?' Things like that," she explained. "I told him that for now, Daddy has to stay with Uncle Gregory and that his Grammy will be with them when he spends the day with his dad."

"It's gotta be tough," Pedone said. "Sorry . . . what were you saying earlier? You sounded like you were about to ask me a question."

Colleen hesitated again. "I've been thinking about getting a stun gun."

Bob paused for a moment. "If you think that will help you feel safer, I can make some recommendations for you. I would go with a Taser rather than a stun gun, though."

"Oh. What's the difference?"

"Tasers eject electrodes that are tethered to the gun and can reach up to fifteen feet. A stun gun requires you to make physical contact with the person," Pedone explained. "You don't want him close enough to get his hands on you."

Colleen replied immediately. "You are absolutely correct. I'm also having a security system installed."

"That's an excellent idea," Bob Pedone said.

"Between going to court, and teaching school, and trying to put Mitchel's belongings together, I'm feeling a bit overwhelmed."

"That's perfectly understandable. But it's important that you take care of yourself," Pedone added.

"Yes, I know." Colleen sighed.

"How about this. I'll pick up a Taser for you and bring it over. Then I can show you how to use it," Pedone offered. "We don't want you hurting yourself."

"That would be great. But I don't want to put you to any trouble on my behalf." Colleen was almost starting to relax.

"Not a problem. I have to go to the shop and pick up a few things anyway. Do you have a budget in mind?"

"I have no idea. What do they usually cost?"

"Anywhere between four hundred and fifty and eleven hundred dollars."

"Wow. Like I said, I had no idea." Colleen was calculating her budget in her head.

"I don't think you need the most expensive model. I'll pick one out, and I'll use my police discount. That should save you a few bucks."

"I can't thank you enough, Officer."

"It's Bob, remember?" Pedone chuckled.

"Right. Bob." Colleen smiled. "I really appreciate this."

"Not a problem. I'll be happy to come by your house without having to arrest anyone."

They both laughed.

Pedone cleared his throat. "He pleaded

47

not guilty at his arraignment, so there will be a hearing. I will be present for that, by the way." There was a moment of silence between them. "I'll be in touch later today after I pick up the Taser. Is there any particular time that's better for you?"

"School is out at two forty-five, and I'm usually home by four-thirty."

"That's fine. I'll see you around four-thirty. Remember, we're here to serve," Pedone added.

"Thanks again. Bye." Colleen hung up the phone, feeling like a huge weight had been lifted from her shoulders. Officer "Bob" Pedone had been truly kind throughout the ordeal.

She thought about how considerate he had been over the past two weeks. He had escorted her home the night of the incident and spoken to her before the arraignment. She was terrified. He was reassuring. She didn't want to see Mitchel's angry face ever again. She knew he could have killed her that night. His rage was out of control. But knowing Officer Pedone was in the courtroom and was keeping an eye on both of them gave her a little peace of mind. She wasn't going to let Mitchel intimidate her with his seething, belligerent anger. No. Not again. Not anymore.

Bail was set at $10,000, which in Colleen's mind wasn't nearly enough. As usual, Mitchel's mother bailed him out, and they left the courthouse shooting all sorts of sneers and dirty looks in Colleen's direction, as if all of it had been her fault. And in Mitchel's twisted mind, it was. It always was.

The judge granted permission for Mitchel to go to the house to pick up some clothes, but he had to be accompanied by a police officer. This time it was Officer Davis returning to the scene of the crime, so to speak. The judge gave him one hour to clear out what he needed until further notice from the court.

With her mother by her side and Officer Pedone in the room, Colleen felt safe and confident — something she hadn't felt in a while. The mental abuse from Mitchel had taken its toll.

At the temporary custody hearing, Mitchel had blown his cool. That little outburst had worked in Colleen's favor. At least for the moment. But she feared that the outcome would inflame his anger toward her even more. The stalking was Mitchel's way of trying to unnerve her. If he couldn't have things his way, then he would torture her mentally.

Within the next couple of days, she would be well armed with a Taser and a security system. She had to make sure she wasn't violating any rules if she took the Taser to school with her. She would also take along a copy of the order of protection. One of the first things she had done was to give a copy to the school principal to put on file, as well as a copy to the guidance counselor and one for the security guard. She was well past being embarrassed. Shame was no longer an issue. Survival was all that mattered.

She glanced toward the counter, where she had left the note from Ellie Bowman. Yes. She would take her up on her offer for Jackson to play in the yard. When Jackson returned to the kitchen with his backpack, Colleen gave him the news.

"Yippee!" Jackson was delighted. It was the first time Colleen had seen his face light up in quite a while.

CHAPTER SIX

Ellie jumped from her seat when her burner phone rang. She had forgotten she had given the number to Colleen. "Hello?"

"Hi, Ellie. It's Colleen. Colleen Haywood. I hope I'm not calling too early."

"No, not at all. I'm always up at the crack of dawn. How are you doing?" Ellie's voice was warm and friendly.

"I'm all right. I wanted to thank you for your invitation for Jackson to play in your yard. He's pretty athletic for a boy his age, so he could always climb the fence, if necessary."

At that moment, Ellie was glad she didn't have an electrified fence, although Buddy was the reason she chose not to have one. She knew she was paranoid, but zapping someone or something could be avoided with the security system she had in place. The motion detector's security beam was high enough above the fence line not to be affected by Buddy, but low enough should someone the size of an adult try to climb over it. She rarely set the perimeter alarm during the day since she had a complete view of the property from her perch in the loft. The system had several zones, depending on what time of day it was.

"Wonderful. I'm sure Buddy will be very happy. Do you want to start today?" Ellie asked.

Colleen thought for a moment. She had to finish putting Mitchel's things together and could use some extra time.

"That would be great. Do you mind if he stays for more than an hour? I have some things I need to do, and I'd rather not have to do them in front of Jackson." Colleen hoped she hadn't said too much.

"No problem. He can stay in the yard as long as he wants. I don't know who will get tired first, him or Buddy." Ellie chuckled softly. "And, listen, I want to apologize for turning down all of your lovely invitations, but I am really up to my eyeballs with work."

"What do you do? If I'm not being too pushy," Colleen asked.

"I work in IT. I'm what you might call a computer geek — one of those people who does online chats when you have a problem with your computer. I also work with software companies, doing beta testing on new programs. Pretty boring stuff, really." Ellie wasn't lying about the computer part. The "boring stuff" was definitely an exaggeration.

"I am not that tech-savvy. Just the basics," Colleen said.

"That's why there are dweebs like me." Ellie chuckled.

"I won't keep you from your geeking. It was nice talking to you, Ellie. And thanks again for the Buddy-Jackson connection." Colleen was surprised at how easy it was to talk to Ellie. She seemed so "normal."

"Nice talking to you, too. Enjoy your day." Ellie hung up and put the burner phone on a shelf. Maybe she would keep this one just for Jackson and Colleen. She hadn't made any other calls with it so far.

Besides her weekly calls to her mom and Kara, and maintaining her fabricated life, she felt a connection to Colleen. Maybe it was because she knew more about her than Colleen realized. Being a crackerjack computer geek, Ellie could be a good hacker when necessary. She knew that what she did was illegal at times, but her life depended on it.

Ellie had over a dozen repair calls that day. *Mercury must be in retrograde,* she thought to herself. A normal day usually brings five or six, lasting about an hour each. That day, it was one huge problem after another. Before she knew it, the buzzer at the gate rang. She looked at her watch. It was 3:20. She looked out the back window and saw Jackson with his baseball glove and a ball and buzzed him in. The gate shut behind Jackson, just as Hector had planned.

Ellie noticed a police car pull up in front of Colleen's house. She hoped there wasn't anything wrong. She pulled out the binoculars and watched a policeman climb the front steps, carrying a package under his arm. Colleen had a smile on her face as she let him in. Ellie was relieved. Now if they could just get that creepy husband to stop parking his car on their block.

Ellie turned to look out the back window again. Buddy and Jackson were running all over the yard. She was glad Hector had cleaned up after Buddy that morning. She'd hate for Jackson to go home with doggie doo-doo on his shoes.

Feeling a bit neglected, Percy jumped up on one of Ellie's desks and started knocking things over. For a feline, he was quite a character. Most cats are agile and can walk around almost anything without disturbing it. Not Percy. It was his mission to disrupt whatever you were doing. And if you weren't paying enough attention to him, he'd find something to bang or slam. As annoying as it might seem, it always made Ellie laugh.

"You are such a goofball!" She picked up his fifteen pounds of fur and rubbed her face in his neck. Even though he had to sit on her lap at every opportunity or lie on top of the very newspaper she was reading, he didn't like to have his four feet dangling in her arms, and he started to squirm. She set him down on the floor, and he immediately jumped back on one of her consoles and tossed a computer mouse onto the floor. "And you know that's called a mouse, don't ya?" He gave her a loud meow in return.

"Now scoot. I have work to do." Percy gave her a look that said, "No way, lady." And he perched himself on one of her drafting stools.

"OK. You sit there, but behave." Ellie talked to her animals as if they were people. She preferred them over most people. And for the past two years, they were all the company she had had.

She leaned back in her chair. Human connection was something she was beginning to miss. At first, she hadn't wanted any contact with people. It was much better that way. But after two years, she was feeling the burden of being a hermit.

She thought about what it used to be like to have a female friend to hang out with. Have tea. Shop. Share a bottle of wine. She had to admit she missed it. Maybe she would invite Colleen over for tea. Just not yet. She'd wait to see how the Jackson-Buddy situation developed. And Colleen was going through a major transition. She probably could use a friend right now, but Ellie was apprehensive about getting too close to someone. Maybe she would limit the contact to phone calls. They could discuss work, school. Nothing too personal.

Her computer chimed. Another confused and frustrated customer. She turned back to the consoles and began to type.

Ellie: Hello. I'm Sheri. How can I help you today?

She never used her real name. Nor the fake one she had been using for the past two years, either.

CHAPTER SEVEN

At 3:15, Colleen sent Jackson over to Ellie's. She was so happy to see him in such a
good mood. But her mood changed when
she went into her bedroom and opened
Mitchel's closet. It was the first time she
had bothered to peer into it since he had
been allowed to take some of his personal
items. Of course, he had left a pile of dirty
clothes, filthy sneakers, and several greasy
baseball caps. She changed into clothes appropriate for cleaning out the rancid items,
went into the kitchen, and pulled out several
large trash bags and rubber gloves. She had
tossed almost everything into the bags when
the doorbell rang. She checked her watch.
Four-thirty already! Officer Pedone —
rather, Bob — was here. She took a quick
look in the mirror. She was a sight. And not
a good one. Her hair was a mess, and she
was wearing sweatpants and a T-shirt. She
didn't know why, but she wanted to make a

good impression. This definitely wasn't the way.

"Be right there!" She took another look at herself to see what she could salvage in less than three minutes. Quickly change her clothes. Run a brush through her hair. Lipstick.

When she got to the door, she was a bit winded. "Hi, sorry. I was in the back, cleaning out a few things. Please come in!"

She opened the door wide, as wide as her smile.

"No problem," Pedone answered. "How are you doing?"

"Good. I'm good. Really." And she meant it. Colleen felt as if her life was beginning to turn around. Yes, it would be a long haul, but she was moving in the right direction. Away from the madness.

"Where's Jackson?" Pedone asked.

"He's at a neighbor's playing with her dog." Colleen nodded in the direction of Ellie's house.

"You mean Ellie Bowman?" Pedone asked quizzically.

"Yes. She's letting Jackson play in the yard." She hesitated. "I know it's none of my business, but do you know why she never comes out of the house?"

"Haven't a clue," Pedone replied. "We like

'em quiet." He smiled.

"I was surprised she invited Jackson to play in the yard. That's a first. I've invited her over for tea, but she's always declined. I thought maybe she was agoraphobic." She shrugged. "But she seems very nice."

"Like I said, we like 'em quiet. And if you say she's nice, that's even better. One person we don't have to keep a constant eye on." Pedone put the package on the dining-room table. "Speaking about people we're keeping an eye on, there's Mitchel Haywood."

"Oh?" Ellie asked. "Any particular reason?"

"We found out that his brother, Gregory, has a gun permit. I don't mean to alarm you, but thought you should know."

"Can't you do something about that?" Colleen was getting nervous.

"Unfortunately, no. Second Amendment and all."

"But what about Mitchel? He was arrested. Is he allowed to be near a gun?"

"Yes, he was arrested, but he hasn't had his trial yet, so he's not been convicted of anything as of now." Pedone wished he could have given her better news.

"So, when he gets convicted, can he still live in a house with a gun?" Colleen tried to remain calm.

"It will depend on whether he's found guilty of a domestic-violence felony."

"Why wouldn't he be?"

"They could find him guilty of a domestic-violence misdemeanor, which would not necessarily require that there be no gun where he lived."

Colleen was starting to shake. Pedone took her by the shoulder and moved her toward a chair.

"Listen, we're a small town. We don't like bad people ruining it for everyone. If he gets convicted of a felony, then his brother has to keep the gun locked up so that Mitchel cannot have access to it. Mitchel's relationship to the gun would then be called constructive possession."

"How can we force his brother to make sure it's in a safe?"

"Another answer that starts with 'unfortunately,' but we can't." Pedone sat down in front of her. "Let's focus on what we can do, OK? I brought you a new toy." Pedone opened the bag and pulled out the box with the Taser and unwrapped the weapon.

"We should probably do this outside." He smiled at her. "Give me a sec. I need to get something else out of the car."

Pedone returned with a torso that looked like a car-crash dummy.

"What is that?" Colleen asked.

"In order to show you the proper way to use this, we need a proper human-type figure."

"Do you always have one of these guys in your car?"

"Not usually." Bob smiled at her. "Let's do it."

Colleen got up and motioned toward the back door. "I don't think anyone will be able to see us if we stay close to the house."

Pedone pulled a chair over to the side of the house, about fifteen feet from where they stood, and set the dummy in the chair.

"If you ever have to use it, it will mostly likely happen when you are least expecting it. The most important thing to remember is to aim at the stomach if he's facing you. Or at the middle of the back if he's facing away from you. That will send impulses to the central nervous system and knock him down." Pedone got behind Colleen and placed the Taser in her hands. He unlocked the safety catch. "Now squeeze." The wire tentacles of the gun flew out so fast she almost fell over with surprise. "Holy smoke!" Colleen was struck by the force and distance the probes flew. "Let's do it again!"

Pedone smiled. "OK. Now let me show you a little finesse. If you are thinking straight during the altercation, turn your wrist and thus the gun slightly to the left or right. This way, you'll have a wider spread of the pins, which will affect a larger part of the body." He took the gun from her and showed her.

He pulled a spare cartridge from his back pocket, reloaded the gun, and then he handed it back to her. "Now you try it."

Colleen followed his instructions to the T. "You're a pretty good shot!" he remarked.

Colleen laughed. "During the summer, I would work at the county fair, at the shooting range. Not *real* guns. The ones where you shoot at moving ducks and try to win a prize."

Pedone found her quite amusing. "I thought you didn't know how to shoot."

"Like I said, not *real* guns." She smiled up at him. "Jackson will be getting home soon, so we should probably put this away." Then she remembered the big trash bags. She grimaced.

"What is it?" Pedone asked.

"Oh, I threw Mitchel's disgusting dirty laundry into trash bags, and I need to get them out of the house before Jackson gets home."

"Why don't you give them to me, and I'll take them over to his brother's."

"Really? I can't let you do that." Colleen was floored at the generous offer.

"Doing my civic duty, ma'am." Pedone nodded.

"Are you sure? I don't want to put you out."

"Positive. Besides, a visit from me may send a message that the police are watching him. Maybe he'll rethink loitering at the end of the street and near the school."

"That would be such a relief. We'd better hurry." Colleen led Pedone down the hall. He picked up all four bags in both hands and headed toward the door. He put them in his trunk just in time, as Jackson was skipping toward the house.

"Hey, Jackson! How are you doing?"

"Hey, Officer Pedone! I'm great! How are you doing?"

"Very well, thank you."

"So whattya doin' here?"

"Just helping your mom fill out some papers." He looked over at Colleen, who was standing on the steps. "Isn't that right, Mrs. Haywood?" He gave her a wink.

"Yes! Just a little paperwork, that's all." Colleen motioned Jackson to go into the house. "Get cleaned up. Maybe even change

63

your clothes. You look like you were rolling around in the grass." She smiled at him. "Did you have a good time with Buddy?"

"The best!" Jackson had a big grin on his face. "He can run faster than I can! But tomorrow, I'm going to win the race around the fence!" He stomped through the door.

"That's the happiest he's been in weeks." Colleen looked relieved. "And you have been such a help to me. I don't know how to thank you."

"Do you bake?" Pedone asked.

"A little. But I'm not Betty Crocker."

"Why don't you bake me some muffins? That'll be thanks enough."

"I'll give it a try."

He gave her a wave and folded himself into the police car.

Colleen watched as he drove away. She had finally noticed him as a man. Not just a police officer. Nice-looking, with dark, curly hair graying at the temples. She figured he was a tad over six feet tall and in excellent shape. She could feel his muscles when he stood behind her and held the gun in her hands. And he made her feel safe. That was something she hadn't felt in a very long time.

CHAPTER EIGHT

Hector was happy to see Buddy with a playmate. The yard was lovely, and the dog had been the only one enjoying it. He felt bad for Ellie. She had to be lonely in that house, all by herself. Sure, she claimed she was fine. But he didn't really believe her. And after two years, he still didn't know why she had asked him to find her a house. Especially one in a remote part of the country.

During one of their many personal exchanges over the Internet, Hector told her he lived in a small town in Missouri over a hundred miles from St. Louis. That's why he was so good at gaming. There wasn't much else to do. He joked that it was like Mayberry. The only difference was they had one sheriff and four police officers. The town had approximately five thousand residents spread over a fifteen-mile area. There was one elementary school in town and a high school in Manchester, the next town over, which also was not heavily populated. The entire county had maybe twenty thousand people. The biggest event was the county fair in July.

He warned Ellie that it was sticky and boring, but she didn't care. She said she needed to find a quiet place. Well, she sure got "quiet," all right. Except for that big hubbub at the Haywoods' house, nothing ever happened in this town.

When she told him she needed his help relocating, he was happy to oblige. Before her request, they had spent many months online playing games, after which they became "cyber-friends." Ellie was a whiz with computers and appreciated Hector's skill and quick mind. She was floored when she found out he wasn't quite sixteen. She was impressed with his aptitude and willingness to learn beyond just playing games.

It didn't take long for them to develop a deeper geek friendship, and within a few months, they had designed a simple game for kids that Ellie was able to sell to a gaming company for a goodly sum.

He scouted around the area for a cottage-type place and came upon the house where she was now living. Years back a carpenter had bought it and made a lot of renovations.

The main floor had two bedrooms, with a connecting bathroom suite. Ellie wasn't concerned about sharing a bathroom with anyone because there wouldn't be anyone. A modern kitchen with a center island opened up to the dining and living area. There was a sliding door on the dining-room wall that led to the screened-in porch. A small laundry room was adjacent to the kitchen, which also had a door leading to the back porch.

The second floor had been a storage loft, but the carpenter had opened up some of the space and made it an open loft that spanned above the first floor, with a railing on one side. It was like a large balcony overlooking the lower level. The carpenter had installed skylights and replaced the windows so that you could see both the yards, front and back.

Ellie had Hector find someone to set up special remote blinds that she could open and close by pushing a button. She divided the upper-level space, placing all of her computer equipment on one end and a small sofa and bookshelves on the other. During the day, Percy would curl up on the sofa, where he could get lots of sunshine coming through the skylights.

From the loft, Ellie had a bird's-eye view

of the block, enabling her to see who was coming and going. That's where she kept several sets of binoculars. The rear of the house backed up against a forest that was protected from future development.

The front yard was enclosed with a four-foot-high, white, Madison-style fence that wrapped around both sides of the house and connected to an eight-foot-high wire fence along the perimeter of the backyard. When Hector worked as a landscaper during the summer, he had access to lots of plants and had made it very homey, as well as animal-friendly. All in all, it was a sweet modern cottage that was perfect for a single woman. Sitting at the end of a cul-de-sac, it was probably the nicest house on the block.

The Haywood house wasn't bad, but it needed some serious updating. It had been built in the 1950s, and very few improvements had been made since. Hector knew that Mitchel Haywood was occasionally unemployed, leaving Colleen to balance the budget on her teacher's salary. Hector also knew that Mitchel was a bit of a drunk, and not the nice kind, like Otis on the *Andy Griffith Show*.

Hector hoped that, someday, Ellie would tell him the real reason she was in Hibbing. All he knew was that at one time she had been in a hospital, and when she got out, she wanted to — or had to — move. He wasn't sure which it was. But he liked her and wanted to help. He was also very protective of her. People in town knew Hector. They also knew he was the "errand boy" for the "shut-in" down the block. Occasionally, people would stop and ask him questions about the mysterious woman, but Hector said she was a nice lady and couldn't leave her house. She could have been in a wheel-chair, for all they knew. But there were no ramps. What there was was lots of speculation.

Every Halloween, there would be several big plastic pumpkins filled with candy for the kids to take. No one ever saw who put it there, but they suspected it might be Hector. And their suspicions would be correct. Under Ellie's direction, Hector would purchase the candy and leave several plastic pumpkins hanging on the front fence.

At Christmas, the front door had a wreath, and lights adorned the front porch. Ellie would bake cookies and cakes and leave them for Hector to take to the church holiday bake sale. For all intents and purposes, Ellie was an active member of the block. Except she never physically came out of her house. Her generosity of spirit was the only thing visible.

Hector's wish was that she would one day invite him into the house and show him all of her cool electronic devices. But for now he had to be satisfied that he was her confidant and assistant.

Hector often rode his bike when he ran errands for Ellie. He had a driver's license, but the family only had two cars, so he had to depend on his legs to get him to and from a lot of places. He was now a senior in high school and had been applying to several high-ranking colleges. He hoped the money he'd earned from the sale of the game would cover most of his expenses. He was making good money running errands for Ellie. He would be happy to do it for free, but she insisted on paying him $200 a week. That enabled him to help with the family bills. He did his own laundry and lots of chores, so his father could get a break on the weekends.

He was not your typical high school kid. Except for the part about him spending time in the basement playing video games. But his parents no longer worried about that. Hector had proved that his hobby could be lucrative. They were very proud of their son.

Hector's grandparents had come to America on one of the last Freedom Flights from Cuba in 1973. His parents were born six years later in Miami and had been raised a few blocks from each other in the area called Little Havana. They had been high school sweethearts and married when Hector's mother turned twenty-one. Hector was born a year later.

When Hector was ten years old, they moved to Hibbing, which was near a manufacturing plant. At first, Hector loved living in a small town, but once he became a teenager, he realized there wasn't a lot for him to do, so he shuttered himself in the basement, where he learned to play video games. When he turned sixteen, he spent his summers mowing lawns and became a part-time employee of a landscaping service. His parents let him spend half of his own money on the games, insisting he save the other half for college. When Hector was in high school, it became clear that the family could not afford to send him and his sister away to college, so Hector decided to look into getting a degree in electronics through an online course of study. At least there would be no room-and-board fees, except what he gave his parents every month from his various jobs. His sister got a scholarship to a state college and worked as a waitress to help pay for her room and board.

The family wasn't poor, but they understood the importance of saving money and not being irresponsible about spending. Besides, Hector actually liked living at home. His mother was an excellent cook, specializing in many originally Cuban recipes, and his father was a great musician, playing guitar and serenading the family on Sunday afternoons. Friends and neighbors would stop by often. Some would bring instruments, and they would have jam sessions on the front porch. If it weren't for the boredom, Hector would have liked it just fine. Miami was too big, and Hibbing was just a little too small, but for now it was home. And he had a friend a few blocks away. Even if he couldn't hang out with her.

CHAPTER NINE

Mitchel Haywood slumped down in his car as the police officer drove past. He guessed that the cop knew he was sitting in the driver's seat, but he didn't want to be too obvious. He couldn't tell if the cop had seen his face. Yeah, the cop could run his plates. But so what if he did? You can't arrest a guy for sitting in his car. Mitchel knew the rules. A hundred yards. He had measured it one night. In all directions. Same thing at the school. He wasn't going to let that wretch ruin his life. And she sure wasn't going to keep him from his kid. No. He'd figure out a plan.

He lit another cigarette and cracked open his thermos of coffee laced with bourbon. He checked his glove compartment to make sure he had the bottle of Listerine handy.

That was how he had gotten out of the past two DUI close calls. The only difference was that both of those times he didn't have an open container in the car. When the flashing lights appeared in his rearview mirror, he had quickly grabbed for the mouthwash and taken a big swig. But he didn't have an opportunity to spit it out so he had to swallow it. Man, did it burn. He had pulled his car over and rolled down the window. "Something wrong, Officer?"

"License, registration, and insurance, please." The cop turned on his flashlight and waited.

"Of course." He slowly reached up and pulled the registration and insurance from the visor clip. "My license is in my wallet. Give me a sec." Mitchel wiggled his scrawny ass and pulled his wallet out of his back pocket. It was a bit of a juggling act, but he didn't want to get out of the car unless the officer instructed him to do so. He fiddled with the wallet and handed his license to the cop.

"I noticed you rolled through that last stop sign." The officer aimed the flashlight toward the back seat, then the front.

"So sorry. My foot must have eased off the brake." Mitchel tried to act composed and sober.

"I see you live a few miles from here. I'll let you go with a warning, but you need to follow the rules." The officer handed back

Mitchel's ID and papers.

"Yes, sir. Thank you, sir." Mitchel proceeded to put the items back into place and waited, hoping the cop would leave before he did. He pulled out his phone and pretended to make a phone call. Since he was parked on the side of the road, he wasn't breaking any laws. At least not for being parked where he was. A few minutes later, the police car moved on. Mitchel gave a big sigh of relief, then smirked. *Dumbass local yokels. Like they got nothin' better to do.*

Now staying with his brother in Manchester, he had better watch himself. Maybe find a bar that was within walking distance of his brother's. He couldn't always depend on Uber or Lyft. Most of those drivers were too drunk to drive. He snickered to himself and took another pull of his bourbon-laced beverage.

It was 8:15 — time for the kid and the old lady to head to school. Technically, the cops could take him in if the kid and his mom walked past his car while he was in it, so he didn't want to take a chance. He tossed his half-burned cigarette out the window, screwed the top back on the thermos, and started the car. He slowly moved away, toward the school and away from the house where they lived. But he knew she knew he was there. Every single day. If he couldn't get near her, he was determined to get under her skin. He needed to think. He needed a plan.

He headed to the bowling alley to kill some time. He wasn't going to bother to find a job. What for? He would figure out a way to grab Jackson and beat it out of town. He'd set them up in a new place. A place where no one could find them. He just had to figure out when and how. As long as his mother was supervising visits, he knew that he wouldn't be able to pull it off. Even though she was his own mother, she would never go along with a scheme like that. She wanted Mitchel to file for joint custody and have them both live with her.

Like hell. She could be a bigger bitch than his soon-to-be ex-wife. Women. He probably hated all of them. The only thing they were good for was sex, and even then there wasn't a whole lot of participation coming from their side. Hookers were the best for him. No-nonsense, and they did whatever you wanted them to do. For a price, of course. But since he had lost his job, he didn't have the cash for the higher end. For now he had to settle for the skanks.

He parked his car in the bowling alley's parking lot and noticed Clay's truck in one

76

of the spots. Clay was the village idiot. Not because he had a low IQ. Although that could be debated. It was because Clay did stupid things like try to swing on a rope tied to a tree, but instead of letting go and jumping in the water, he swung back and slammed into the tree. Or the Tide Pod Challenge. He bet $50 he could eat five of them. He won the bet, but he also ended up in the emergency room. Or trying to see what would happen if he lit firecrackers inside a metal bucket turned upside down. He was hoping for a mini bucket launch, but all he got was a bunch of flying scraps of metal and thirty stitches in his head. Of course, Clay had to see what a battery tasted like, and what would happen if he put a screwdriver in an electric socket. The guy was an idiot. And he would go along with any stupid idea anyone suggested.

Mitchel thought for a minute. Clay just might come in handy at some point. He'd keep it in mind as he was formulating a plan. For the moment, he had to behave until the hearing following his arrest. *Domestic violence. That was bull.* She was a nag. If only she had shut up, he wouldn't have grabbed her. If only she had stayed put, he wouldn't have tried to punch her.

He knew he had to face the judge again at

a hearing. His lawyer told him that if he would plead guilty, he wouldn't have to go to trial and would probably get probation and community service. That could possibly blow any chance of joint custody. He knew he had messed up at the temporary custody hearing, so he had to play it cool. That was going to be a tough one. But he knew that he had to present himself as a model citizen. Otherwise, there was no way out of this. Maybe parking at the end of the block every day wasn't such a good idea after all. He had to think on it.

CHAPTER TEN

Ellie watched Jackson and Buddy running around the yard. It gave her a sense of peace and calm. But she had to remind herself that she needed to be vigilant in her routine. One wrong move could be dangerous. She didn't want to end up in a hospital again. Or the morgue.

She picked up a pair of binoculars and peered down the street. She couldn't help but notice Mitchel's car parked there every morning until just before Jackson and Colleen left for school. At least he didn't try to violate the order of protection and break into the house or sit there long enough for them to come closer than a hundred yards. But his continued presence had been unnerving. The guy was sleazy. She worried for Colleen and Jackson, but was glad she could offer some relief to the little guy. Once again, she thought about inviting Colleen for tea. But she needed a little more time to get comfortable with the idea of having someone else in the house. If she did have her over, where would they sit? She would have to leave the door unlocked and have Colleen let herself in.

Her computer buzzed, signaling another person in techno-despair. This one turned out to be an easy fix. A woman had bought a new computer and could not get her built-in video camera to work. Ellie typed:

Ellie: Run your finger over the top of your monitor. There should be a very tiny button in the middle.

Customer: I don't feel anything.

Ellie: If you can, take a look. It's very small. Like a pinhead.

Customer: Oh yes. I see it now.

Ellie: Gently push down on the pinhead. The camera should pop up from the screen.

Customer: Oh, for heaven's sake. I'm so stupid! I had no idea that's what I had to do!

Ellie: No worries. Unless someone tells you or you read through a PDF file, it's not easy to see or figure out. Is there anything else I can help you with?

Customer: No. I'm fine now. Thanks so much.

Ellie: My pleasure. Enjoy the rest of your day.

Ellie was often amused at the simple

things that appeared so complicated to people. But then again, technology was changing every day. It was even hard for professionals to keep up.

She checked her watch. Almost time to make some dinner.

She heard the buzzer, indicating that Jackson was ready to go home. This time, when she buzzed him out, he looked up at her window and waved. That was a first. She smiled. She could tell that Jackson was starting to ease into the new routine.

Once Jackson was past the front fence, Ellie opened the laundry-room door. There were two doggie doors for Buddy. One went from the laundry room to the porch, the other from the porch to the yard. He came galloping in her direction, practically knocking her over. Meanwhile, Percy was rubbing against her legs. "I think you guys are trying to kill me!" Ellie laughed and snuggled Buddy. She scooped up Percy, and the three of them headed into the kitchen.

"So, what shall I serve for dinner?" She looked at Percy, then peered at the cans. "Do you want the salmon pâté, or do you prefer the shredded tuna?" Percy gave her an "I don't care, just feed me" look.

"Well, then, it shall be salmon tonight." Ellie took the can from the pantry cabinet.

Looking at Buddy, she said, "And you, sir? Chicken or duck?" She patted him on the head. "Did I hear you say 'duck'?" Buddy gave her a soft woof. Ellie laughed out loud. It struck her that she had been laughing and smiling more than usual lately. Maybe she was finally relaxing in her own skin, finally feeling at ease with her surroundings and her cottage on Birchwood Lane. It had been two years. It was about time. But she caught herself again in doubt. *Don't get too comfortable. Things could change in an instant. Like the last time.* She shook off the cloud that was about to surround her and focused on the task at hand. Feeding the three of them.

Ellie opened a bottle of a crisp white wine and poured herself a glass. She fixed Buddy and Percy's plates and turned on the news. More bickering in Washington. What else was new? You would think that, after going through that horrible pandemic, people would just try to be nice to each other. It's easy to be nice when things are going well. Only when people are nice during hard times is it a testament to their character. But times were better now. Weren't we *all* supposed to be better people?

She felt like she was a better person. In some ways, that is. She was more compassionate, for sure. And she was grateful. Grateful that she hadn't been in a major city during the outbreak, especially grateful she wasn't in a hospital at the time. She was also grateful that her mom was OK. She missed her dearly. She hoped she would see her again, but it wouldn't be until she was finished dealing with the trauma. Not until she was safe.

She jumped when the phone rang. She had forgotten again that she had designated that one for Colleen and Jackson.

"Hello?" Ellie said.

"Hi, Ellie. It's Colleen. I remember you said that the phone number was only good for a few days, so I wanted to first say thank you for letting Jackson into the yard. He has been so happy. And tired! He's finally sleeping better." Colleen was almost out of breath.

"I'm so glad to hear it." Ellie waited for Colleen to continue.

"I know there's been a bit more activity on the block lately, and I wanted to explain what happened." Colleen took a big breath.

Ellie had a pretty good idea about what was going on but feigned not knowing anything. She took a gulp of her wine. Aside from her weekly conversations with her mother and Kara, the quick exchanges with

Hector, and the occasional person who insisted on "speaking to a human," talking to Colleen was the only real human-to-human contact she had, even if it was over the phone. The truth was that even her conversations with Kara had been getting mundane. There wasn't much to tell her friend or her mother, if anything at all. She felt that her whereabouts had to remain secret, so there was no talking about Buddy in the yard and Jackson. For the most part, she just listened to the latest news from her mother and the family, and Kara's accounts of her latest dustups with other members of the Junior League. Poor Kara. She was always interjecting her opinion when it wasn't wanted. The frustrating part was that Kara was usually right. Except for one thing. And that one thing was part of the reason that Ellie had ended up where she had and, now, where she was. But she never blamed Kara for it. Ellie had made her own choices.

"Ellie?" Colleen wanted to be sure she was still on the line.

"Oh, yes. Sorry. It was looking like Buddy was going to steal a biscuit off the counter." *Gosh, I'm becoming a stellar liar.*

"I was saying that I am sure you heard and saw the police car the week before last?"

Colleen paused.

Ellie replied with, "Uh-huh."

"It's no secret. Mitchel went booze-o-gonzo on me, and I had to call the police."

"Wow. Are you OK?" Ellie was genuinely concerned.

"For the most part, yes. We still have a ways to go. There's Mitchel's hearing, and perhaps trial, depending on what happens at the hearing, then the custody situation."

"Sounds like a lot to deal with," Ellie answered.

"Yeah."

"What's the next step?" Ellie asked.

"Well, there is a restraining order against Mitchel. He can't come within a hundred yards of me or Jackson except for when he gets to have Jackson for a supervised visitation. Everything is kinda up in the air, but I feel like I'm making some progress." Colleen paused. "I put most of his clothes — his dirty clothes, by the way — into a few garbage bags, and Officer Pedone hauled them away for me."

"What's he going to do with them?"

"I'd like to say 'burn them,' but I don't want Mitchel to have anything negative to say about me. Officer Pedone was going to drop them off at Mitchel's brother's house. That's where he's staying now. His mother wanted him to stay with her, but she can be a real pain in the butt. Anyway, we have several more steps before everything is settled, and it can take a really long time."

"I can only imagine." Ellie had had her own experience with red tape.

"So, if Mitchel pleads not guilty, there will be a trial. If he pleads guilty, they will probably knock the charges down from felony domestic violence to misdemeanor domestic violence."

"There's a difference?" Ellie knew there was. "That was sarcasm, by the way. I cannot believe that they can actually consider any act of violence a misdemeanor. It's infuriating."

"It sure is."

"So what will happen in each case?"

"If he pleads guilty, and they reduce the charge, he'll get probation and community service."

"That hardly seems right." Ellie was starting to steam.

"Yes, indeed. And if he pleads not guilty, he'll go to trial, and the jury will decide." Colleen explained further. "And going to trial could take months. Even a year."

"Jeez. Sounds awful."

"So the present custody arrangement is in effect, as well as the temporary restraining order, until the hearing. That's when we'll know how he pleads and what comes next."

"How are you holding up?" Ellie sipped on her wine.

"Not too bad, really. Our marriage had been in a severe downward spiral for a couple of years. I'm actually relieved."

"Sometimes it takes a monumental eruption to move us forward." Ellie spoke from experience.

"You got that right. Anyhoo, I had a security system installed and bought a Taser."

"A Taser?" Ellie was curious. That was one of the first things she'd purchased when she had left the hospital. One can never be too safe. Or maybe she was just being paranoid. She chuckled to herself.

"Yep. Wow. Those things are impressive. Officer Pedone showed me how to use it." Colleen felt herself blush. "He's been extremely helpful."

"Glad to hear it. Sometimes it can be very frightening when you're faced with so much stress with little or no backup." Ellie spoke from experience.

"And Jackson seems to be doing so much better. I cannot thank you enough for your kindness." Colleen almost started to get weepy. She had been keeping herself in check for Jackson's sake, trying to hold back the tears.

"I'm glad he and Buddy are friends." Ellie paused for a moment. *Was this the right time to invite her?*

"Listen, I've gotta go and put dinner on the table. Jackson is washing up. Oh, and, if you ever need anything, say, an errand to be run, please let me know."

Ellie was slightly stunned. "Why, thank you. I appreciate it."

"I know Hector does a lot for you, but just in case, please know you have backup."

"Thanks, Colleen. I'll certainly keep that in mind. Thanks for calling. Have a good evening."

"You, too."

The two clicked off at the same time.

Lots of thoughts rushed through Ellie's head. Had she found a friend? For the first time in two years, she felt that there was someone she could relate to. Even if it was just over the phone.

CHAPTER ELEVEN

Mitchel had tried to keep his cool the evening Officer Pedone delivered the rest of his clothing. He was very polite to the man, but what he really wanted to do was punch his face in. *Delivery boy.* And who the hell was she to have a cop bring his clothes? "Yes, Officer. Thank you, Officer." Mitchel was seething at his own impersonation of Eddie Haskell. He signed the receipt and grabbed the bags. As soon as the officer was out of sight, he went outside and threw them in the trash.

"Hey, Mitch?" his brother, Gregory, yelled from the basement. "What's up with the cops?" He had seen the police car leave as he looked through the small basement window.

"He was making a delivery. And it wasn't pizza." Mitchel was almost spitting, he was so mad.

Gregory climbed the steps, wiping his

hands on a towel. "What was that all about?"

"The rest of my stuff."

"Like what stuff? All your junk from the garage and basement?"

"Nah. Just my clothes." Mitchel lit up a cigarette.

"Hey, man, you know the rules. No smoking in the house," Greg reminded him.

"Yeah. Whatever." Mitchel stomped out the kitchen door and sat on the back step.

"What's going on, bro?" Gregory was right behind him.

"What's going on? You're kidding, right?" Mitchel threw him a look.

"No. I mean I know there's a lot going on. But what was the visit from the cop all about?"

"I told you. He delivered my clothes." Mitchel flicked the cigarette butt onto the sidewalk.

Gregory went over and picked it up and put it in the metal ashtray. "See, you do it like this," Gregory instructed his brother. He was getting worn-out by Mitchel's attitude, especially since he and his wife, Elaine, were letting him stay there for, well, they didn't know for how long. But it was becoming apparent the arrangement wasn't going to last very long. Even after a few days, Elaine was getting annoyed at Mitchel's sulking, smoking, and drinking.

"Buzz off." Mitchel went back inside and popped open a can of beer. Greg followed him in.

"Listen, I know this is not easy, but you're going to have to take control of your emotions." Gregory had become used to Mitchel's mood swings. He didn't like the idea of having to deal with his brother's emotional state, but at the moment, there wasn't much he could do other than abandon his brother in his time of need.

"Yeah, right. Control my emotions." Mitchel took a swig of his beer and wiped his mouth with his sleeve. He pointed to the can with his other hand. "This, my brother, is how I control my emotions." He chugged the rest of the beer, opened the refrigerator, and grabbed another one.

Greg put his arm on his brother's shoulder. "Maybe you should slow down, eh?"

Mitchel pulled away from Greg violently. "Don't *you* be telling me what to do also!"

Greg could see Mitchel's anger increasing, and he had to defuse the situation before it got out of hand. And especially before Elaine got home. If she saw Mitchel in this frame of mind and on his way to a bender, both men might be out on the street.

"Come on. Let's go watch some baseball. I just finished putting the new console together for the TV downstairs. I wanna see how it looks from the sofa." Gregory opened the basement door and gestured for Mitchel to go down.

When Greg and Elaine had bought the house, it had a finished basement that Greg had converted into a game and TV room. He built a bar on one side and arranged a seating area on the other, with a pool table in the middle. It was supposed to be a playroom for the kids they had planned on. But after several attempts, Elaine had been unable to carry a pregnancy to full term, so they gave up on trying to have a family. Elaine sought solace by working at a children's art center that focused on kids with learning disabilities. Several evenings a week, she would volunteer at the library.

Greg and Elaine had led a relatively quiet life until they opened their home to Mitchel. One of their bedrooms was for guests, another was a den. Elaine was uneasy with Mitchel sleeping in the room next to theirs, so Greg set up an area in the basement where Mitchel could have his privacy and leave them with theirs. He put up a couple of bookcases as a room divider and moved one of the futons over. The only rule was no smoking in the house, a rule that Mitchel seemed to forget every time he lit up.

Mitchel begrudgingly descended the steps to his new temporary home. "How about a round of pool instead?" Before Greg could give him an answer, Mitchel started racking up the balls. He had a cigarette dangling from his mouth. "It ain't lit," he said through clenched teeth. He pulled a cue stick and hit the ball with such force it flew off the table.

"Whoa! Easy there!" Greg walked over to where the ball landed and picked it up. "You sure you want to do this?"

"Screw it." He threw the pool cue on top of the table and headed toward the bar. He pulled out a bottle of scotch and poured himself a large dose.

Greg knew Mitchel had gone beyond the point of reason and decided to leave him alone with his miserable mood. By now, the scotch seemed like a good idea to him as well, so he poured himself two fingers' worth and headed toward the stairs.

"Where you goin'?" Mitchel was being snarky.

"I need to clean up before Elaine gets home. I promised I'd heat up the manicotti. You want any?"

"Nah. I'm fine." Mitchel had his back to

Greg, and he waved his glass in the air.

"OK. There's plenty if you change your mind." Greg knew Mitchel wouldn't change his mind. He'd get totally smashed and pass out on the sofa. That seemed to be the routine since he had come to stay with them. He never once made it over to the futon that Greg had unfolded into a bed.

Greg knew that Elaine was going to be asking how much longer Mitchel would be staying with them. She had argued that he could stay with their mother, who was alone, in a much bigger house. But Elaine also knew that Vivian Haywood could be as impossible to deal with as Mitchel. At least she knew where he got his attitude from.

Gregory and Mitchel's dad had been a farmer. He worked at least twelve hours a day until late one afternoon, when he didn't show up for supper. The boys were only ten and twelve years old at the time. Greg, the older of the two, was sent out to look for him. After an hour spent searching the property, he found his father crushed by a tractor. It appeared he had been trying to fix something when the tractor engaged and ran right over him, then stopped a foot away from his trampled body. It was clear that he was dead.

Smashed like a pumpkin. Greg was never

able to forget that image. It had humbled him for life. Greg often thought about what effect it would have had on Mitchel if their roles had been reversed? Would Mitchel be less aggressive and angry? He would never know the answer. What he did know was that his brother was on the fast track to either jail or a hospital. He was hoping neither would be Mitchel's fate, but one or the other seemed inevitable.

CHAPTER TWELVE

Ellie cringed as she watched her ninety-year-old neighbor, Andy, hobble to his big 1959 Cadillac Coupe DeVille. Unlike Andy, his car was in pristine condition. In fact, Andy had several classic cars that he kept in a storage facility on the outskirts of town. What he planned to do with them was something she could not imagine. She supposed everyone should have a hobby, but a man in such frail condition probably shouldn't be behind the wheel of a car.

Andy was a pleasant old gentleman. As far as she could tell. Each morning, using a cane, he would navigate his way to his automobile. Slowly and carefully, he would back out of the driveway and, Hector had told her, head to Sissy's coffee shop, where he would have breakfast. It was almost embarrassing to her that someone at his age and his state of health had the guts to get out and do something every day, while she was homebound.

An hour or so later, the huge car would return and gingerly inch its way back into the driveway. Andy would get out of the car, open the trunk, and pull out one or two grocery bags. She watched with trepidation as he managed his way back into the house. She prayed every morning that he wouldn't fall. If he did, she would have to call 911. That would make Birchwood Lane quite the hot spot for police activity.

At one time, she suggested to Hector that he should go over and talk to Andy and offer to run errands for him for free. She offered to pay Hector out of her own pocket, just to avoid the anxiety caused by watching him, but Andy politely declined Hector's offer. He said that going shopping gave him something to do. And every morning, watching Andy gave her something to do as well. She wanted to be sure he was safe and not lying on the ground with a carton of milk at his side. What happened after he got into his house was another story. She knew from doing a little surreptitious checking that not only did he not have Internet service; he didn't have cable, either. He had an old antenna on the roof, which she assumed provided whatever he needed for entertainment.

She put down the binoculars and moved toward the "control panel" area of the loft and began to type. Ever since her release from the hospital, she had been on a mission to acquire information — information that could save her from the prison in which she was living.

Before she finished with one of her searches, her computer dinged. It was Hector. He needed some advice on a project he was doing for one of his classes. He had another idea for a game that would be somewhat like the one they had developed together. It was called Catch Me. The premise was for people to pretend they were running from something and for players to find ways to catch them.

Hector's game was all about finding someone who was running from the law or had simply gone missing. A "missing person" type of game for kids. Something like super-sleuthing but without a lot of technology. Good, old-fashioned, gum-shoe detective work. It would be a simple game. Not a lot of special effects. It was more of a puzzle-solving game that required thinking skills instead of the skill of pushing buttons. Granted, games required thought, but quick reaction was how you won.

When she read the premise, it freaked her

out a little. Was Hector trying to dig into her past in reverse? No. Hector wouldn't do that. Though maybe, subconsciously, the idea had come to him because of her mysterious background. In any event, it reminded her of the old episodes of *Columbo* that had recently been running on a cable network. It was the little clues that led the shrewd detective to solve the case. This would be similar, except you had to locate the person by following a set of clues. There was a sprinkle of Choose Your Own Adventure involved as well. The player got to choose which door, street, alley, room, town, or place to explore. If they hit a "dead end," they would have to start all over, but the clues would be different, and the situation would change. Someone could get all the way to where they think they have caught the "runner," but one bad choice would send them back to the beginning, to a new case with new clues.

There were several similar games on the market, but it was a growing genre. If Hector could develop it fast enough, Ellie would pitch it to the clients for whom she did the beta testing.

She typed a message to Hector:

Ellie: Would you personally own it and be able to sell this game, or would the school take ownership?

Hector: Good question. I'll check with my teacher. Thanks for the heads-up. And the help!

Ellie: No prob.

She sat back in her chair. This could help her out a lot. Not the money but the game. She would help Hector make it sophisticated enough that it would attract young people with a high intellect. The kind who watch *Jeopardy* every night. She liked the idea and would discuss it with him at some point. But he had to do the basics before she could get involved.

The rest of the morning ran as usual. Slow. Steady.

She went downstairs to fix some lunch. Buddy was getting antsy. He was getting so used to his playdates with Jackson that it seemed as if he knew what time it was.

"Are you waiting for your friend?" She patted him on the head. "Just a couple more hours." He snuggled against her in response. Percy jumped on the counter, as if to say, "Excuse me, but I'm here, too."

"Oh, you goofball. I love you, too!" Ellie scratched Percy's ears and rubbed his face. "I know. It's time for a treat."

Percy's meow almost sounded like he was saying "treeeeeet."

That always made Ellie laugh out loud. Ellie reached into the pantry and took out some dental treats for her cat. After the incident, Ellie thought getting a cat and a dog would be good therapy for her. She had gone to the local shelter, where she found both of them. They were each around two years old and had grown up in the same house. Unfortunately, the owner could no longer care for them and had surrendered them to the shelter. Ellie couldn't think of separating them, so she adopted both. That's when the veterinarian suggested that Ellie brush Percy's teeth. As if that was ever going to happen.

Ellie fixed herself a roast-beef-and-cheddar sandwich and stood at the kitchen counter. Spring had come a couple of weeks early, and the daffodils, crocus, and tulips were peeking their heads above the ground. She had to admit, Hector was a kid of many talents. Not only was he a computer genius, he was an excellent gardener. Ellie felt that was a good combination for a balanced life.

She knew about his parents and his strict upbringing — strict in an old-fashioned way. Everyone in the family had dinner together every night, and without being tethered to an electronic device. They went to church together every Sunday and celebrated holidays with friends and relatives. And if someone was alone, they would be invited to join.

Ellie had been invited to dozens of dinners and celebrations, and had declined them all, until she felt she needed to explain.

Dear Mrs. Cordoba,
I want to thank you for your many generous offers for dinner. I appreciate the invitations greatly; however, there are circumstances beyond my control that makes leaving my home extremely difficult. I hope you understand, and perhaps one day we shall meet in person, and I will enjoy one of the wonderful dishes Hector has bragged about.
Sincerely,
Ellie Bowman

After she had written the note and given it to Hector, she chuckled to herself. *What if they think I'm under house arrest?* She mulled it over and decided that was much more interesting than the truth.

In the generous and kind manner the Cordoba family always displayed, Hector's mother prepared a special dish and sent it to Ellie via Hector.

"My mother asked that I bring you this."

Hector had smiled with delight. "Lechon asado and papas rellenas. Marinated pork and Cuban potato balls."

"Oh, Hector. That was so kind of her." Ellie's mouth had been watering. Aside from her bland chicken and fish dishes, and occasionally pasta, Ellie wasn't a very good cook. It was ages since she had savored something this good. "It looks and smells delicious."

"Oh, it's one of my favorites! Good thing my mom let me use her car; otherwise, it would be Cuban goulash if I had been on my bike!" Hector joked through the window.

"Please tell her how much I appreciate it. I can't wait to dig in!"

"I will tell her. She is quite proud of her cooking, so I hope you like it. Have a good night."

Buddy nudged Ellie's knee, bringing her thoughts back to the kitchen in which she was standing. She looked at her roast-beef sandwich. "You're no ropa vieja, either."

She washed down a bite with a swig of what was left of her morning coffee. It didn't matter that it had been sitting around for a couple of hours. She didn't mind it at room temperature. It was like iced coffee without the ice.

Buddy watched her in anticipation of a

taste of the sandwich. "OK, you beggar. But this is it." Ellie tore off a small piece of her sandwich and made Buddy give her his paw before she rewarded him. "Good boy." She gave him a smooch on the head. Percy was still sitting on the counter, looking bored to tears.

After finishing the last bite, Ellie washed the dish and coffee mug. "Why do I even bother to use a plate?" she asked out loud. "I don't even sit down." She shook her head at herself.

"OK, guys. Back to work." Ellie headed back upstairs, with Buddy at her feet and Percy meandering at his own speed.

She logged in, letting her client know she was available for customers. Within minutes, one of her computers dinged. It was an e-mail coming in on her other screen.

kkarak@squibmail.com. It was from Kara. This was something out of the ordinary. They rarely exchanged e-mails. Ellie had told her that her work was top secret and that she should only contact her in case it was an emergency.

The e-mail read:

Call me ASAP.

Ellie jumped up and grabbed a new burner

phone package. She tore it open, made sure it was charged, and dialed Kara's number.

"Hello, is that you?" Kara breathed heavily into the phone.

"Yes. What's going on?" Ellie tried to mask the panic in her voice.

"Christian heard from Rick." Kara gasped.

"Oh my God." Ellie sat back down in her chair.

"How? Why? Where is he?" It had been two years since she had heard her ex-boyfriend's name. She was starting to shake.

"Why? Because he needs money, that's why." Kara could barely keep her composure.

"Where is Rick?" Ellie couldn't help but ask.

"Who knows. He asked Christian to send it to a PayPal account."

"How much money does he need?" The hair on the back of Ellie's neck was standing up.

"Five thousand dollars," Kara barked.

"Five thousand dollars?" Ellie was stunned.

"Yep. Five grand. Five smackeroos. Five big ones."

"Is he going to send it?" Ellie asked.

"Not if he plans to stay married to me, he isn't," Kara replied.

"Did he say what he needed it for?"

"Are you kidding? That would be too much to expect from him."

"What did Christian tell him?"

"He said he'd see what he could do."

"Did he give him a phone number to call him back?" Ellie was hoping for a "yes" answer, but didn't really expect one.

"No. He said he was using someone else's phone and that he would call again tomorrow." Kara took a gulp of air. "Can you believe that guy? After all this time? Talk about gall!"

"Was there a phone number on the caller ID?" Another disappointing response followed.

"Only if 'Out of Area' counts. I can't believe that guy!"

"Wow." That was all Ellie could muster at the moment.

"Sorry if I upset you, but I had to tell you. I just couldn't wait until Sunday."

"No. It's fine. I'm glad it wasn't some kind of health emergency."

"Oh, it will be if Christian sends that jerk one penny! I will kick his ass."

Ellie had to laugh at Kara's remark. And she knew Kara was just the type who would do it.

"I will never forgive him for skipping town

106

when you were in the hospital," Kara said.

Ellie had a completely different opinion.

"Well, don't be surprised if Christian tries to send him something." Ellie wondered if she should pursue the conversation further.

"I mean it. I will throw his sorry ass down the stairs," Kara said plainly. "If Rick can't tell us where he is or why he needs the money, you have to think something is rotten in Denmark."

"Yeah, especially if Rick is there." Ellie needed more comic relief from this shocking call.

"Oh, aren't you funny?" Kara hadn't heard Ellie crack a joke in a very long time.

"I'm not really on a secret mission. I'm at a comedian school." Both women broke out laughing.

"You do sound a bit more chipper," Kara noted. "Anything or anyone tickling your fancy?"

"As if," Ellie replied, remembering to keep up the deception. "All a bunch of geeks, dweebs, dorks, and propeller heads." She looked down at Buddy and mouthed, "I don't mean you," and she patted him on the head, hoping he wouldn't bark. That would draw a lot of suspicion, so she thought she had better get off the phone fast. On Sunday, when she normally called her mom and Kara, she would do it from the bedroom closet, keeping Buddy locked in the hallway. Sitting on the floor underneath her clothes created a great sound barrier, just in case the bell rang.

"Listen, I have to go. Keep me posted. Love you." Ellie quickly ended the call. Had she not been shaken by Kara's e-mail, she would have placed the call the way she normally did. Ellie let out a huge sigh of relief. She didn't know how much longer she could keep up the charade with her mother and her friend.

She pulled the SIM card from the phone, cut it in half with a wire cutter, and put the small particles in the garbage disposal. She wondered how many times she could get away with that before the disposal crapped out on her. The SIM card was as small as her thumbnail, so half of that shouldn't screw up the blades too much. She hoped. That thought led her to another: *What if I need something fixed? It's bound to happen.* She tried to keep calm and not have one of her panic attacks.

Maybe it was time to invite Colleen over. Or maybe let Hector in? Her head was spinning. She had to lie down. She didn't want to take another pill.

Ellie jumped when the buzzer rang. She

must have dozed off as she fought the panic attack. She checked her watch. It was 3:30 already. Time for Jackson and Buddy. She gave that kid a lot of credit.

Even if it was raining, Jackson never missed a day.

Ellie thought about her conversations over the past couple of days. Colleen, then Kara. She surely missed girlfriend companionship.

Chapter Thirteen

Andy Robertson had lived on Birchwood Lane for the past twenty-five years. The house he had moved into was the oldest one on the block. When he moved in, there were only three houses on the street. Over the years, he had watched two more houses be built and families come and go. The houses were modest cottages, ranging from twelve hundred to sixteen hundred square feet. Many of the homes were considered "starter homes" for new families or people wanting to invest in their future. He had weathered all the ups and downs of the housing market, happy that his house had long ago been paid for. While the exterior of the house was pristine, inside it needed some work. He felt almost guilty that his five cars were in better condition. Almost. Once a week, he would drive to the other side of town to visit the four-car collection he had in storage there. He wasn't sure why he kept them.

Obviously, he could only drive one at a time. He thought about selling them at an auction, but that would mean he was surrendering to his age. He didn't feel like ninety, except when he had to get out of a chair.

Andy had once owned the only antiques store in the area, and it had a steady clientele. When he turned eighty, his friends convinced him to sell the store. Ten years later, he couldn't remember why he had agreed to do so. At least when he had the store, he got to see the people who came in to shop. Now he had to *go* to see someone, anyone.

Making his way to the kitchen, he navigated between the piles of fabric, newspapers, and magazines that had piled up over the years. Trying to get from one part of the living room to another was like charting a course through a maze. Some of the stacks were so high he couldn't see over them, and he was over six feet tall. The very thought of sorting through so much stuff made him weary. He occasionally worried that if anything happened to him while he was inside, there would be no way out. Not easily.

He ambled into the kitchen, another room in dire need of a dumpster. It wasn't so much that it was garbage — just a lot of unnecessary things. How does one sort through years of *Time* magazine or *Life*? He knew there was nothing on those pages except nostalgia, but he just wasn't ready to part with the shiny pages that chronicled the last twenty-five years of his time on Earth. He was also afraid that looking back would catapult him into the present, a place that he didn't want to depart anytime soon. But he also did not like how the world was unraveling. He yearned for calmer, more peaceful, and cordial times. Times when people actually got out of their pajamas when they went to the store. Times when people greeted each other with "Good morning." Times when everyone stood up for the national anthem. If he thought about it for too long, it would make him weep.

Even though he barely participated in most social gatherings, he enjoyed visiting the neighbors for summer barbecues. He was always invited, and he appreciated the opportunity to mingle with others, something he missed since he had shuttered the antiques store. He had no family, no significant other. Life could be lonely. He often wondered why that young woman at the end of the block was a shut-in. He thought that if he was still in his thirties, he would be painting the town. To him, her situation was incredibly sad. She had no idea what she was missing, and if she lived to be his age, she would most likely have regrets. He recalled a quote often attributed to Mark Twain but in reality Jackson Brown, Jr. said it:

Twenty years from now you will be more disappointed by the things you didn't do than by the ones you did do. So throw off the bowlines! Sail away from the safe harbor. Catch the trade winds in your sails. Explore. Dream. Discover.

He knew it so well from memory. It was on a plaque that had once hung in his antiques shop. He looked around at all the clutter. He knew the plaque was somewhere under one of the piles. He chuckled. "Twenty years? What I wouldn't give to have those years back."

He thought again about the woman down the street. She could use that plaque. He made a decision. He was going to find it. With any luck, it wouldn't take too much time. Now, if he could only remember which stack it might be under. For the first time in ages, he felt he had a purpose besides making it back and forth to Sissy's without sideswiping someone's car.

CHAPTER FOURTEEN

Jackson was adapting well to the new situation at home. He was no longer anxious about what kind of mood his father would be in. Even though he didn't fully understand the word "anxiety," he knew what fear was. His father had never beaten him, but Jackson was not sure when the day would come that he would. His mom also seemed to be more relaxed. He was happy to see her smile. She was even singing when she was baking cookies. His mom had a nice voice. She used to sing at the church, but his father had made her stop. He wanted his bacon and eggs on Sunday morning when he got up, which was more like lunchtime.

After his big breakfast, his father would go down in the basement and fiddle with something. Jackson never really knew what he was fiddling with because he never came upstairs with anything to show for the time he spent down there. And if Jackson asked, his father would say, "Son, it's man stuff." Once Jackson pressed the issue, and his father exploded. "Don't you ever question me, boy. You understand that?" Jackson never asked his dad a question again. He tried to remember when things were better, but it made his brain hurt to think so hard. He used his birthday parties as a point of reference. The last one was OK, but his father hadn't shown up until most of the cake was gone, and everyone had left. His father got really mad at his mom for not saving him a piece. She tried to reason with him. "Mitchel, there is plenty left. Have some."

"I ain't eating no leftovers," he bellowed.

"They're not leftovers. We just cut it less than an hour ago," Colleen said calmly.

"Well, you shoulda waited for me." He took a fork and dug into the last piece on the serving platter, then threw the fork in the sink. "Next time, show me some respect." Then he stormed down the steps to his private sanctuary in the basement.

Jackson counted on his fingers how long ago that was. His next birthday was soon, so maybe it was a year. He wasn't sure, but he kinda thought he might be right. He then thought about Christmas. Christmas came halfway between his birthdays. That much he knew.

He recalled going with his mom and dad to get a tree. His mom had picked out a super pretty one, but his father didn't like it. "They dry out too soon." Finally, they let Mitchel pick what he liked. It wasn't much different than the first one, but it was better than listening to them complain to each other in the car. His mom sat quietly during the drive home.

Once they got back to the house, Mitchel turned to Jackson, and said, "Well, son, you want to see how a real man puts up a tree?"

Jackson watched as his father cut the lower branches and trimmed the trunk. He placed the base on the trunk and tightened the screws. He reached over to the top end of the tree and pulled it up so it was vertical. But it was crooked, so his father kicked the tree over and stomped down the basement stairs. Jackson immediately began to cry.

He remembered his mother running into the living room. "What happened, honey?"

"Daddy got mad at the tree and kicked it." He was hiccuping at this point.

His mother rocked him in her arms. "It's going to be OK." He had heard the same words since his birthday. "Come on. Let's have some hot chocolate; then we'll see if we can fix the tree." When he got up the next morning, he was happy to see that the tree was standing upright in the corner.

Jackson was going to have his first visit with his father the next day. He was extremely nervous. He kept reminding himself of what his mother said about none of this being his fault. But how come he still felt that way? He knew his mother would never lie to him, but still, his dad hadn't been the same since his last birthday. It had to be his fault, even if it was only a little bit. Was it because they didn't wait for him to light the candles? Sure looked that way.

Jackson deliberated about what he should wear because he didn't know what the plan was for the day. He knew Grammy Haywood would pick him up, but he didn't know what they would be doing. Going bowling? Playing ball? Taking in a movie? Should he bring his bat and glove? No one told him anything, which was making him nervous.

He walked down the hallway into the kitchen, where his mom was making cookies for the school bake sale. "Hey, Mom?"

"Yes, honey."

"Do you know what I'm going to be doing tomorrow?"

"You'll be spending the day with your

father. But you know that."

"Yeah. But what will we be doing all day? I don't know if I should wear my good pants, school clothes, or my jeans."

Colleen realized she hadn't been told any of the details.

"Let me call your grandmother and ask her." She dreaded speaking to the woman.

When she phoned, an abrupt "Yes?" came through the phone line.

"Hello, Vivian. Jackson would like to know what the plan is for tomorrow."

"Mitchel said he wanted to take him to see some new space movie, but I don't remember the name. Why? Is there a problem?"

"No. No problem. As I said, Jackson was wondering, that's all." Jackson could see that his mother was not happy talking to his Grammy. He knew Grammy could be cranky, like his father, sometimes.

"Well, as far as I know, it's lunch and a movie. Unless you have any objections," Vivian replied.

"That's fine. As long as the movie is suitable for Jackson's age. But please don't take him to any fast-food places."

"We'll take him to wherever we want. It's our time with him, not yours!"

"Gotcha. Eleven o'clock?"

Jackson watched as his mother rolled her eyes. He started to giggle. Then his mother gave the phone a funny look. He guessed Grammy had hung up because his mother didn't have a chance to say goodbye.

"Looks like it's going to be a movie," his mom declared. "Some space thing."

"Yippee!" He was excited to know that there was going to be at least one thing he would enjoy that day. He knew it was going to be weird going to the movies with his father and grandmother. He couldn't remember if any of his friends went to the movies with grandparents. Yep, it was going to be weird all right.

The next morning, Jackson was up at the crack of dawn. He was both excited and anxious at the same time. He wished he could go over to Ms. Bowman's house and run with Buddy before his grandmother picked him up, but then he would have to change his clothes, and he didn't want to upset his mother. He could tell she was in one of her "worry moods." Jackson came up with that term whenever his father didn't come home for dinner and his mother didn't know where he was. Once, when his father was absent from the dinner table, he blurted out, "Mom? Are you in a worry mood?"

"A what?" she asked.

"A worry mood. You know, when you worry." Jackson thought he was making perfect sense. She smiled at her astute son then, so he decided to ask her again now.

"Mom?"

"Yes, honey."

"Are you in a worry mood?"

She wiped her hands on a paper towel. "To be honest, I am a little worried."

"What about?"

"Oh, that you'll have a good day with your father. And Grammy."

"We're going to the movies!" Jackson said it as if there was no doubt they would have a good day.

"Yes, you are. And you're going to have some lunch, too."

"Will Dad bring me home?"

"Not this time. Grammy will drop your father off somewhere, then she'll bring you here."

"How come Daddy won't bring me home?" Jackson still didn't know why his father wasn't around.

"Remember the big argument when the police came?"

"Yes." Jackson was getting uneasy. He had

tried to keep the memories of that evening at bay.

"Well, there are a few things that need to get fixed and figured out. I don't want you to be in a 'worry mood,' OK?" She gave him a hug, and he giggled because she had used his word.

"OK!"

CHAPTER FIFTEEN

Mitchel decided to clean himself up for his big day with his son. Besides, he didn't want any flak from his mother and wanted to make a good impression on his son. For a fleeting moment, he was feeling a little guilty about the morning when he had yelled at Jackson from the porch. If Colleen hadn't dragged him away, maybe things would have turned out differently. He tried to move his thoughts to a better place, but he was stuck. He was stuck in a state of loathing. He couldn't think of anything that was OK in his life, except for his son, and even he had been taken away from him. Mitchel gripped the sides of the sink and looked in the mirror. He needed a shave, for sure, but there wasn't anything he could do about the bags under his eyes. He knew he had Visine eye drops in the glove compartment of his car. They were almost a daily routine. It would help with the bloodshot eyes but not the bags under them. He splashed cold water on his face, combed his hair, and took out the shaving cream and razor.

Ten minutes later, he took another good, long look. It was an improvement. He pulled the freshly ironed shirt from the hanger.

Elaine had been kind enough to wash and press a shirt for him. Little did he know she had ulterior motives — to get him the hell out, and if helping him clean up his act would facilitate his moving out, she would iron all of his shirts, pants, and underwear. Well, maybe not the underwear, but surely his socks. Maybe not those either, but desperate times called for desperate measures. If she could write him a check to get out, she would. It had been only two weeks, but she was at her wits' end. The drinking was out of control. He had practically wiped out Greg's entire bar stock. He hadn't once cleaned the bathroom in the basement and always left a pile of dirty clothes on the futon. Since he wasn't using it as a bed, he was using it as a laundry hamper. And it was going to stay that way. Ironing a shirt for when he was going to see his son was one thing. Being his personal maid was something entirely different. Elaine wondered how Colleen had been able to put up with him for as long as she had.

Mitchel climbed the steps, looking like a different person. He was showered and clean-shaven, and his hair was combed. He had on a clean pair of jeans and the shirt Elaine had ironed. His shoes needed a little work, but Elaine wasn't going to mention it. "You look very nice, Mitchel," she offered.

"Thanks to you." Mitchel could turn on the charm when necessary. But it seemed as if he didn't think it had been necessary for a while. "And thanks for putting up with me." Now he was pouring it on thick. He knew he had been teetering on the edge of getting thrown out on his ass, and he surely didn't want to go live with his mother. Spending the entire day with her was bad enough. At least he would have Jackson with him.

"What are your plans for today?" Elaine asked, as if she cared.

"We're going to grab some lunch, then go to a movie. Maybe stop at the bowling alley if we have time."

"Sounds good." Elaine poured herself another cup of coffee.

"What time is your mother coming over?" She hoped it was soon and that she would

125

only stay long enough to pick him up.

"In about fifteen minutes. She's picking up Jackson at eleven."

"Will she stay for coffee? I can put on a fresh pot." Elaine held her breath, waiting for an answer.

"Nah. We'll want to get moving."

Elaine sighed in relief. Her mother-in-law could be one nasty old hag.

"After your visit, what do you think you'll be doing?" Elaine was praying he would say "looking for an apartment," but she knew that miracles rarely happened.

"If we go bowling, Ma will drop me off, then take Jackson home."

"You're coming here right after?"

"Not sure. Playing it by ear." Mitchel reached for a cigarette and winked. "Going out back."

As Elaine watched Mitchel exit the kitchen door, she thought how sad it was. He was, or at least had been, a nice-looking man. Tall, thin, sandy-brown hair, green eyes, and a big smile. He had had an excellent job at an auto-repair shop and was considered their best mechanic. That was until he started arriving late and not showing up a few times. Then, when he got arrested, Otto, the owner, couldn't deal with him anymore. His life was in shambles at age thirty-six.

Such a waste.

Elaine remembered when he had met Colleen. She was a sophomore at the state college and was home for the summer. She was working the arcade at the county fair when Mitchel first approached her. They started dating, and the rest, well, the rest had turned into a calamity. Mitchel's mother didn't like Colleen from the get-go. She thought Colleen was a bit uppity, being a college student and all. In turn, Colleen's mother didn't much like Mitchel. She thought Colleen "could do better." Mrs. Griffin was right. Colleen could have and should have done better. Her mother-in-law, on the other hand, should have been kissing Colleen's feet. Mitchel might have been good-looking and charming, but there was something about him that had never sat right with Elaine. And her instincts had turned out to be spot-on. Mitchel had become a train wreck, and the rest of the family was having to clean up the mess. Mitchel certainly wasn't going to lift a finger to help himself.

The doorbell rang, and Elaine called out the back to Mitchel. "Vivian is here." She refused to refer to her mother-in-law as mom, mother, or any other type of endearment.

Mitchel came in and walked to the front door. "Hello, Mother." He gave her a peck on the cheek.

She nodded hello. "Mitchel. Elaine. You look well, dear."

Vivian secretly blamed Elaine for not giving her more grandchildren, but Elaine had a fairly good idea about how Vivian felt. She would admonish Elaine for working while she was pregnant. "You should be at home, where you belong." Did Vivian really think Elaine was being irresponsible? Elaine wanted to wring her neck at the time. She *could* claim hormonal imbalance.

"Thank you, Vivian. As do you. Enjoy your day with Jackson." Elaine turned and went back into the kitchen. She looked out the window, and, sure enough, there were two cigarette butts on the patio. The ashtray was only a few feet away. *You'd think he'd have the sense or courtesy to use it.*

Mitchel sprinted to the car. "Jackson, my boy! Come give your daddy a hug!" He reached for the handle of the car door and swung it open.

Jackson unbuckled his seat belt and jumped out of the car into his father's arms. He smelled good. His face was smooth, and his breath was clean, too. This was the daddy he remembered. This was the daddy he wanted.

Fortunately, Jackson was tall enough and old enough to ride without a booster seat, but he had to be buckled into the back seat.

"Dad? Can you ride in the back with me, please? Grammy? Can he? Please?"

Vivian couldn't say no to the child, but she resented being a chauffeur. "Very well."

"So, son, tell me what's been happening with you?"

"Uh, like lots of stuff. I have a new friend. His name is Buddy."

"Buddy?"

"Yeah. Buddy the dog. He lives down the street. Remember?"

"Sure. I remember Buddy the dog. I thought you were talking about another kid in school."

"Nah. I have gobs of friends at school. Buddy is my friend for after school."

"You mean the crazy lady lets you play with Buddy?"

Vivian looked in the rearview mirror. "Crazy lady? What crazy lady? Colleen lets him play with a crazy lady?" Vivian was sounding a bit crazy herself.

"No, Grammy. She's not a crazy lady. She's very nice."

"She never leaves the house," Mitchel interjected.

"That's because she has a sickness," Jackson informed them.

"What kind of sickness?" Vivian was peering into the mirror again.

"I dunno. Mom just said she wasn't well. So I figured she was sick."

Vivian couldn't stop herself. "Mitchel, you need to put an end to this right away. I don't want my grandson hanging around someone who is sick or crazy."

"Easy, Mother. She seems harmless. I doubt Colleen would let Jackson go over there if it wasn't safe, right, pal?" Mitchel patted Jackson on the knee.

"Right, Grammy! She's really nice. For real. She leaves candy inside pumpkins for us at Halloween and bakes cookies for things."

"Well, if she doesn't leave the house, who does all her shopping for her?" Vivian was being a pill and throwing a wet blanket on the day.

"Hector. He's kinda her assistant, I guess," Jackson replied.

"Mother, can we please change the subject?"

"Fine. So what do you want to talk about then?"

"Baseball!" Jackson yelled.

Vivian shrugged her shoulders. "Fine. You

boys talk about whatever you like. I'm just the chaperone here."

Mitchel gave Jackson a nudge with his elbow. "So you think the Cardinals can pull off another World Series?"

"Maybe. They've won eleven so far, but nothing since 2011." Jackson was proud of his knowledge of baseball.

"Maybe the Kansas City Royals will be the big winners this year," Mitchel suggested.

"Nah. They had a good season in 2015, but nothing good since." Jackson was a whiz at stats.

"Very impressive, son. You sure know your baseball." Mitchel had started tossing a ball with Jackson as soon as he could stand up. After Jackson grew out of T-ball, Mitchel had tried coaching one year, but he got into too many arguments with other parents and was asked to resign. That was when things started to sour in Mitchel's life. Had Mitchel's forced retirement from coaching influenced his drinking? Or was it the other way around?

No matter. He was with his kid that day, and would be permanently if he had anything to say about it.

"I thought we'd grab a couple of burgers before the movie. Whaddya say, sport?"

"Sure thing, Dad!" Benny's Barbecue and Burger Grill was a bit of a drive from Hibbing, but it was near the movie theater. They continued to talk baseball while Vivian drove them to the restaurant.

After about thirty minutes, they pulled into the roadhouse restaurant, and Mitchel unhooked Jackson's seat belt. Both jumped from the car and headed toward the door.

"Excuse me! Do you mind if I join you?" Vivian screeched at them.

Jackson stopped in his tracks, turned around, and ran toward his grandmother. "Sure, Grammy! Come on!" He grabbed her hand and pulled her toward the door.

They looked over the menu, and Mitchel was about to motion for the waitress when he realized he had made a big mistake in choosing that restaurant.

"Hey, Mitchel. Long time no see. How ya been?" The name tag said LUCINDA. She was wearing a bright yellow uniform with pockets in the front.

Vivian shot him a look.

"Hey, Lucinda. Yeah. Been busy. How ya doing?" Mitchel was trying to be cordial. He had forgotten that Lucinda worked the day shift on Saturdays. It had been months since he had seen her last. And done much more than see her. He thought their fling had ended OK, both of them being married and all. She seemed to have taken it well, but there was an edge to her voice. Or was that the way she normally spoke? He wondered. He really couldn't remember much except for some extramarital shenanigans in the parking lot after several rounds of anything over eighty proof.

"This here your boy?" She pointed her pencil in Jackson's direction, cracking her gum.

"Yes. This is Jackson. Jackson, this is Lucinda." Mitchel was starting to squirm as the rise in Vivian's blood pressure was starting to show on her temples. "And this is my mother, Vivian."

"Well, nice to meet cha all. Jackson. Vivian." She smiled at both of them, revealing a few gaps between her front and back teeth.

"What can I get you folks?" Another crack of gum. Mitchel wondered if it ever got stuck in the spaces.

Jackson ordered a burger from the kids' menu. His father ordered one from the adult side and a draft beer. Vivian gave him a dirty look.

"Don't start," Mitchel growled. "I'm only having one."

"It's barely past noon," Vivian growled back.

"Please, Mother. Can we just enjoy our lunch?"

"Fine." That was Vivian's most commonly used response to most things, especially those of which she disapproved.

Lucinda stood there while mother and son bickered.

Jackson was starting to get antsy. "Dad? Can I get a milkshake?"

"Sure. Whatever you want. This is *our* day today. Right, Mother?" He gave her a stare that could kill a snake.

"And you, Miss Vivian? What would you like?"

"I'll have a BLT, mayonnaise on the side, and a Coke." She paused. "Please."

"Comin' right up!" Lucinda stuck the pencil back behind her ear and wiggled her way to the kitchen.

Mitchel gave his mother another look as if to say, "Don't ask."

Jackson was oblivious to the veiled exchange between the adults. He was enjoying being in a new place, having a burger with his dad.

Lucinda returned with their drinks. "Food will be coming out in a jiffy." Another wiggle back to the kitchen.

Vivian could not hide her horror, imagining her son carousing with such a loose woman. Colleen was looking good in comparison. So what if she thought Colleen was an educated snob? At least she had all of her teeth and a respectable job. The thought of her baby boy playing rumpy-pumpy with that trailer trash made her lose her appetite.

The gum-smacking waitress returned, carrying a big tray above her shoulder and setting it down on the table next to where they were sitting.

"Your BLT, Vivian, burger for Jackson, and a burger for Mitchel, well done, if I remember correctly."

Vivian was about to vomit. Mitchel wasn't too far behind. He finished off his beer as if he were in a guzzling contest.

Jackson slathered his fries with ketchup, not having a clue.

After they finished, Lucinda cleared the plates. "Can I get you anything else?" She put her hand on Mitchel's shoulder.

He was horrified. Vivian thought she might faint. Jackson innocently asked, "Ice cream? Please, Dad?"

"Not right now, son. We have to get to the movie theater. We'll have ice cream later. Check, please?" Mitchel really meant, *"Please! Now! Not a minute longer!"*

Lucinda slapped the check on the table. "Y'all come back here real soon!" Then the final wiggle back to the kitchen.

Mitchel pulled out his wallet and threw two $20 bills on the table. The check was only $26, but he didn't want to wait for change. "Let's go." He moved as fast as he could.

Jackson skipped to the car, while Vivian waddled her way to the driver's side door. She couldn't get over what she had just experienced. She slammed the door shut and shot Mitchel another stink-eye look in the rearview mirror. So far, the day had been awful.

The ride to the movie theater took ten long minutes. It seemed like an eternity for both Mitchel and Vivian. Fortunately, Jackson was oblivious and was getting excited about seeing the movie.

"I think I'll skip the movie and go to the outlet shops." Vivian thought she was going to jump out of her skin. She knew they would be violating the "supervised" part of the visitation, but she didn't think a movie with just the two of them would do any harm. Besides, she had to get away from Mitchel for a bit.

"Good idea, Mother," Mitchel said with relief. He opened his wallet and handed her several twenties. "Buy yourself something nice."

"I don't need your money to buy myself anything. Besides, you need to hang on to your cash. You don't have a job, remember?" She was seething.

Mitchel held his breath and didn't respond. Besides wanting to scream at her, he wanted to strangle her as well.

"Come on, Jackson. Let's go watch the movie." He helped Jackson with his seat belt, and they both got out of the car.

"Movie runs for almost two hours. See you at three."

Vivian didn't answer.

"See ya later, Grammy!" Jackson waved, but his grandmother pulled away without returning his wave.

Mitchel walked up to the ticket window and handed the cashier one of the twenties his mother had refused. Mitchel leaned down, looked straight into Jackson's eyes, and said, "We won't tell anyone that Grammy went shopping. OK, sport?"

"OK, Dad!" He gave him a thumbs-up.

Anticipating Jackson's next request, Mitchel intervened. "No popcorn. You just had a big lunch, and we're getting ice cream later. I don't want you to get sick. Then your mother will be really mad at me, and we don't want that, do we?" He sounded reasonable for a change.

"OK, Dad, but I might have to have two scoops. With sprinkles!"

Mitchel chuckled for the first time in a while. His son was having a good time. Mitchel couldn't remember the last time the two of them had had a day together. They went into the theater, and Mitchel let Jackson pick out their seats. Of course, it was all the way down in front, but Mitchel didn't mind this time.

Vivian was furious. She didn't care about the outlet stores. She just had to get away from the situation. Everything was unraveling. If Mitchel was cheating on Colleen with that, that woman, Lord knows what else or who else he was up to. And the drinking. She pulled over to the side of the road and burst into tears. Not since her husband had died had she felt like her calm and well-controlled life was slipping out of her grasp.

She must have been sitting there for several minutes because a patrol car pulled up behind her. "Oh Lord, now what?"

The officer walked up to her window. "You all right, ma'am?"

"Oh, yes, thank you. I just got a little weepy thinking about my late husband and thought it best to pull over." Vivian could be a good liar when necessary. Well, it was partly true.

"You OK to drive? Do you want me to call anyone for you?" the patrolman asked.

"No, I'm fine. Really. I have to pick up my son and grandson at the theater in an hour. I might do a little shopping before I go. Retail therapy I think is what they call it." She smiled at the officer.

He smiled back. "Sorry for your loss, ma'am. Try to enjoy the rest of the day."

Vivian started her engine and headed toward the outlet shops. She failed to mention that her husband had been dead for twenty-six years.

Vivian stopped at the Cheesecake Factory and bought some cookies and cupcakes. She didn't know why, but it seemed like a good idea. Then she spotted a shop that sold scarves and gloves and went inside. She picked a pink floral print and wrapped it around her neck. It brightened her face. The price tag said $35. She looked around for something less expensive and found one for $18. Glancing around the shop, she noticed that the two clerks were engaged in conversation. The price tags were secured with a simple gold safety pin, so she switched the price tags, taking the one she wanted to the cash register. If they spotted the incorrect price, she could fake it. How was she to know the tags were on the wrong items? Neither clerk noticed, and she handed them cash and walked out the door. Not only did the scarf brighten her face, it brightened her mood. She had given up on the Lord twenty-six years ago, and after what she had witnessed at the restaurant, she decided it was no more Mrs. Goody Two-Shoes for her.

She checked the clock on the bank building outside the shop and decided it was time to skedaddle and head back to the movie theater.

As she pulled into the parking lot, she saw Mitchel and Jackson waiting in front of the ice-cream shop. She parked the car and walked briskly toward them.

"Grammy! A new scarf?" Jackson yelled out. He had never seen his grandmother wearing anything that pretty before.

"Yes, Jackson. I thought I should treat myself." She shot Mitchel a look.

"It's lovely, Mother, but I wish you would have let me treat you," Mitchel broke in.

"You need to hang on to your cash, son. I am perfectly capable of treating myself." That much was true. Between Gregory Sr.'s life insurance policy and his Social Security, she was financially stable. The house had been paid for before her husband died, and the property taxes were minimal, owing to a special farm rate. Her only monthly expenses were utilities, food, and gas for the car. She had offered Mitchel his old bedroom, but he had chosen to stay with his brother, saying it was closer to Jackson. That, too, was true. Still, she felt that Mitchel would have a better chance at gaining joint custody if he had a more permanent environment. She wondered what Mitchel was going to do about that. She knew he couldn't afford an apartment without a job. She also knew that she was particularly hard on her sons, but with her new attitude, maybe Mitchel would change his mind.

They went into the ice-cream shop, and Jackson ordered a scoop of cherry vanilla and a scoop of chocolate. "With lots of sprinkles, please," Jackson said politely to the young girl dressed in the pink-striped jumper and funny hat that looked like an ice-cream cone turned upside down.

"Absolutely!" She smiled at him.

Mitchel and Vivian both ordered a scoop of coffee ice cream sans sprinkles.

"So, my man, we still have a couple of hours. How about we go bowling?" He looked at Vivian for approval after he addressed Jackson.

Vivian sat back and folded her arms across her chest. She reminded herself that *that* Vivian was the old version. Then she relaxed and smiled.

"That's if Grammy doesn't mind driving us around a little more." He looked over at his mother. She was smiling. He was surprised.

"Oh, I don't see why not. We *do* have lots of time. As long I don't have to participate. You know how much I hate renting bowling shoes!" She chuckled. Mitchel did a double take. *Who is this woman?*

Jackson laughed out loud. "Grammy, you're funny!"

Vivian fiddled with her new scarf. "I'm simply happy to be with two of my favorite men. Of course, Gregory is a favorite, too, but he's not here today."

Jackson was taking the final lick from his cone as the others got up from the table. "Finish up before we get in the car, please." Mitchel was giving Jackson a warning.

"No problem, Dad." Jackson began crunching on the sugar cone. A minute later, he showed that his hands were empty. "See?"

Vivian chimed in. "I see you should probably go wash your hands." *She's still smiling. How odd,* Mitchel thought.

142

The restroom was only a few feet away from the table, so Mitchel let Jackson go in by himself. While Jackson was in the bathroom, Mitchel leaned over to his mother. "Everything OK?"

"Of course, Mitchel. Why do you ask?"

"You seem, well, I guess the word is 'relaxed.'" Mitchel chose his words carefully.

"I am, dear."

Mitchel blinked. *Dear?* She hadn't called him that since he was in the fifth grade.

"Well, good. I'm glad to hear it." Mitchel let out a big exhale. He hadn't realized that he was holding his breath.

"Listen. I really appreciate you babysitting both of us today."

Mitchel was as sincere as he could be. He knew that little encounter with Lucinda had put his mother over the top. But in the past few hours, her entire demeanor had changed. *Maybe it's a magical scarf.* He snickered to himself.

"It's OK, son. I know you're going through a rough patch. Remember, my house is always open to you and Jackson. At some point, you might have him for an entire weekend. It would be nice if he had his own room. You don't want to impose any further on your brother, now, do you?"

Mitchel could hardly believe this was his mother talking in such a kind and compassionate manner. He was going to savor it even if it was only temporary.

Jackson returned to the table and showed both of them how clean his hands were.

"Good job, my man. C'mon, let's get rolling," Mitchel said.

The three left the shop and got back in the car. "Are you sure you don't want to bowl with us, Mother?" Now Mitchel was teasing her.

"What? And use stinky shoes that were on someone else's dirty feet. No, thank you." She looked into the rearview mirror and grinned at both of them. "I'll be just fine watching the two of you." She turned on the radio and put the volume on low. She found a classic rock station and sang along with Neil Diamond's "Sweet Caroline."

Jackson nudged his father, and whispered, "I didn't know Grammy could sing so good."

"She used to be in the church choir but quit after your grandfather died," Mitchel explained.

"Hey, Gram! You sound really good!" Jackson yelled over the seat.

Vivian turned the volume down. "Sorry, boys. I was reminiscing about my youth.

Bap-bap-baa," she continued to sing along.

Mitchel often forgot that his mother had once been a young woman. He was only ten when his father died, so he didn't have a lot to go on. Ever since that terrible day, his mother had been morose and dour. But since dropping them off at the movie theater, she was a different person. He decided that whatever it was, he was glad. It was as if a heavy cloud had been lifted. At least one of them.

Jackson joined in the singing. "Bap-bap-baa!"

Mitchel felt his shoulders relax for the first time that day. He realized he hadn't had a cigarette since he left the house that morning. Maybe things were turning around for him.

The ride to the bowling alley took about twenty minutes, with Vivian singing along to all the songs she recognized. By the time they arrived, the three of them were in a fine mood.

Jackson grabbed her hand. "You sure you don't wanna put on some stinky shoes?" He giggled. She laughed. Mitchel was in a state of disbelief.

The rest of the afternoon went smoothly. No ex-flings, no more beer. Mitchel was on his best behavior. At least for the moment.

They bowled a few games, then headed for home.

When they finally reached Gregory's house, Jackson was a bit teary-eyed. This was the dad he wanted. This was the dad he needed. As they got out of the car, he wrapped his arms around his father's waist. "I miss you." Then he burst into tears.

Elaine heard Jackson crying and flew out the front door. "What's going on?" she demanded.

Vivian took the reins. "We had a lovely day. I think Jackson is upset that he has to leave his dad now."

"He'll be all right, won't you, Jackson?" Mitchel spoke softly to his son.

Jackson sniffled and wiped his nose on his sleeve. Vivian dug into her purse and retrieved a tissue. "Here you go."

She motioned for her and Elaine to go inside to give the boys some private time.

Elaine was a bit apprehensive, but Vivian nodded, indicating it was OK to leave them alone for a few minutes.

When they got in the house, Elaine couldn't help but ask, "So how did it go?"

"Very well. They had burgers, went to a movie, had ice cream, and then we went bowling."

"How was the movie?" Elaine asked innocently.

Vivian caught herself just in time before revealing she had gone shopping. "Oh, I . . . I dozed off. Those kinds of pictures don't interest me."

"Dozed off? With all that noise?" Elaine was half-serious.

"I guess I was tired from the drive," Vivian said, keeping up the ruse.

"New scarf?" Elaine couldn't help but notice that Vivian was wearing something cheery.

"Oh, yes, I bought it at one of the outlet shops." Vivian realized she was about to give her secret away and continued, "I got it a few weeks ago but didn't have an occasion to wear it. I thought today would be a good one." She was getting rather good at thinking on her feet. *Must be the scarf,* she thought to herself, and smiled.

"What?" Elaine asked with a puzzled look on her face.

"What? What?" Vivian repeated.

"You had a funny smile on your face." Elaine had noticed the change in Vivian as well.

"Must be the scarf," Vivian finally said out loud.

Jackson and Mitchel sat on the front step

while Jackson regrouped. "I'm sss . . . sorry, Dad."

"For what?"

"Crying like a baby." Jackson sniffed.

"It's OK. To tell you the truth, I wanna cry myself." Mitchel put his arm around Jackson. "But we'll get together again next weekend. You can decide what you want to do, OK?"

"Sure. Does Gram have to come with us?"

"Yes, for the time being. But we'll have fun. Maybe she'll even sing to us again." Mitchel ruffled Jackson's hair. "C'mon. We gotta get you home."

Mitchel opened the front door. "Mother, I think it's time to get Jackson back home." He put his hand on Jackson's shoulder. "Right, kiddo?"

"Right-o, Dad." Jackson gave his father another hug. "Bye, Aunt Elaine! Bye, Daddy!" He held back the tears until they got into the car. He was in the back seat, sniffling.

Vivian turned to him. "Honey, I know this is hard now, but it will get better. We just need to figure out a few things."

"That's what my mom said." Another sniffle. "I hope it doesn't take too long." He sighed and settled into the seat.

Fifteen minutes later, Vivian pulled into

Colleen's driveway and walked Jackson to the front door. "Now you be a good boy this week, and we'll have some fun next Saturday." She leaned over and gave him a hug. He hugged her back with all the strength he could muster.

"Thanks, Gram. I had a really nice day."

CHAPTER SIXTEEN

Ellie watched from her perch. Jackson's grandmother was dropping him off from a day with his father. Ellie wondered how it had gone. She looked at the clock. It was almost 7:00. She doubted that Jackson would come over at this late hour. Buddy had been pacing the floor all day. "He'll visit you tomorrow," Ellie kept reassuring her dog. He would look up at her with those big eyes, as if to say, "But I wanna play now!" He must have gone in and out a dozen times, looking for Jackson. Ellie thought it was sweet. She also thought about calling Colleen to see how she was doing, but she figured Jackson probably had a lot to tell his mother.

Ellie walked over to the console and sat down. She pulled up an Internet search engine and typed in the name *Rick Barnes.* There had to be hundreds of them. She then tried *Richard J. Barnes.* Still dozens, including Richard J. Barnes Sr., Rick's father. She knew he would be no help.

She hoped she could figure out where he was. Not that she wanted to see him. If anything, the opposite was true. If anything, it was for her sanity.

She tried several other iterations of his name and came up short. When she glanced at the clock in the lower corner of her monitor, she realized that she had just spent the last two hours trying to locate her former boyfriend. *Hasn't he already used up enough of my time?* she asked herself.

She stretched and spun around on her drafting stool. Percy was lying on the sofa. "Are you bored, sir?" she asked her cat. He yawned and stretched in response. *Animals are really smart.*

Ellie went downstairs to get ready for the rest of the evening. She was off duty that night. Oftentimes, she would be asked to take a late shift since many of her clients offered twenty-four-hour online help. But she had already put in almost sixty hours that week and was computer-weary, especially after wasting so much time looking for Rick.

She put the kettle on and went into her room to change into a different set of clothes. This time it was her pajamas. That was one of the advantages of being a shut-

151

in. No one knew what you wore each day. If she wanted, she could wear the same clothes, including her pajamas, twenty-four/seven, but she wasn't the type. In fact, she would put on a little makeup and blow-dry her hair after her morning shower. She didn't know why she fussed even a little, but it reminded her of a semblance of normalcy. She hadn't quite resigned herself to being like this forever. She *hoped* it wasn't forever, but it was what it was for now.

Two years had been an exceedingly long time. The idea that she was entertaining the thought of inviting someone in was almost like passing a milestone, but it was still only an idea. She hadn't made it happen yet. As her therapist would remind her, "Baby steps."

The teakettle was whistling in the kitchen, and Percy was on the counter, expecting a snack. Ellie poured some water over two chamomile tea bags and let it steep. In the meantime, she opened the pantry and grabbed two dental treats for her cat.

"Here you go, Mr. Bossy Pants." Buddy's tail was pounding out a rhythm on the floor. "Oh, I suppose you want one, too?" His tail thumped harder. Ellie reached into the cookie jar and took out a Bully Stick dog bone. "Don't eat it all at once," she told him. "Sit," she instructed. He obeyed. "Paw." He held up a paw. "Now the other one." He looked at her. "Please." Then he lifted it. *Yep, animals are very smart.*

Once the tea was ready, she grabbed a book she had started and headed to the bedroom. She fluffed up the pillows and pulled down the comforter. That was another thing she did every day. Make the bed. In essence, she appeared to be a normal person, doing normal, everyday things. That was because if she allowed herself to go down a rabbit hole, she might never return. Routine was a good stabilizer.

Buddy jumped up and made himself at home at the foot of the bed. Percy strolled in and perched himself on the chaise lounge in the corner of the room. Ellie turned on her reading light and flipped to where she had left off in the book, but she found it hard to concentrate. Ever since her phone call with Kara, she hadn't been able to stop thinking about Rick and their relationship before the episode, the very thing that had blocked her memory. She was told it would come back to her, but after two years, she still strained to remember. There was a gap in her memory from when it, whatever it was, had happened to when she woke up in the hospital. She couldn't remember any details except that when she woke up, there was an IV drip in her arm and her mother and Kara were sitting in her room.

She flipped through a few more pages and decided it was futile, so she put the book down, turned off the light, and tried to sleep. It was 3:00 A.M., and she was still tossing and turning.

Buddy was snoring, and Percy had moved from the chaise to the pillow next to Ellie's face. He peeked at her. "I could have been working and getting paid. Darn!" she said to him.

He gave her a look that said, "And I could have been sleeping."

She laughed at the idea that she was having conversations with her animals.

At first, she thought talking to Buddy and Percy was just another "symptom," but she'd read that talking to your pets is a sign of intelligence. The same with inanimate objects. When Ellie had read that, she thought she must be a genius. If she bumped into a chair, she would say, "Excuse me." The article had been published by a zoological anthropology professor, so she felt that she had permission to converse. *And they laughed at Dr. Doolittle.*

CHAPTER SEVENTEEN

After Mitchel's mom dropped him off at the end of his outing with Jackson, he went into the kitchen to grab a beer. Greg was sitting at the table, reading a golf magazine.

"How did it go?" Greg asked.

Mitchel popped the top and placed the beer on the counter. He leaned back and crossed his arms across his chest, something his mother often did — that is, up until today. "It was really great." Mitchel uncrossed his arms. "Well, except for running into an old friend." He used air quotes around "old friend."

"Oh?" Greg opened the refrigerator and pulled out a beer for himself. "Let's go outside. You can tell me all about it."

Greg opened the door for Mitchel to walk outside, figuring Mitchel would want to light up a cigarette. He was surprised when he handed the ashtray to Mitchel and Mitchel refused. At first, Greg thought it would turn out to be an argument and was stunned at Mitchel's response.

"Nah. But thanks." Mitchel pulled out one of the patio chairs from the table and took a seat. Greg did the same.

"So?" Greg clinked beer cans with his brother. "Spill."

"OK. So you know a while back I was kinda misbehaving myself."

Greg interrupted. "Which 'while' are you referring to?" Greg knew that Mitchel had not been on his best behavior for over a year.

"Hah. Funny guy." Mitch took a pull of his beer. "In Clarkston. Benny's Barbecue and Burger Grill." He raised his eyebrows.

"Oh, yes. Benny's Grill. I recall a young lady waitress worked there?"

"You got two things wrong. She ain't young, and she ain't no lady." Mitchel guffawed.

"Well, you seemed to think so at the time, if I recall." Greg was egging him on in a brotherly way.

"Aw, c'mon. I never said anything about her being a lady. Far from it, my brother." The two guys burst out laughing.

"Touché." Greg tapped Mitchel's beer can again with his.

"So what happened?"

"OK. So, you know Ma, she was in her

usual mood."

"Let's not overstate the obvious. Get to the good part." Greg sat back in the chair, waiting for the juicy bits.

"Yea. So we get to Benny's, and I had totally forgotten about Lucinda until she appeared at our table. I should say flew to our table on her broomstick."

"How could you forget she worked there?"

"It's been a year, and I had forgotten that she works the Saturday day shift. She always said she was a night owl and liked getting off at eleven. She'd say, 'That's when all the fun begins.' " Mitchel reached in his pocket for a cigarette but thought better of it. He had only smoked one the entire day. Maybe he was on his way to stopping. "Anyway, she comes sauntering over to our table, cracking her gum. She leans into the table and puts her face so close to mine I almost had a heart attack. I thought she was going to smack her lips all over me. So, she starts, 'Helloooo, Mitchel, long time no see.' You should have seen Ma bristle. I mean, Lucinda could not have been more obvious. I think she even brushed her breast against my shoulder, but I was frozen in place."

"Oh, man, Ma must have been having a cow!"

"Several." Mitchel laughed. "And then

Lucinda keeps wiggling her ass every time she walks away."

"Oh, you managed to catch that, did you?" Greg asked.

"Stevie Wonder would have been able to catch that!" Mitchel almost spit out his beer at his own joke.

"Holy smoke. So what did Ma say?"

"Not a whole lot. She didn't have to. The looks she was giving me and Lucinda could have stopped a freight train," Mitchel answered. "I couldn't wait to get out of there. Then, when I asked for the check, she draped her arm over my shoulder. Man, I thought I was going to have a heart attack. I had no idea what Lucinda might do or say next. It was really bad."

"And did you get away unscathed?" Gregory pressed.

"Thankfully. But Ma was in such a mood that she refused to go to the movie and wanted to go to the outlet shops."

"So you skipped the movie?"

"No. Hey, don't tell Elaine, or anyone. But Jackson and I went to the movies alone."

"Wow. You were taking a big chance, brother."

"Yeah. But I wasn't thinking straight, and you know how Ma can be. She was *not* going to that movie. I could tell she wanted to get as far away from me as possible. But then the strangest thing happened. When she came back to pick us up, she was in a great mood. It was like she was a totally different person. Somebody I had never seen before. Not just from her mood this morning, but a different person altogether."

"Retail therapy can do that for a woman." Greg finished off his beer and got up to get another. He turned to Mitchel. "You want one?"

"Nah. I'm good. Thanks."

"Speaking of a different person, are you all right?"

"Yeah. Why?" Mitchel asked.

"Because I don't remember you ever turning down a beer, and you haven't had a cigarette. Don't get me wrong. I think it's great. Hold that last thought. I'll be right back."

Greg went into the house to get himself another beer. Elaine was in the kitchen. "What's going on?" she asked casually.

"Mitch is telling me about his day and how Ma was like a different person by the time" — he stopped short of revealing how Mitchel had violated the visitation rules — "they were on their way back."

"Funny you should say that. I thought she

159

was in a very un-Vivian mood when she dropped him off. She was smiling and genuinely nice. What's up with that?" Elaine asked. "Not that I mind. But if we can figure out what put her in a good mood, maybe we can buy a hundred of whatever it was." Elaine chuckled.

"I'm about to find out. What are you up to?" Greg asked.

"Working on a proposal for some funding for the school."

"You are the best." Greg gave her a kiss on the cheek. "I'll fill you in later."

Greg went back outside to hear the rest of this most interesting story about his mother. Greg and Mitch only referred to her as "Ma" when they were alone together. She had made it abundantly clear that she was to be called "Mother." Period.

"Continue, please."

"Yeah, so she gets back, wearing this pink, flowery scarf. Something I had never seen on her before. I mean it wasn't just that particular scarf, but you know how she dresses. Anything dark, boring, dowdy." Mitchel finished what was left of his beer. "Then, get this, she turns on the radio and starts singing along to 'Sweet Caroline.' "

"Are you sure that was our mother? Is it possible that some alien from Mars or somewhere took over her body or something?" Greg leaned in closer.

"Right? Crazy. But anyway, we had ice cream, then went bowling. I'm kinda pooped, to tell you the truth."

"So all went well with Jackson?"

"Yeah, man. The movie was awesome. I mean, like the special effects. Then, when we were having ice cream, she was still in a great mood. I was waiting for her mood to change, but it never did. It was so bizarre. She even joked about bowling shoes." Mitchel was shaking his head. "Jackson was getting such a kick out of her. He even sang in the car. 'Bap-bap-baa.' It was a great day, for sure."

Greg gave his brother a high five. "Way to go! So, what's next?"

"We do it again next Saturday." Mitchel crushed his beer can in his hand. "I told Jackson he could decide what it will be. Let's just hope it's something Ma will want to do."

"By the sound of it, she may be fine. Elaine just told me the same thing. Ma was in a good mood and unusually nice when she brought you home."

"I guess miracles can happen." Mitchel gave his brother a pat on the shoulder and went back inside. "You mind if I make a sandwich? I'm getting a little hungry."

"Help yourself," Greg called from the yard. Then thought. *Odd. Mitchel's never asked if he could do anything before.*

Mitchel fixed himself a cheese sandwich and poured himself a large glass of water. It felt wonderful to feel good.

Mitchel woke up the next morning without his usual hangover. He had even slept on the futon instead of the sofa. He rubbed his chin, feeling for morning whiskers. Not too bad. *Must have given myself a really good shave yesterday.*

Then he thought about the outing yesterday with Jackson and his mother. It had started out a bit rocky, but ended up being a great day. He still could not get over the change in his mother's behavior, but he wasn't going to question it. He was going to pray that, whatever the reason for the change, it was permanent.

CHAPTER EIGHTEEN

Ellie bolted upright and started gasping for breath. The nightmares had returned. Her pajamas were soaked in sweat. She was shivering. Buddy jumped up and started to woof softly. He nudged her arm. "It's OK, pal. Mommy's OK." She hugged him close to her neck. He kept nudging her, begging for reassurance. She wasn't sure who needed it more, Buddy or her. Even Percy was disturbed by Ellie's sudden jerk. As aloof as he appeared, Percy was a big mush and would pace and meow if he felt anything was amiss. "It's OK, guys." She rocked back and forth, clutching her dog. "It's OK, it's OK, it's OK." She tried the deep-breathing exercise her therapist Zach Meyers had taught her. That was helping a bit. She didn't panic. That was a step in the right direction, in spite of the nightmare. When the nightmares began after the episode in New York, she would wake up screaming.

Now she could stop the horror as soon as she woke up. Baby steps. Progress.

She checked the clock on her nightstand. It was five in the morning. She got up, went into the bathroom, and ran a hot shower. Maybe she could get in a little more sleep once she washed off the terror.

By the time she had finished the shower and dried her hair, it was almost 6:00. She debated whether she should try to get a little more shut-eye or check her client list for the day.

Buddy gave her a woof, indicating he was ready to do his morning duty. "OK, pal, let's go." She shuffled into the kitchen and disarmed the alarm system, unlocked the interior laundry-room door, and let Buddy go through the doggie doors to do his business.

Percy was already on the counter waiting for his food when she heard Buddy barking. It was a bark indicating he knew who it was. But who could it be at this hour? Hector usually didn't get there until 7:00. She looked out in the yard and saw it was Jackson, standing outside the front fence. *What is he doing here so early? Does his mother know?*

She went to the security console and pressed the intercom. She hoped he could hear her from the speaker next to the door. He was about twenty feet away.

"Jackson?" she called, and saw him jump. He wasn't expecting to hear her voice this early either. "Is everything all right?"

"Oh, hi, Miss Bowman. Yeah, everything is fine. I'm sorry if I disturbed you. I didn't know what time Buddy came out in the morning. I just wanted to pat him on the head."

"That's quite all right, Jackson. I'll buzz you in."

"That's OK, Miss Bowman. My mom might be worried if she can't see me."

"She knows you're out this early?" Ellie was wondering if Colleen was aware that Jackson was out of the house.

"Yeah. I told her I wanted to see if Buddy was up. I missed seeing him yesterday."

"Well, he missed you, too. Do you want me to call your mom and see if it's OK for you to come into the yard?"

"That would be swell," Jackson replied.

"OK. You hang on a minute." Ellie took the steps two at a time and retrieved the phone she had designated for Colleen.

A startled Colleen answered. "Hello?"

"Hi, Colleen. Sorry for calling so early, but Jackson is here, and I wanted to know if it was all right to let him into the yard."

"I hope he didn't disturb you," Colleen said.

"Not at all. I was up already."

"Well, if you don't mind, that would be super. Jackson had a good day with his father, but then he had a bad night and woke up with nightmares."

"I can relate to that," Ellie said casually. She felt at ease speaking to this woman. "I'll buzz him in. You can call me when you want me to send him home." Ellie remembered telling Colleen about the time frame of the phone number.

"Is that same number good?" Colleen asked.

"Yes, for another day." Ellie had to come up with some other plan for communication with Colleen. Changing phones every five days for Colleen and Jackson seemed a bit extreme. Not that "extreme" wasn't a part of her norm.

"Thanks very much. You can send him home anytime. Talk to you later."

"OK." Ellie signed off. She would actually like to talk to Colleen later.

Ellie spoke to Jackson again over the intercom. "Go to the side gate, and I'll let you in. Your mom said it was OK. She'll call me if she needs you to come home."

Jackson gave the thumbs-up to the speaker

and shrugged. He had no idea if she could see him or not. But she could. He was a bit too young to be scoping the area for surveillance cameras. He trotted to the driveway, where a small Mini Cooper sat. No one had ever seen anyone drive it. He wondered if it even worked. But Ellie had Hector start the engine once a week just to keep it running. She didn't know if she would ever need it to run, and if *she* had to run, could she?

Ellie buzzed Jackson into the yard and began tossing the ball to Buddy. She watched from inside the kitchen. She and Jackson had a lot in common. They both suffered from nightmares, and both of them didn't mind spending hours with a dog.

Ellie spent the rest of the morning working with a few customers when she realized it was getting close to noon. She looked out the window again. Jackson was sound asleep on the swinging bench in the garden, and Buddy was lying under it. It was a sweet scene. Ellie wondered if she should disturb them when her phone rang. The only person it could be was Colleen.

"Hey," Ellie answered.

"Hey," Colleen replied. "I hope Jackson hasn't been a pest. He's been there for hours."

"He's fine. In fact, he's curled up on the

bench, taking a nap. Buddy is lying under it, keeping guard." Ellie chuckled.

"Oh, good. I was worried he was overstaying his welcome."

"Not at all. Do you want me to send him home for lunch?" Ellie wished she could offer the kid a sandwich, but she knew she couldn't.

"Good idea. Besides, he shouldn't be sleeping in your yard." Colleen stifled a laugh.

Then Ellie realized that Jackson wasn't within earshot of the back-porch intercom or the one at the gate. "I just thought of something." Ellie hesitated. "He won't be able to hear me from the bench. It's set back in a garden area."

"I can come and get him," Colleen said, as if everything about the situation was normal.

"Great. You can come through the front gate and walk around to the back." She didn't tell Colleen that opening the front gate sent a chime signal to the security panel.

"What about Buddy?" Colleen asked. "Will he be all right with me sneaking up on them?"

Ellie thought about it. Maybe it was better if Colleen came to the side gate. That's where Hector and Jackson entered and exited. Ellie had no experience with anyone walking through the front gate and walking around the yard. Better not take any chances. "I have a better idea. Come around to the side gate and ring the bell. I'll buzz you in."

"Thanks. I'll be over in a couple of minutes." Colleen was excited to have so much interaction with the mysterious woman at the end of the block. Besides, she was curious about the landscaping. If it was as nice as the front, it might be pretty special.

Ellie heard the bell from the gate and buzzed Colleen in. She spoke into the intercom. "Just push the button when you're ready to leave. Jackson knows the drill."

Colleen gave the thumbs-up to anyone who might be watching.

Must run in the family. Ellie laughed to herself.

When Birchwood Lane and the surrounding area was first being developed, the local council decided to make sure it didn't become a suburban cluster of cookie-cutter homes with little room in between. Each house had to be on an acre, allowing families to plant vegetable gardens and have room to raise children. It was a quiet neighborhood, with large trees lining the street. When Hector had sent Ellie the photos of the cottage, she knew it would be perfect for her needs at the time, and for as long as necessary. The rear of the property had some trees, but Hector assured her that he would make it as private and as serene as possible.

As Colleen entered through the gate, she was in awe of the backyard. It was a half-acre of beautifully manicured shrubs, dogwoods, silver maples, an eastern redbud, and a magnolia that was on the verge of blooming. Toward the back of the property was a garden of azalea bushes and peonies, with a small fountain. A swing bench with a canopy was on one side of the fountain, and two Adirondack chairs were on the other. No wonder Jackson loved to come by every day. It was an oasis compared to their scraggly yard with the rusty swing set. Colleen couldn't help but wonder why Ellie wouldn't want to spend time in such a lovely place. Hector had certainly done a marvelous job. Buddy had already raised his head when he heard the buzzer at the gate. He wagged his tail, but remained on guard. Colleen was slowly approaching the swing when Jackson sat up, rubbing his eyes. "Mom. What are you doing here?" Buddy got up and greeted Colleen with one of his soft woofs.

"I came to get you for lunch." Colleen looked around.

"I can see why you like to come here. It's beautiful. And peaceful." She sat down on the bench next to Jackson. "How are you doing, kiddo?"

"I'm good." He stretched his arms over his head. "I guess I conked out." He rubbed his eyes.

"You certainly did." She put her arm around him and rocked the swing. Jackson put his head on her shoulder. "You ready for some lunch? You hardly had any breakfast."

"Yes! I'm starved!" Jackson was surely ready for something to eat. "Tuna fish?"

"Coming right up. Let's go." Colleen took him by the hand, and Buddy followed them to the gate.

"Thanks, Buddy." Jackson patted him on the head and pushed the buzzer for Ellie to release the gate. "Thanks, Ms. Bowman," Jackson said to the air around him.

"You're welcome." Ellie's voice came from the speaker next to the gate.

"See you tomorrow." Ellie realized the irony in what she had just said. Or was it a dichotomy? She could see them, but they couldn't see her. She had almost forgotten the dynamics. Seeing Jackson sleeping so peacefully with Buddy had helped to ease her mind after the nightmare that had wakened her that morning. She finally made up her mind. She would invite Colleen over. But first, she had to invite Hector into her house. That would only be right. After all, he was the reason she was there. She owed him that much. That is, assuming he cared. She thought about it again. Of course he cared.

Lunch had sounded like a good idea, so she went to the refrigerator and peeked inside. Time to make a shopping list. She took out a few eggs, some milk, cheddar cheese, bacon, and butter. There was a package of crescent dinner rolls in the refrigerator door. She checked the expiration date. There were still a few days left.

Sunday brunch sounded like a good idea. She looked for a split of champagne in the wine refrigerator and some pear nectar. Perfect. She'd make herself a Bellini.

That was something she missed — Sunday brunch with Kara. They would go to a restaurant, have a leisurely brunch, then go to an art exhibit. In the summer months, they would go to the park and listen to live music, usually a jazz combo or an ethnic band from the Caribbean. Once, there was an accordion player with a real monkey. The accordion player wasn't all that great, but the monkey provided plenty of entertainment. He was a feisty little thing, trying to look up the ladies' dresses. They wondered who the bigger pervert was, the player or the monkey. Someone must have taught that monkey his tricks. One of his favorites was picking a man's wallet out of his pocket. But the player would never let the monkey keep the wallet, although once it was returned to its rightful owner, most owners felt compelled to give the monkey a reward. Seemed odd and contradictory, getting a reward for returning something that you had stolen. But it was all in good fun. Those were happier days, for sure. Maybe one day she would have happy days again. Baby steps.

She took her Bellini and one of the burner phones into her walk-in closet and made her weekly calls to her mother and Kara. Mom was first.

"Hey, Mom! How are you?" Ellie was feeling pretty chipper.

"Hey, sweetie. I'm doing fine. How's my super-spy daughter doing?"

"Mom, I'm not a spy." Ellie laughed.

"Well, with all the secrecy, you'd think you

were working for the CIA."

Ellie was quiet for a moment.

"Honey?"

"Yes, Mom, you'd think that, wouldn't you?" It occurred to her that a CIA gig wouldn't be such a bad cover. She'd use that if things ever got out of hand.

"So, when is this secret mission of yours going to be over? We miss you."

"I miss you, too. I wish I had enough information to give you, but I honestly don't know. Once I'm finished here, they're going to send me somewhere else." She was running out of countries in her head.

"Well, I hope they're not sending you to some ungodly places with terrorists and all."

"Now, Mom, we discussed this before. I am not in any physical danger," she lied.

"I should hope not. But I've heard some of these government contract jobs are in remote areas of the world. In uncivilized areas."

Ellie moved a few pair of shoes to get more comfortable. This was going to be a long make-Mom-feel-OK conversation.

"I can assure you I am not in an uncivilized area." She picked up one of her sneakers, gave it a disgusted look, and tossed it aside. "It is remote, but not in a bad way."

"Can you explain further, or would that

be a breach of your contract?" her mother prodded.

"I'm not in Antarctica. That much I can tell you." At least that much was true.

"That's reassuring." Her mother laughed quietly. "Do you have any idea how much longer this is going to be?" Ellie's mother asked the same question week after week, hoping Ellie's answer would change.

"Maybe a couple more months," Ellie lied. She had no idea how long it would be, but that was better than telling her mother it was yet to be determined. It would also make her mother relax if she thought it would be over soon.

"So what else is happening?" Ellie took a sip of her brunch beverage. "Any local gossip?" She wondered if her mother knew that Rick had been in touch with Christian.

"The library is putting the summer reading programs together. They want to have more than one a week, but I told them it's not worth the effort. Kids want to play outside, go swimming, camp, and all that."

"You're probably right, Mom."

"And Kara agrees with me. She got into it the other day with Mrs. Wilson."

"Uptight Willie?" Ellie remembered the sourpuss from the local library. It was people like her who gave librarians a bad rap. And most librarians were a lot hipper and cooler than people gave them credit for. Ellie had dealt with many of them before the incident and found them to be fun and often wild. *Who knew?*

"Yes. Apparently, she doesn't think fresh air is important."

"Well, one could argue she suffers from a lack of oxygen."

"More like too much hot air!" Both laughed.

"Anything else to report?" Ellie didn't want to mention Rick.

"Nothing else, dear."

"OK, Mom. I'll give you a buzz next week. You take care of yourself. Love you!"

"And you take care of yourself, too, honey. Love you, too."

They ended the call. Ellie took another sip and dialed Kara's number. She was anxious to hear if there was any more news about Rick. She cared, but not in the way an ex-girlfriend would care. This was different.

"Hey, girl!" Kara's bright voice said over the phone.

"How did you know it was me?"

"That weird area code. I know it's one of those disposable phones, my friend."

"Correct. But it's not as if I haven't been

using one for the past two years."

"True, but you asked!" Kara giggled.

"What's the latest?" Ellie held her breath. "Any more news from Mr. Wonderful?"

"Yeah. He called last night. Christian asked him what he needed the money for. He said it was a project he was working on and he needed funding for it."

"What kind of project?"

"Well, that's just it. He told Christian it was some kind of proprietary thing and he had to sign a nondisclosure agreement."

Ellie was dubious. "Interesting. What did Christian tell him?"

"Like I told you the other day. If he gives him one penny, I will send him to the moon without a rocket ship."

"You gave up on the idea of kicking his ass down the stairs?" Ellie teased.

"Whichever one provides the better opportunity!" They burst into laughter.

"I really miss you, Kara."

"Miss you, too, my friend. Anyway, Christian told him that he really needed more information before he could float it past me."

"Christian ain't no dummy!" Ellie smiled.

"Seriously. I think Christian wasn't buying his story. Since when was Rick an entrepreneur?"

"Beats me. He was able to go a long way with his good looks and charm." Ellie remembered what it was like when she had first met him.

"And let's not forget that bankroll he blew."

"Boy, was his father pissed. I guess when they set up that trust, there were few or no stipulations. A hundred grand when he turned twenty-five. And another when he turned thirty."

"Yeah. That's just crazy. Imagine what most people could do with that kind of money?"

"I hear ya. I guess his father thought he would invest the first chunk and have backup for further investments. I suppose it made sense at the time, considering his father was a very successful real-estate investor. He probably thought good business sense ran in the family," Ellie observed.

"When you met him he was what, thirty?"

"Yes. He had just gotten the second pile of cash. Remember, he wooed me by taking me to the Bahamas for a romantic weekend?" Ellie thought back to the time when she had dated Rick.

"He surely won you over with the gifts, dinners, trips."

"It wasn't about the stuff. It was about his

damn charm. And his wit and intellect. He was a smooth operator, that's for sure."

"You know I've always felt a little guilty introducing you to him and pushing for you to date him," Kara confessed for the zillionth time.

"Well, don't. I made my own choices. It was fun and romantic. How could one resist?" Ellie sighed.

"True. But when his father cut him off after he spent all the money, he was no longer so charming," Kara noted.

"No kidding. Boy, did he turn into a total ass." Ellie remembered that much.

"And then leaving town while you were in the hospital? That was the worst." Kara opened the wound again.

"Good thing I don't remember much, or I'd really be pissed," Ellie said soberly.

"Let's change the subject. We don't need to be wasting our time talking about that jerk."

"I don't suppose he mentioned where he was?" Ellie had to ask.

"Nope. Just that it was all 'under wraps.' He's as mysterious as you are, girl. But I know *you're* not lying."

Little did she know, Ellie thought.

"So, I hear Willie Wilson is giving you guys a hard time about the summer library

179

program?" Ellie changed the subject, but she couldn't erase from her mind her concern about Rick and his whereabouts.

"I wanted to offer summer reading at camps, but Willie said she did not want to be responsible for bringing books to places with dirt," Kara said.

"If she only knew what kids did when they got their library books home." Ellie laughed, remembering using them to sit on when there was nothing else between her butt and the ground.

They both cackled at that remark. Kara added, "I offered to pay for any damages out of my own pocket, but she said that was against the rules. Something about violating government funding."

"That's ridiculous. You mean to tell me that people can't make donations?" Ellie asked.

"You just gave me an idea. I am going to buy a dozen books and donate them with the stipulation they be used for summer-camp reading programs. That ought to put her panties in a wad."

They were hysterical at this point. "That's a sight I'd rather skip," Ellie said.

"You mean the look on her face?"

"No, the tighty whities!" Ellie was snorting with laughter, and Kara echoed her glee.

"Whew. That was funny," Kara added. "It's so good to hear you laugh."

"It *feels* good to laugh." Ellie had to admit to herself that it really did feel good.

"OK, girlfriend. I'd better get going. I don't want to burn up all my minutes," Ellie said. "Next week?"

"Same bat time? Same bat channel?" Kara snickered.

"You got it! Take care of yourself and keep laughing. Love you, my friend."

"Love you, too," Ellie said, and disconnected the call.

She couldn't stop thinking about Rick. The money. His location. *Where can he be? And what is he doing? Why does he need $5,000?*

Ellie got up and took the sneakers with her. She opened the bedroom door, where Buddy had been waiting for almost an hour. He knew the routine, but he didn't like it. Buddy would get anxious if he didn't have access to her. "Hey, pal. All done. My mom is good, so is Kara." He looked at her as if he knew exactly what she was saying. He woofed in approval. He nudged her leg. "What?" She patted him on the head. She knew he could feel her anxiety, too. Why did she have to bring him up? She knew the answer to that question. She wanted to know where he was. She *needed* to know where he was.

She took out a garbage bag and tossed her sneakers in it. She was horrified that she still had those old things. Why hadn't she thrown them out already? Then it dawned on her. They were the sneakers she was wearing the night she was taken to the hospital. At least, that's what they put in the bag with her personal belongings when she was discharged. They were her size and looked familiar when the nurse handed the bag to her. But the situation that put her there was still submerged somewhere in her subconscious. Perhaps she thought the shoes would help her remember. On the other hand, maybe it was better if she couldn't.

She rinsed her glass and put it in the dishwasher. Percy was in his usual spot on the counter, expecting something. "You are too much!" Ellie laughed and gave him a treat. She knew that if she gave him a treat every time he got up on the counter, he would never stop. But it was too late. She had done it over a hundred times. Plus, Percy liked to be close to her eye level instead of always being on the floor. The floor was good for getting oneself from one part of the house to the other, but when it came to sitting, Percy wanted to be able to look you in the eye. He was quite a character.

Ellie headed up to the loft and promised herself she would not do any cyber-sleuthing about Rick. But as soon as she sat down, she logged into her access point to the dark web. You could find anything there if you knew how to navigate and access the sites. People in the tech world referred to it as going for a deep dive when someone wanted to get the nitty-gritty details on someone. That's how so many hackers succeeded. They went through the back door, so to speak. No system was foolproof or hack proof. She should know that. Very often, she tested systems for possible security breaches.

Ellie usually avoided going to certain sites for her own purposes, but occasionally she would have to do it for a client. It was often part of the testing process. While she didn't have access to bank records, getting public records was a snap. Most people would go to one of those "people info" websites and have to spend money to get background checks, often turning up nothing.

Ellie could get all the details with one or two clicks.

She started with the area where she had

last seen Rick. At least, where she remembered seeing him last. In an instant, a sharp, searing pain passed through her head. She began to get dizzy.

She stumbled over to the sofa and lay down. This was the second time it had happened in just a few days. Both times, it had happened when she tried to find Rick. Maybe she should take it as a big hint from the universe — leave it alone. But she could not. She decided to rest a bit until the buzzing in her head subsided. The migraines had been frequent when she was in the hospital and had continued for a few months afterward. Since moving to Hibbing, the migraines were few and far between. She tried to recall the last one she had had. Except for the other day, she realized that it had been almost a year. Hibbing had been good for her in a very unconventional way.

CHAPTER NINETEEN

Rick Barnes had led a charmed life for a long time. He had good looks, charisma, and a wad of money, money he didn't mind spending on whatever he wanted. But, at the moment, he was broke and a thousand miles from home. He hated the idea of calling one of his old buddies and asking for money, but he certainly couldn't ask his old man. His father had, for all intents and purposes, disowned him. Rick knew he was a fool to have blown through all that dough, $200,000, but he couldn't help it. The parties, the cocaine, the women. Yeah, the women loved to drink Dom Perignon, and he loved to be able to order it just by snapping his fingers.

Fortunately for him, after blowing the first hundred grand, he had been on a winning streak at various casinos. Hotel suites, single-malt scotch, champagne, and megastar shows were at his disposal. As long as he kept winning, the casinos were happy to pick up his tab, hoping they would eventually get their money back. It had worked for him for a few years. He would win an average of $50,000 over a weekend and was smart enough to take it home. With his winnings, and the casinos comping him, he was having the time of his life.

When he turned thirty, the second $100,000 was released to him, much to his father's dismay. His father had never expected his son to blow the first $100,000. Richard J. Barnes Sr. thought his son was smarter than that. He was correct to believe that his son was smart; unfortunately, his son had not an ounce of common sense. Richard J. Barnes Sr. knew that his son was ambitious. What he did not realize was that his son had no work ethic, as in zero. Only when Rick had graduated from college, with a grade-point average that reflected his partying rather than his studying, did that realization take hold.

His father gave him a job working as a project manager for his real-estate development company. But all Rick managed to do was come in late, miss meetings, and totally lose track of the timeline for the job.

Rick thought his father was being too hard on him. *What was the big deal anyway?* he thought. There were so many projects in the works, and his father was loaded. What was the problem with one job being a week late? Except one week turned into two, then a month. The client was aggravated and frustrated and asked that Rick be removed from the project. Having no choice, and at risk of losing a valued client, his father put someone more competent on the job and gave Rick something easier to handle.

Unfortunately, Rick also proved unable to manage anything simple. Finally, his father relegated him to managing the office. His only job was to keep track of supplies. But he didn't do that very well either. The copy machine was out of paper. The postage-stamp machine had expired. The cleaning people hadn't been paid in weeks and threatened to stop working. But Rick always had an excuse. Lost paperwork. No one told him they needed certain things. The list went on and on. Rick had an excuse for every failure on his part. He could write a book on it; he was *that* good at shifting blame. Rick's dad was starting to feel the eyes of his employees burning holes in his back when he walked into his corner office. He knew deep down that hiring Rick had not been the best idea he had ever had, but Rick's mother insisted that he be part of the family business. Why he listened to that woman when it came to business was a mystery. Maybe it was because her father had started the business? But even if that was how Richard Barnes began, he had earned his way to the top, tripling his father-in-law's revenues in less than four years. No, Richard J. Barnes Sr. had earned every penny. It was sad that he couldn't say the same for his son.

So, despite his wife's wishes, he had to find other gainful employment for Rick. Having Rick in the business was not working out, for him, the business, or even Rick.

Richard Barnes arranged for Rick to work for a small computer start-up in which his father had invested some money. That should hold Rick for at least a year, provided he didn't screw up in the meantime.

As predicted, after a year, the computer company's management realized that Rick was an albatross, but at that point the company was well on its way to being profitable, and Rick's salary was a minuscule expense, given their bottom line. But that was then, and things had changed.

Rick was currently unemployed and in a place where he didn't want to be found. There was only one thing that could change his situation. Finding her. But until then, for him, there was no way out.

After his conversation with Christian, asking for a "loan," Rick thought about how they had all met. Christian had been on a committee that organized a fund-raising gala for underserved urban communities. The goal was to be able to provide some type of technology to these kids, either a tablet or a computer.

The night of the event, Chris brought his wife, Kara, and Kara's best friend.

Rick was intrigued, probably because the friend seemed a bit aloof. She was a striking woman. Five-foot-seven, long auburn hair pulled into a ponytail, with big, wide eyes. She wasn't gorgeous like the models he was used to dating. There was a different type of beauty about her.

She was wearing a cobalt-blue jumpsuit. She wore very little makeup but exuded confidence. She was confident without being arrogant.

He couldn't help but notice her. She was laughing as if no one was watching, throwing her head back in sheer exuberance. Christian's wife was almost as stunning, but there was something about *this* woman that struck him in the gut.

He sauntered over to where the two

women were standing.

"Good evening, ladies." He made a small bow. "Judging by the sound of your laughter, you seem to be enjoying yourselves quite a bit."

Kara knew Rick through her husband's affiliation with him. She didn't know him well, but she knew he was good-looking and charismatic. "We are indeed."

Rick was impatient and wanted an introduction, pronto. "Richard Barnes at your service." He took a slight bow. It was almost comical. "And whom do I have the pleasure of meeting?"

As she introduced herself, she had held out her hand, but within a blink of an eye, he took her hand and kissed the back of it. "So nice to meet you. What brings you to our event this evening?"

Kara thought he couldn't be soppier, but nonetheless, she found him amusing.

The mysterious, auburn-haired beauty explained that she worked in computer technology and was a guest of Kara and Christian. Within a noticeably short time in conversation, he realized she was quite witty and intelligent.

"You ladies look like you could use a refill. Shall I?" he offered.

They both gave an approving nod, adding, "Why not?" and, "That would be swell."

He nodded, snapped his heels together, and departed toward the bar.

Kara said, "He's kinda cute, and I think he might like you."

"Oh, puleeze . . ." she replied.

"No, seriously. I think he might be smitten," Kara said.

"Smitten? Did you just get off a Victorian stagecoach?" she teased her friend.

Seeing Prince Charming returning with filled champagne glasses, Kara said, under her breath, "Here he comes. Be nice. You never know."

He handed both women fresh glasses filled with champagne.

The women took the glasses from his hands. "Thank you" and, "How lovely, thank you."

Rick was intrigued by the auburn-haired woman. She was witty and articulate.

"What brings you to our soirée?" he asked.

"I work as a beta tester for several tech companies."

"You must be quite a brainiac," he replied.

"More like a 'super-geek,' " she answered.

"You are too beautiful to be considered any kind of geek." Rich was pouring on the charm. It was borderline schmaltz.

He thought he caught her blushing, even

if it was just a little.

She smiled warmly, murmured, "Thank you," and gave a little nod in his direction.

The conversation continued when Kara politely excused herself, giving her friend an opportunity to see how things might pan out.

The gala was being held at an art gallery, a type of venue she always enjoyed visiting. She and Rick walked through the exhibit together, discussing the various artists and their styles. Rick had offered to fetch them another refill when Kara spotted them. She hurried over before Rick could return with their glasses.

"So?" Kara asked eagerly.

"So, what?" she replied, acting as if she had no idea what her friend wanted.

"How's it going?"

"Fine. He's very nice. He likes art."

"Oh my God. Do I have to pull it out of you?" Kara was getting impatient, but in a teasing sort of way.

"No. Ssshhh. Here he comes."

"Kara!" He handed the glass to his new companion. "I would have gotten you a fresh glass. I thought you would be fluttering around like a social butterfly."

"I've already made my cameo appearances for those who needed to see me." Kara smiled. She glanced over at a group of people, recognizing someone else she needed to greet. "Oops. Spoke too soon. Be right back. Kara swooped over to the other group, leaving her friend alone with Rick again.

Rick also had to make the rounds. He realized that he had spent almost an hour with this woman, neglecting his duties as one of the hosts. "Listen, I also have to say hello to a few people, especially the ones who wrote out big checks." He hesitated, but then asked, "It's been a pleasure meeting you this evening. In case we don't run into each other before the end of the evening, would you care to have dinner with me? They're having a private late-night supper after this. The hors d'oeuvres were good, but not enough."

"That would be nice, but I have plans for later tonight. A rain check?"

"A rain check it is, then." He fished into his breast pocket and pulled out his business card. "Call me when you're free."

She put the card in her purse. "I shall. Thank you." She put her hand out to shake his, but he took it in his and looked into her eyes. "I hope to see you very soon." Then he kissed the back of her hand, as he had earlier that evening.

A week later, she called him, and they made a date for dinner. He chose one of the most expensive restaurants in the city. He picked her up in a limo town car. This way, no one had to be concerned about drinking and driving, and a cab was just too shabby if he wanted to impress her. That was one talent Rick did have. He knew how to impress people — until they were no longer impressed.

CHAPTER TWENTY

Colleen was pleased that Jackson had had a good day with his father. She was stunned by the way Jackson described her mother-in-law, laughing and singing. Vivian rarely smiled. As long as it was a good experience for Jackson, Colleen was happy. What she was concerned about was the nightmare he had had that night. When she heard him screaming, she flew out of bed and dashed into his room. Once she had calmed him down, he said he couldn't remember anything except that a yellow monster with no teeth kept sticking his face in Jackson's, and Gram was trying to pull the monster off him.

Colleen had no idea what it could have meant, but she suspected it had something to do with his outing with his father. But Jackson had been in a fine mood when he got home. He admitted that he got a little sad when Gram dropped his dad off at Aunt

Elaine and Uncle Greg's, but he insisted that he had had a great day.

She was also incredibly happy that Ellie had been up early and let Jackson into the yard. Colleen wished she had taken a photo of Jackson sleeping on the swing with Buddy underneath. Clearly, there were no nightmares there.

Colleen fussed around the kitchen, assembling Jackson's requested tuna fish sandwich. She looked in the pantry for sweet relish. There was none. She wondered if she could call Ellie and ask if she had any. Isn't that what most neighbors do? Of course, Ellie wasn't most neighbors, so she dropped the idea. "Honey? I'm sorry, but I don't have any sweet relish to put in your tuna."

"That's OK, Mom. Just put some extra celery." Jackson seemed refreshed after playing with Buddy and taking a siesta on the bench swing. Colleen chopped up a bit more celery and tossed it in the mayonnaise-and-tuna mixture. She finished making the sandwich and handed it to Jackson on a plate, with a napkin.

"Ms. Bowman is a really nice lady, Mom." Jackson dived into his lunch like he hadn't eaten in weeks.

"Easy there. You don't want to choke."

Jackson made a smacking sound as he chewed, knowing that his mom would say something. She gave him a look, then smiled. Jackson did the same, then continued to eat like a normal person. "I was pretending to be Buddy. He chomps on his Bully Stick like that."

"You really like going over there, don't you?" Colleen took the seat across from him at the kitchen table.

"Yes. Like I said, she's a very nice lady." He took another bite. "I wish she would come out and play with us sometime. I bet Buddy would like it, too."

"Maybe one of these days." Colleen wished it were true, too. "So what are you going to do this afternoon?"

Jackson shrugged. "Probably ride my bike over to Billy's, if that's OK with you."

Billy Warren lived on the next block. Their streets were parallel dead ends, and the connecting road had light traffic. Jackson knew that once he got to the end of his block, he had to walk his bike over to Billy's street. It seemed silly, but Colleen was wary about Jackson's being on a bicycle where there were cars going in both directions. One slip, and he could be in harm's way. Birchwood Lane only had five houses, so the only cars coming down the street were those owned by the people who lived there, delivery people, or friends and family. Everyone knew there were children in the neighborhood and minded the speed limit. Except for Andy. He drove as slow as molasses, but no one cared. His car was big enough to see from one end of the street to the other, and everyone knew to get out of his way.

Andy's house was across from Colleen's. The house next to his, which was catty-corner to hers, had been on the market for two months. There would be an occasional open house, which was the only time Colleen worried about traffic on their street.

She heard a car door open and close, and went to the window to see who it was. It was Marjorie Stiles, the real-estate agent, exchanging the FOR SALE sign with one that said SOLD.

"What's up, Mom?" Jackson was still working on his lunch.

"Looks like we're going to be getting new neighbors."

"Do they have kids?" Jackson asked.

"I don't know, honey. The agent just put up the 'sold' sign."

"Maybe we should go ask?" Jackson wouldn't mind another kid on the block. At present, he was the only one.

Colleen thought about it a minute. It

wouldn't be a bad idea to find out who was going to live on her street, so close to her house and son. "OK. Let's go! Are you finished with your lunch?"

Jackson wiped his mouth and turned his plate over to show her.

"Put it in the sink, and we'll go over."

Jackson obeyed and grabbed his baseball jacket. Colleen pulled a wrap around her shoulders. It was spring, but there was still a bit of a chill in the air. She put her cell phone in the back pocket of her jeans. It was always a crapshoot getting cell service. It depended on where you stood, but it was never consistent. Colleen thought she was incredibly lucky it had worked the night of the domestic disturbance; otherwise, she and Jackson would have had to climb out the window.

They crossed the street and greeted Marjorie Stiles. "Hey, Marge! I see you sold the house," Colleen said.

"Hey, Colleen. Hey, Jackson. Yes. A very nice, youngish family. They have a son who is around twelve and a daughter who's a little younger than Jackson."

Jackson was getting excited about the idea of having a boy on the street to play with.

"When is the closing?" Colleen asked.

"Next week," Margie answered.

"So soon?" Colleen asked.

"Yes, they had the cash. They'd put a deposit on another house, but the deal fell through. And now they have to move out because the person who bought their house was promised a move-in date. Since it was a cash deal, we were able to put a rush on it. They'll be moving in very soon."

"Wow. That is fast," Colleen said.

"Yeah. The Bentleys were anxious to close. It's been on the market for way too long. I kept telling Mr. Bentley that he was asking too much, so when the cash offer was put on the table, he couldn't snap up the money quick enough."

Margie leaned over and whispered in Colleen's ear. "I've heard that the older kid had a run-in with the police, so keep an eye on Jackson."

"Great," Colleen said sarcastically. That's all she needed. More trouble. "Anything serious?" She held her breath.

"Shoplifting, I think." Margie stood back, looking at her handiwork.

"Do you know what kind of shoplifting?"

"I think he stole a motorcycle."

"What? That's not shoplifting." Colleen was beside herself.

"Because he's a minor, they went easy on him."

Colleen shook her head in dismay.

"Don't worry. His mother told me that he's been on his best behavior since they put him in juvie for a weekend."

"Kind of a scared straight thing?" Colleen asked.

"I guess you could call it that."

Colleen knew all too well about juvenile detention programs, having been in the teaching profession for over a decade. She had to admit that there wasn't a whole lot to do in Hibbing. "Well, I hope you're right about his good behavior. I have enough problems right now."

"Gotcha," Marge replied. "Take it easy, Colleen. See ya, Jackson." Marge got in her car and waved as she drove away.

"What did you mean about problems, Mom? You and Dad?"

"I guess you could say that. Come on. Let's go back into the house." Colleen was fit to be tied. She really did not need to have to worry about someone being a bad influence on her son.

"Mom? Are you mad?" Jackson asked innocently.

"No, sweetie. I just need to figure out a few things."

"You keep saying that. How long do you think you'll be figuring things out before you figure them out?" Jackson was a smart kid, but sometimes the grown-up stuff was more than he could understand.

"I know." She let out a big sigh. "Are you going over to Billy's?

"Yep. If it's still all right."

"Sure thing. You know the rules."

"Yes. Walk my bike on Clifton Avenue until I get to Billy's street."

"And be home before dark."

"Right-o." Jackson walked over to the side of the house, where he kept his bike under the carport. He wheeled it out onto the street and hopped on. "See ya later, alligator!"

"After a while, crocodile." She waved him off and marched back into the house.

She was unnerved at the idea of a new family with a bad kid moving across the street. Jackson already had enough to deal with, let alone someone who could be a bad influence on him. She really needed someone to talk to.

Colleen picked up her landline and dialed the number that was on the original card Ellie had sent over inviting Jackson to play in the yard.

The phone rang five times before Ellie picked up.

"Hello?"

"Hi, Ellie. It's Colleen. I am sorry to bother you, but I need someone I can talk to."

Ellie was surprised to hear what sounded like distress coming from Colleen.

"Sure. What's up?" Ellie didn't mind lending an ear.

"I don't know if you noticed, but the house that's been up for sale has just been sold. I just saw the real-estate agent today."

"What happened?" Ellie thought selling a house in the neighborhood couldn't be such a bad thing.

"They have two kids. A twelve-year-old boy and a seven-year-old daughter."

"That might be good for Jackson, no?"

"No. The kid was in trouble with the law."

"Oh, that could be a big problem." Ellie now understood Colleen's concern. "What kind of trouble?"

"He stole a motorcycle. Can you believe that? A twelve-year old stealing a bike, as in the motor type." Colleen was pacing in her kitchen. "And they only charged him with shoplifting! Amazing."

"I assume that's because he's a minor and they didn't want him to have a serious record."

"Sounds that way. Ellie, I don't know if I can handle any more trouble right now."

"I totally understand."

"They put him through that scared straight program. You know, when they're supervised but exposed to all the horrible things that can happen to you in jail."

"Yes. There was a movie about it a number of years ago. I didn't know it was something they did here."

"Our state has some issues with drug abuse. Unfortunately, it seems to start in junior high school. Kids overdosing on opioids."

"That appears to be a national problem among adults as well." Ellie sighed.

"Yes, apparently kids steal their parents' prescriptions, but what's worse is that someone is making bootlegged pills, so who knows what they're taking."

"Colleen, please try to calm down," Ellie urged. "You don't know what the circumstances were. Maybe he was just going for a joyride. Kids do that. Not that I know a whole lot about kids, but . . ."

"I guess I'm just frazzled," Colleen confessed. "All the legal stuff with Mitchel and worrying about Jackson. Now I have a juvenile delinquent moving across the street."

"I know this has been a very upsetting time for you, but try not to jump to any conclusions." Ellie could hear the panic in Colleen's voice.

"You're right." Colleen's anxiety seemed to have eased somewhat. "I guess we'll find out sooner or later."

"And you may be pleasantly surprised," Ellie said, offering more encouragement.

"Thanks, Ellie. You've been a real help."

"I didn't do anything."

"You listened," Colleen said. "I don't have a whole lot of people I can talk to. My mother is on one of her 'I told you so' kicks. I can't speak to Mitchel about any of this, and my mother-in-law, well, who knows what kind of mood she might be in."

"She's pretty tough, eh?" Ellie knew little or nothing about Vivian Haywood except that she was a widow and lived on a farm.

"You have no idea. She blames the world for all her suffering."

"Many people do." Ellie knew all too well what that was like. Not that she blamed anyone for what had happened to her except herself, but she had dealt with enough people to understand that blaming someone else is often much easier than taking responsibility. It was a national epidemic, along with stupidity and partisanship.

"Although Jackson told me that Vivian was in a great mood yesterday. She was smiling and singing. I don't think I ever heard that woman sing a note. Never mind smiling." She gave a little chuckle.

"People *can* change." That was something she had hoped would happen with Rick when his father pretty much threw him out on his ass. "But they have to want to change. And even then, wanting doesn't mean doing. People have to do the work."

"You are so right, Ellie."

"Maybe she's had an epiphany of some sort," Ellie joked.

"I cannot imagine what that could have been. But Jackson was simply delighted about her new attitude."

"So he had a good day?" Ellie asked, trying not to pry.

"He did. He told me he got a little weepy when his grandmother dropped Mitchel off at his brother's, but he was excited to tell me all about the burgers, movie, ice cream, and bowling."

"Sounds exhausting." Ellie laughed lightly.

"It must have been. I didn't have to coax him to go to bed. But he woke up in the middle of the night with a nightmare."

"Well, that's not good."

"That's probably why he conked out on the swing," Colleen added. "By the way, your yard is absolutely stunning."

"Thank you. Hector has done an incredible job." Ellie wished she could go out and enjoy it, but for now she had to be satisfied with looking at it from the windows.

"Seriously. He's got a lot of talent," Colleen said.

"Yes, he's quite the computer whiz, too. But you probably know that. He's won a few science awards."

"Very smart kid. And a particularly good one. His family is lovely, too."

"They are. His mother sent an invitation for me to join them for dinner, but as you have already guessed, I don't leave the house." Ellie knew that might open a can of worms for unwelcome questions, but Colleen didn't push the issue. "Instead, she sent over a wonderful Cuban dish. It was marvelous, a real treat for someone whose cooking skills are as rudimentary as mine." Ellie remembered how much she had enjoyed that meal.

"Did you know that Hector's father is a musician? Not professionally, but his guitar playing would blow you away. He and some of his friends play at local events to help raise money for various groups. It's always a lot of fun. You should come to one of them." Colleen stopped dead in her tracks. "Oh, I'm so sorry." Colleen was embarrassed that she had overstepped.

"It's OK. Really. You were caught up in the moment," Ellie reassured her. "Perhaps one day."

"Well, I've already taken up too much of your time. Thank you for talking me down from the ledge." Colleen was bringing the conversation to a close. She was afraid she might say something out of line again.

"No problem, Colleen. Glad I could help. Call if you need to talk. I'm not going anywhere." Ellie actually laughed at that last remark.

"Thanks again." Colleen hung up. She looked for Marge Stiles's phone number. She wanted to get the name of her new neighbors. Maybe Officer Pedone could give her some information without violating some law. While juvenile records are generally sealed, it was still possible that a story about the incident had appeared in a newspaper or somewhere online.

Chapter Twenty-One

Andy wasn't sure if he was happy about the house next door being sold and having to get to know new neighbors. It had been vacant for almost a year, and he had gotten used to the quiet. The woman on his left never left her house, so that was also a plus. At least it was as far as he was concerned.

He shuffled to the kitchen, easing past the piles of newspapers. He had to walk sideways to get from one room to another. He was beginning to think that maybe he should call someone to help him go through his things. But he had no idea what was in the house. He couldn't see anything over the piles of newspapers. He knew there was a vast collection of silver in the cherry dining-room cabinet, but he hadn't seen the front of the cabinet in, well, he couldn't remember when.

He boiled a cup of water in his microwave, the only appliance, other than the refrigerator, that worked. He tossed in some instant coffee and milk. Once he had finished the poor excuse for a cup of coffee, he hobbled back to his bedroom to get dressed. He knew he should probably get dressed before he made his coffee, but then he would have to fill in the time he'd save from making the trip back. That was another problem: he had too much free time on his hands despite knowing that he didn't really have much time at all. It was depressing.

He took out a freshly pressed, button-down shirt and slacks. That was another part of his routine — going to the dry cleaner's every other week. His house might have been an unsightly mess, but he refused to be one. No one would ever think he was a hoarder based on the way he presented himself in public. When it came to dressing himself, he always looked quite dashing.

Before he had retired and opened his antiques shop, Andy had worked for a fine department store in St. Louis. He started as a tailor for the rich women who would come in for fittings. It was back in the day, when they would come in by appointment and sit in a lounge area as models came out, one by one, to show off the latest styles. Once the customer picked out the style she wanted, Andy would either tailor the dress to fit or make one from the vast selection of fabric the store kept in its tailoring shop.

At age sixty-five, when his eyesight was failing, he decided to leave the world of fashion, move to a small town, and open an antiques shop in a space that he rented for practically nothing. With all of the connections he had made working at the department store, he had a nice list of people who would become his clientele. They would venture out to the country on weekends and visit his shop, browsing the big and small finds Andy had accumulated during the early part of the week. Between Social Security and his pension, he was able to live quite comfortably in his modest two-bedroom house in Hibbing. The additional income from the antiques shop was gravy. It was an extended hobby that kept him busy and afforded him the opportunity to interact with people. When he turned eighty, fifteen years after starting in the antiques business, friends convinced him that it was time to give up the shop. He could no longer travel long distances to scout for furniture, and keeping the shop organized was a chore.

Some of the neighbors helped him with a garage sale the likes of which the town had rarely seen. It was maybe not the biggest, but it was surely one that offered the finest items, not old rusty lawn chairs and broken lawn mowers. But even with the number of antiques he had sold, there were more that had not sold. He and his friend Stuart moved the remaining items into Andy's house and garage, thinking that one day they would go through it all, do an inventory, and try to sell it as one big lot. But as time went on, Andy started to feel more and more attached to the things he had so lovingly collected. So he kept putting off the task. In addition to that, ever since he had retired, he had gotten into the habit of keeping every piece of paper that came through the mail, even junk mail.

The exterior of his house was similar to the way he dressed — simple but impeccable. The landscaping company where Hector worked was in charge of mowing his lawn and trimming the trees. Colleen would stop by and water the few flowers he had growing in containers on his front porch. She wouldn't take money, so he would rummage around the house, trying to find things he thought she might like. But as the months went by, it became more difficult for him to navigate from one room to another, let alone find something buried under the piles.

Neighbors would check in on him if they

didn't see his car leave the driveway, which wasn't often. He was determined not to waste away in the heap of stuff he had collected.

He hoped his new neighbors were as kind and considerate as the other families on the block. There weren't many of them, and it was a dead-end street, so it was important that they all get along or keep themselves locked up in their houses like his neighbor. Andy had no ill will toward the woman, just curiosity about her circumstances.

He knew next to nothing about her other than that she had a dog and a cat. The dog's name was Buddy, and the cat was Percy. He never saw Percy, but Buddy spent a lot of time in the yard. He was a well-behaved pooch and only barked when a strange car or unfamiliar people came down the street. Buddy was almost everyone's watchdog.

His owner seemed nice enough. She'd leave candy for the kids on Halloween and modestly decorated her house for the holidays. Andy knew it was actually Hector doing the labor, but Andy appreciated the idea that the woman wanted to be part of the neighborhood, if only in spirit. She also made sure that her yard was immaculate. Andy liked that she was letting Jackson play in her yard. Clearly, she wasn't one of those crazy-hermit types. Or maybe she was. From his point of view, she seemed rather normal except for that one little thing about never leaving the house. Yes, Andy decided she was a good neighbor, even if an invisible one.

There were dozens of mirrors hung all over the house, but there was only one he could actually see himself in. All the others were behind some pile of something or other. Andy put on his blue blazer and inserted a four-square handkerchief in the pocket. He was pleased with his attire. Picking up his cane, he wiggled through the maze and found his way to the front door. Checking that he had his keys, he ambled toward his car. He thought he might visit his car collection and trade the Cadillac for one of the others. Maybe the light blue Lincoln Continental Mark V. It was spring, and it seemed fitting to have something a little more colorful.

He donned his cap and slowly meandered toward the car. He gingerly folded himself into the driver's seat, turned over the engine, put the car in gear, and carefully pulled out of the driveway. As he made his way to the end of the block, he saw Colleen and Jackson heading to school. He would have offered them a lift, but he didn't want to be responsible if he got into a fender bender. His luck had been with him for a long time now. No scrapes, scratches, tickets, or accidents. He wasn't necessarily a superstitious person, but he didn't want to press his luck. As he passed them, he honked the horn and waved. They both waved back, and Andy proceeded to the stop sign at the end of the street. He waited so long that Colleen and Jackson caught up to him. He rolled down his window. "Good morning! And how are we today?"

"We're just fine, Mr. Robertson. How are *you* doing?" Colleen asked.

"I'm as good as can be."

"Did you hear about the new neighbors?" Jackson asked.

"I did," Andy replied. "I also heard there will be two more children on the block. More fun for you, Jackson?"

"I sure hope so, Mr. Robertson," Jackson said.

"And I suppose you'll have the little girl in your class?" he said to Colleen.

"Probably, but no one has spoken to me yet."

"Well, I think it will be nice to have some new people around. Not that I don't appreciate all of you!" Andy always made sure not to offend anyone. "We can use a little excitement."

Then he realized that Colleen had probably had her fill of excitement.

"I'm sure you mean the good kind?" Colleen flashed him a smile.

"Well, of course. We never want to confuse excitement with agitation." Andy gave her a little salute.

"No, we don't." She smiled again.

CHAPTER TWENTY-TWO

Jeanne and Frank Chadwick lived on the other side of Colleen and Jackson. Frank was a retired military officer and Jeanne a retired nurse. Frank had been in Special Ops, and Jeanne had worked in the emergency room. Both had served their country and communities for twenty years.

Frank and Jeanne had met during a blood drive Jeanne was supervising. After dating for a year, they decided to get married. Frank was constantly being deployed, to parts both known and unknown. Depending on how long he would be gone, Jeanne would often follow and get a job in a local hospital. Nurses were always a hot commodity, and she never had trouble finding work.

After several years, they decided it was time to put down permanent roots, so they moved to Hibbing, and Frank took a job at Fort Leonard Wood, while Jeanne went to work at the local hospital. When Jeanne was twenty-nine, she knew her biological clock was ticking, so they decided to have a child. It was a boy, and they named him James after their favorite folk-music hero, James Taylor.

They lived a normal midwestern life on Birchwood Lane.

James played football in high school and went on to the University of Missouri, where he studied architecture. After graduation, he married an engineering major, Ophelia Larson. They were both interested in urban planning. Unfortunately, neither Columbia, where the University of Missouri was located, nor Hibbing afforded them many opportunities in their chosen field, so they packed up and moved to Arizona, where they were offered positions with the city of Tucson.

Jeanne was very unhappy with their decision to move. "But it's hot out there!" she exclaimed when James and Ophelia told them about their plans.

In unison, they replied, "But it's a dry heat."

Neither Jeanne nor Frank were thrilled with the idea. They thought James and Ophelia could find work somewhere close. Somewhere within a few hours, at least. But

Tucson wasn't a hop, skip, and a jump. It was a good twenty-two hours, or a bad twenty-five, on the road, depending on construction.

They were both turning sixty-two and felt it was time to start doing things they enjoyed. They planned trips to visit family and to travel to places they actually wanted to visit.

After being gone a month, they were due back from Arizona. It was a good thing they had not been around the night the police came for Mitchel. Frank would have been on Mitchel's butt in a heartbeat. Even though the houses were over a hundred feet apart, Mitchel's cursing and shouting would have brought Frank over with both barrels loaded.

Despite his background in the military, not to mention his imposing size and demeanor, Frank was actually a likable, easygoing guy. Still, one did not want to piss him off. Don't let him see someone bullying anyone or being cruel to another human being or an animal. Jeanne was also feisty in her own way.

Both had seen enough death over the years, which gave them an appreciation of life and living. If they weren't gallivanting about, they would host cocktail parties in the winter and barbecues in the summer. Frank was the supreme grill master, and Jeanne's potato salad was matchless. Guests would bring side dishes, beer, wine, or someone's latest alcohol concoction. Hector's family would arrive with special Cuban delights, and his father would provide Afro-Cuban and salsa music. It was always a festive occasion.

Jeanne would joke that it was her potato salad that brought so many guests, while Frank would boast it was his special barbecue sauce. But most of their guests agreed that it was Emilio Cordoba's swinging group of musicians that drew the crowd.

Ellie would watch from her loft as people arrived, carrying their hostess gifts and food. But leave it to Jeanne to fix a plate for her and send it over via Hector, who would leave it on the back porch.

Ellie would follow up with a thank-you note that Hector would deliver to the Chadwicks. Everyone on the block accepted Ellie's absence from all activity without judging her. She didn't come across as strange or weird other than the fact that she never left her house. People would wave in her direction, never sure if she even saw them. It became very normal for everyone who lived on the block.

A week before Frank and Jeanne were to return, Jeanne would give Colleen a heads-up. While they were away, Colleen would take in their mail, and Mitchel would keep an eye on the house. Once a week, he would run the faucets, and after a big rain, he'd check for leaks. Of course, Mitchel's role ended after the domestic disturbance.

Colleen was glad the Chadwicks would be home soon, although she was distraught that she was going to have to explain what had happened the night Mitchel had gone bonkers. She knew that Frank would blow a gasket and Jeanne would have a fit. But she also knew that the information had better come from her, rather than anyone else. It wasn't as if Andy would say anything, and Ellie wasn't going to blab it to anyone. Who would she tell who didn't already know? Frank was very fond of the Haywood family, especially Colleen and Jackson. He wouldn't think twice about hunting Mitchel down and giving him what-for, though he wouldn't lay a hand on him unless Mitchel threw the first punch. That was highly unlikely if Mitchel knew what was good for him. No, Frank wouldn't touch Mitchel. Instead, he would put the fear of God in him.

Colleen knew that Frank and Jeanne were

due back that day. Before she went to the store, she brought in the mail and opened the windows. Her grocery list for the Chadwicks was usually milk, eggs, bacon, bread, coffee, juice, cheese, and crackers. She would check to see if they needed beer and wine. A bottle of Chardonnay and a six-pack. The only thing she didn't do was change the linens. At one time, she had actually given it some thought. But then she realized that was getting a little too personal. The Chadwicks appreciated the gesture. It was nice to walk into a house that didn't smell like it had been locked up for weeks. It was also nice to open the refrigerator and have some basic supplies, including a bottle of wine and a six-pack of beer.

As she was emptying the grocery bags, Colleen heard their car enter the driveway. She had hoped to be finished with the sprucing up before they got back, but that's not how it went down.

Colleen opened the front door as they were getting out of the car! "Welcome home!"

She walked over to Frank, and he gave her a big bear hug. "How's our young lass and her tribe?" Colleen stiffened a bit. "Everything all right?" Frank asked.

"Fine! So glad to see you!" Colleen said.

"And look how tan you are! Play a lot of golf, did you?" she said, addressing Frank.

Jeanne walked over to Colleen and gave her a big hug. "I'll have you know that I beat him in a round of golf." Jeanne wrapped her arms around her neighbor.

"Lucky break. My shoulder was bothering me that day," Frank said defensively.

"Your shoulder is always bothering you," Jeanne shot back in a fun-poking way. "Face it, Frank. You're just a sore loser."

Frank muttered something under his breath. Jeanne threaded her arm through Colleen's. "Don't mind him. He hates losing, especially to a girl." The two women giggled and went inside the house.

"You are such a peach, Colleen. The house always smells fresh when we get home." Jeanne took in a deep breath. "Don't tell me you stopped at the market?" Jeanne approached the refrigerator, knowing what the answer would be. "Really, Colleen. You are such a darling. You and Mitchel take such good care of things when we're away. We don't have to worry about anything while we're gone." Jeanne pulled out the cheese and opened the box of crackers while Frank brought in their luggage.

"Oh, sure. Let me do all the work while you fix yourself a snack." Frank loved to tease his wife. He would never expect her to haul their suitcases out of the car. He told her that carrying her pocketbook was strenuous enough.

"Yes, I'm just lollygagging around, fixing us some snacks." She took out a bottle of beer and poured it into a frozen mug she retrieved from the freezer and handed the mug to Frank. "Here you go, my liege lord."

He placed the suitcases in the hallway and took the mug. "Nothing like a crisp, cold one after fourteen hundred miles of highway."

"You can thank Colleen for providing this pleasure." Jeanne cut some of the cheese and placed it on the plate with the crackers. "Let me know how much I owe you for all of this. Please sit."

"Yes, thank you, sweet Colleen. It is much appreciated." He took another sip of his beer and put the half-filled mug in the refrigerator. "I'll be back for the rest of this as soon as I empty the trunk." Frank proceeded to move the suitcases and boxes from the car to their appropriate spots. Boxes went in the garage for sorting. Luggage went into the den for unpacking.

Jeanne turned to Colleen. "I'm going to open the wine, and you can catch me up with what's been happening in our quiet hamlet."

A glass of wine sounded like a good idea, given what Colleen was about to tell them. Or should she wait? The decision was made for her when Jeanne asked, "How are Jackson and Mitchel?"

"Jackson is doing great. He's made good friends with Buddy."

"Ellie Bowman's dog?" Jeanne sounded surprised.

"Yes. And get this. She's been letting Jackson into the yard. He's there every day."

"Seriously?" Jeanne's eyes widened. "How did that happen?"

"You know, Jackson shot up in height this year. Well, one day Mitchel and Jackson were on the street tossing a baseball. Jackson was at the end of the street in front of Ellie's house." Colleen paused, realizing Mitchel would be the next subject. "Jackson was finally tall enough to see over the fence. Buddy was just sitting there, watching and wagging his tail. Jackson walked over to the fence, Buddy jumped up, still wagging his tail, and ever since Jackson petted him on the head, they've been BFFs."

"But how did he get *inside* the fence?" Jeanne prodded.

"Oh, yeah. You know how I invited her a

dozen times for tea, but she always declined."

"Yes. She never leaves the house."

"Right. I guess she was feeling guilty. I really don't know, but one day, out of the blue, I got a note asking if it was all right for Jackson to play in the yard. I almost fell over. After what happened with Mitchel —" She stopped immediately.

"What happened with Mitchel?" Jeanne sat up straight. Frank came down the hallway and repeated what Jeanne had just said. "What happened with Mitchel?"

"Is he OK?" Jeanne asked.

Colleen looked over at Frank. "You better sit down. But first, get your beer."

Jeanne looked genuinely concerned. "Is Mitchel OK? Is he sick?"

"No. And no." Colleen answered. "It's no secret that Mitchel was drinking more than he used to. I don't know what got into him, but his drinking was getting worse."

"I have to be honest," Jeanne said. "I thought he had gotten a little bit too sloshed at a few parties. I'm no one to talk, but at least I'm still *able* to talk when I'm drinking. I may not make a whole lot of sense, but I can usually enunciate my words."

Frank broke into the conversation. "Jeanne's right. I noticed it a couple of times, but I wasn't really paying that much attention. But I guess you're right about it escalating. The last party he got a little snarky with Andy. He called him a 'dandy. Dandy-Andy.' Andy didn't seem the least bit offended, but it was rude and disrespectful. The man is ninety years old, for God's sake, and he dresses better than almost anybody in the state of Missouri. Heck, pretty much anywhere."

"I had no idea Mitchel had spoken to him that way. That's terrible." Colleen was upset, but not surprised about Mitchel's behavior. At the rate Mitchel's drinking had been escalating, it was amazing that terrible evening hadn't happened sooner. *Poor Andy. He didn't deserve that.*

"Never mind all that. I don't think Andy really minded. What happened with you and Mitchel?" Jeanne reached out and touched Colleen's hand.

"Just so you know, everything is under control. No one got seriously hurt," Colleen reassured them.

"Well, that in itself isn't very reassuring," Jeanne said.

Frank interjected. "So start from the beginning. What happened?"

Colleen started with the same information she had already given them. Mitchel's drinking had escalated. One morning, he was on the porch yelling at Jackson to come and talk to his father. They were late for school, so Colleen and Jackson continued on their way. That evening, Mitchel got home late, and he was very drunk. And he "got physical."

Frank interrupted. "What do you mean 'physical'?"

Colleen continued, fearing that Frank might do something irrational. Even though she knew Frank was not the irrational type, this might be a bridge too far. "He grabbed me and threw me down on the bed. I squeezed out from under him. He tried to hit me, but I ducked, and he punched a hole in the wall. I went into Jackson's room and called the police."

Both Frank and Jeanne sat back in horror. Jeanne was first to respond. "Did he hurt you?"

Then Frank. "Did he hurt Jackson?"

"No. I mean yes. He threw me against the wall . . . listen, do we have to go into the gory details?"

"No, of course not." Jeanne put her hand on top of Colleen's. "Just tell us what you are comfortable with."

Frank could not hold back. "If he ever touches you again, he will be the sorriest son of a bitch on the planet."

"Thanks. But wait." Colleen wanted to defuse Frank's anger. "I was able to get out of the room, went to Jackson's, barricaded the door, and called the police."

Jeanne was almost out of her seat. "You barricaded the door? How badly did he hurt you?"

"I was OK. Mostly scared and rattled. The police were great. Came right away. Dispatcher stayed on the phone with me." Colleen caught her breath.

"My God!" Jeanne exclaimed. "That's horrible. When did this happen?"

"Just over two weeks ago."

Frank leaned in. "You must be very shaken by all of this. Is there anything we can do for you?"

"I'm OK. Really. I have a temporary restraining order until he goes for his hearing on the domestic violence charges next week. I'll apply for a permanent one, if necessary."

"If necessary?" Jeanne was appalled.

"Yeah, well, Mitchel was really out of it that night, but he took Jackson out for his one-day-a-week supervised visitation on Saturday."

"You let him take Jackson?" Jeanne was still appalled.

"Yes, but his mother had to accompany them. It's part of the temporary visitation order. He can't have Jackson alone without supervision."

"Well, that's a good thing," Frank observed. "Where is Mitchel staying now?"

"At his brother's. Greg and Elaine's."

"Nice people," Frank said.

"Yes, but . . ." Colleen wasn't sure if she should mention Greg's gun, but at this point there was no reason to leave anything out. "Greg has a registered firearm."

Frank folded his arms and grunted. "Your TRO isn't good against a bullet."

"Frank. Don't." Jeanne didn't want to cause any more alarm for Colleen than necessary.

"Well, it's important to have all the details and not be emotional about it."

"It's OK." Colleen reassured them. "I am somewhat prepared."

"In what way?" Frank asked.

"I have a Taser and was given instruction as to how to use it."

"OK. That's a start. What else?" Frank was borderline interrogating her.

"I had a high-tech security system installed."

"What about when you're not home?" Frank pressed.

"I have permission to take my Taser to work with me. I don't know what else I can do."

"You can learn how to shoot a real gun," Frank added.

"I really don't want to do that, for a number of reasons."

"Like what?" Frank asked.

"First, I don't like them. Second, I don't want to have one in the house. Third, I really, honest and truly, don't think it's necessary."

"And why do you think that?"

"Just say it's woman's intuition."

"Don't give me that crap." Frank was almost snapping at her.

Jeanne intervened. "Let her finish, please."

"Mitch had never been violent before." She put up her hands in anticipation of their protests. "Believe me, I am not trying to defend him. I am really trying to get a realistic view. I have my son to consider."

"Fair enough," Frank commented.

"Vivian took them to a burger place, a movie, ice cream, and bowling."

"That old witch?" Frank wasn't a fan of Vivian.

Colleen laughed. "Yes, and apparently she was in a fine mood. Jackson was delighted that his gram was so much fun."

"Are we talking about the same woman?" Frank looked shocked.

"So it seems," Colleen replied. "Barring body snatching. According to Jackson and Elaine, Vivian was a totally different person."

Invasion of the Body Snatchers." Jeanne guffawed, and the other two followed.

"Seriously, I have no idea what got into Vivian, but I'm not about to question it. If my son had a good day, well, that's all that matters to me."

"So what's next?" Frank asked.

"Mitchel has a hearing to make a plea."

"Well, he's guilty, of course," Jeanne added.

"Yes, and if he pleads guilty, they will most likely reduce it to a misdemeanor rather than a felony." Colleen was matter-of-fact.

"How is that right?" Jeanne asked.

"It's the system, Jeanne."

"What will happen then?" Frank asked.

"He'll probably get probation, be required to get therapy — anger management — and maybe they'll even send him for alcohol rehabilitation." Colleen paused. "And he'll have to do some community service."

"How will that affect the visitation?" Jeanne asked.

"As long as I have a restraining order, he

will most likely need supervised visitation. At least for a while."

"This must be very nerve-racking for you," Frank said.

"Yes, but I'm getting better at handling it." Colleen continued. "I bought a Taser, and Officer Pedone showed me how to use it."

"You should get a gun. I'll teach you." Frank was firm.

"I don't want a gun in the house."

"You said that Mitch is staying with his brother, right?" Jeanne asked.

"Yes. For now."

"Why not with Vivian?" Frank asked. "She has that big old house."

"Hah. Would *you* stay with Vivian?" Colleen snickered.

"Good point," Frank answered.

Jeanne continued to prod Colleen. "OK, so if he pleads not guilty, then what happens?"

"Then it will go to trial. That could take up to a year, and I don't think Mitchel can afford a trial lawyer." Colleen pursed her lips. "We just have to wait and see."

"What can we do to help?" Frank asked.

"Nothing at the moment, but thanks. I had an exceptionally good security system installed. With that and the Taser, I'm feeling pretty safe. Besides, I don't think Mitch would want to blow his visitation rights or end up back in jail if he violated the order. But he was parking the car at the end of the block every day for the first two weeks. It was really creepy."

"Isn't he supposed to keep away from you?" Jeanne asked.

"One hundred yards, which is almost exactly the distance from our yard to the end of the block. As soon as we started walking in his direction, he would drive off."

"He knew you saw him, right?" Jeanne asked.

"Oh, yeah. That was the whole point," Colleen answered. "I don't know if he plans on continuing to stalk us. He was really in a rage that night, and after getting locked up, well, that just pissed him off even more."

"But you said the visit went well?"

"Yes, much to my surprise."

"Maybe he's wised up," Frank noted. "But if I see him parked at the end of the block, I might have to do something about it."

"Frank, please don't," Colleen implored. "I don't want to get him riled up again."

"Fair enough," Frank answered. "But if I see him setting one foot on the property, he will be one sorry guy."

"I certainly wouldn't want to mess with

you." Colleen laughed nervously. She knew that Frank was well intentioned, but she also knew how protective he was of her and Jackson. "My hope is that he can straighten himself out so he can have a relationship with his son. Mitch was only ten when his father was killed, so he missed a lot." Colleen sighed. "I know he loves Jackson, and I hope and pray that he will want to be a better person for Jackson and himself."

"Mitchel wasn't a bad guy when he was sober," Jeanne noted.

"Yes, I know. What I *don't* know is what happened to him over the past couple of years. He had a good job; we were doing fine. Then he started drinking more, and that created so many problems. He even lost his job."

"Oh no!" Jeanne exclaimed. "How? Why?"

"He was on probation because he was screwing up at work. Not showing up on time, leaving early. His boss had had it up to here, and when Mitch was sent to jail, that was it. His boss canned him."

"Now that's kicking a man when he's down. But I understand his boss's point, too. Such a shame." Frank shook his head.

"What is he going to do for money? Can he collect unemployment?" Jeanne asked.

"Yes, but that isn't going to cover child

support and put a roof over his head. I don't know how long Greg and Elaine are going to let him stay there. Elaine told me that Mitch was acting like an ungrateful ass, and she was going to throw him out the door if he didn't straighten out," Colleen said.

"That must be causing a lot of stress on Elaine and Greg's relationship, too," Jeanne mused.

"I don't doubt it. But Greg has always looked after Mitch, ever since their father died. Mitch is his little brother." Colleen sighed.

"Well, you keep your chin up and know that Frank and I are here for whatever you need. You have a built-in babysitter if you need us to watch Jackson." Jeanne patted Colleen's hand.

"Speaking of Jackson, I better get his dinner started."

"Where is he right now?" Frank asked.

"Over at Ellie's, with Buddy. That seems to be his routine when he gets home from school. Homework, Buddy, dinner."

"It's wonderful that she's letting Jackson play with him so much," Jeanne said.

"Oh, and you should see her backyard! It is absolutely magnificent!" Colleen exclaimed.

"*You* were in the yard?" Jeanne was incredulous.

Colleen leaned back in her chair and folded her arms. "Yes. I. Was." She smiled.

Jeanne leaned in as if Colleen had a big secret to reveal. "Whoa. How did that happen?"

"Jackson went over there yesterday morning. It was really early. He'd had a nightmare and was restless, so he got up and walked over to Ellie's to see if Buddy was out. She must have woken up early, too, because she called me at seven to check that it was OK for Jackson to go in the back."

"Wait. She called you? As, like, on the phone?" Jeanne was intrigued.

"Yes, she did."

Jeanne turned to Frank. "We were gone a month, and look at all the things we missed."

"He was there all morning. Ellie noticed he had fallen asleep on the bench swing and called me around lunchtime. She didn't think he could hear her over the intercom, so she suggested I come over and get him."

"Wow. This is incredible." Jeanne was dumbstruck.

"I know, right?" Colleen continued. "So she told me to ring the buzzer on the side gate, and she would let me in. I walked over, rang the buzzer, and she let me in." She took a breath. "I was blown away. The trees and the perennials are just gorgeous. And there is a garden area in the back where she has a swinging bench, two Adirondack chairs, and a fountain." Colleen exclaimed, "It's stunning."

"Too bad she can't enjoy it," Jeanne said. "So what else have you discovered about our secret neighbor?"

"Not much. She seems so normal when you talk to her." Colleen shrugged. "She's a computer whiz is all I know."

"Very interesting." Jeanne thought a moment. "Do you think she's agoraphobic? Afraid to leave the house?"

"I have no idea. I'm just glad Jackson has something that makes him happy. I don't know what I would do if he freaked out on me."

"Jackson is a good kid." Frank got up and helped himself to another beer and another frosted mug. "You ladies want a refill?"

"No, thank you. I really must get back."

"Like I said, honey. You just let us know if you need anything."

"I will. And thank you for listening and your understanding."

"Thank you for making sure we didn't go hungry." Jeanne smiled.

"Or thirsty!" Frank raised the mug in Colleen's direction.

Jeanne got up and gave Colleen a big hug. "Thanks, sweetie. You take care."

Frank walked over and gave her one of his famous bear hugs.

"Remember, we are here for you."

Colleen whispered, "Thank you, Frank."

After Colleen left, Frank turned to Jeanne. "I told you something was going to happen. That Mitchel was going off the rails."

"Take it easy, Frank. We don't know what was really going on with him. Maybe it's a phase."

Frank grunted. "Men don't go through phases, Jeanne. They're either on the bus or under the bus, as far as I'm concerned."

Jeanne reached over and patted him on his butt. "You're such a macho dude. That's why I love you so much."

Frank gave her a kiss on the top of her head. "As I said, he better keep his distance, or he'll have some shrapnel in his ass."

CHAPTER TWENTY-THREE

It was just about dinnertime, and Mitchel wanted Greg and Elaine to have a quiet evening together, so he headed to the bowling alley. When he got there, he spotted Clay's truck in its usual spot. "Jeez, doesn't that guy have a home?" Mitchel muttered under his breath.

Clay actually had a home, but it was the kind you could hitch to the back of a truck. It was more like a camper, with a two-burner propane stove, a small toilet area, and a small sofa bed. What Clay did about showering was a mystery. Although there were plenty of times when it was obvious he hadn't had one in a few days. He'd been thrown out of the bowling alley more than once for "stinkin' up the joint," as the manager proclaimed as he showed Clay the door.

Mitchel figured he'd grab something at the food vendor, whose menu ranged from hot dogs and hamburgers to the ever-popular nachos. Pete ran the junk-food part of the place, which also served beer in wax-coated paper cups. He was wiping down the counter as Mitchel approached. "Pete. What's up?" Mitchel greeted him.

"Same old same old. How about you?" Pete anticipated Mitchel's wanting a beer, so he poured some into a cup and set it down in front of him.

"Not much," Mitchel responded. "Thanks." He took a swallow. "Man, are you ever going to get real mugs, cups, somethin'? These cups are disgusting. And didn't they phase them out years ago?"

"Yep. Sure did. I got myself a pallet's worth for practically nothin'."

"I guess you get what you pay for." Mitchel snickered.

"What brings you here durin' the week, and at dinnertime, no less?"

"I wanted to give my brother a break. He and Elaine needed some private time."

"That was nice of you." Pete almost sounded sarcastic.

"Hey, they've been really good to me through all of this. I'm surprised Elaine hasn't kicked my butt out the door by now. I have to admit, I haven't been the best houseguest."

"Do tell." Pete threw the towel over his shoulder.

"Pete, you've known me a long time. I know I've been off a bit lately."

"You ain't lyin' about that."

"Yeah, yeah. But the other day, when I was with Jackson, I realized how important he was to me."

"You guys seemed to be having a good time. Even your mother. I can't recollect the last time I seen her smilin' like that."

"Believe me, we were all in shock. I don't know what got into her, but I hope that whatever it is, it stays there." Mitchel took a pull of his beer. "Cripes, this is disgusting. Come on, man, I know you have some other kind of container you can pour a beer into."

"It never bothered you before. When did you get so particular?" Pete reached under the counter and pulled out a white coffee mug.

"Oooh . . . now *that's* real fancy," Mitchel snarked back at him.

"No, seriously, man. What's up with you?"

"Nothin'. Just evaluating things, that's all." Mitchel poured the beer from the waxy paper cup into the mug and took a swig. "Ah. Much better. Thanks."

"So, what's happening with you and your old lady?"

"Man, I wish you wouldn't call her that." Mitchel reached for a napkin in the metal container sitting on the counter.

"And fussy, too?" Pete gave him a shocked look. "Don't tell me you started goin' to church."

"Don't be funny. Like I said, I'm evaluating things."

"Uh-huh." Pete grunted. "Ya want somethin' to eat?"

"Got any specials?" Mitchel was kidding him.

"Yeah. I got new corn chips for the nachos," Pete retorted.

"Perhaps I'll try the mystery-meat sandwich," Mitchel kept up.

"One filet mignon comin' up." Pete chuckled and yelled into the window behind him. "Tony! Slap a burger on the grill for our friend here." He turned back to Mitchel. "Would you like fries with that, sir? A pickle to tickle your fancy? And what about cheese?"

Mitchel was in a funny mood. "Perhaps a fine Gruyère?"

Pete burst out laughing. "You ain't gonna find no greeyare anywhere near this place! That's fer sure."

"I guess whatever you have in the back that isn't green will have to do," Mitchel shot back.

Pete wiped his hands and put the towel behind the bar. He took Mitch's mug and gave him a refill. "On the house."

"What's gotten into *you,* being all nice and stuff."

"Must be contagious," Pete bellowed.

Mitch gave him a wave of the mug. "Thanks, mate!"

Pete leaned across the counter. "So, tell me, what is going on with the missus."

"Huh. Well, it's no secret we got into a thing a little over two weeks ago. It was bad. Really bad." Mitchel started to explain, with as little detail as possible. He didn't want people to think he was a wife beater, although a description of what had happened would eventually get into the local news outlets as soon as he had his hearing and there was an outcome. "We got into a fight. I was in a wild kind of mood and scared the heck out of Colleen. And Jackson. Then, if that wasn't enough, I trashed the kitchen." Mitchel looked forlorn. "She called the cops, and they cuffed me and dragged me out. I spent two nights in jail."

"Wow. Did she press charges?"

"Why do you think I was in jail?" Mitchel gave him a "you dumbass" look.

"Right. So, now what? What about your

boy? You guys seemed to be having a good time the other day."

"I have supervised custody until things get sorted out."

"Is that why your mother was here?"

"Yep."

"I was wonderin' what the heck she was doing here. I know she's not the bowlin' kind."

"She surely is not."

"But she was all smilin' and stuff."

"Yeah. Like I said, we don't know, and we ain't asking." Mitchel chuckled.

"How often do you get to see your boy?" Pete seemed genuinely interested.

"Just once a week. For now," Mitchel said with resignation.

"Where you gonna live?"

"I have no idea. First, I gotta get a job." Mitch nodded.

"Got anything in mind?"

"I don't suppose they need someone to set up the pins?" Mitchel joked.

"Now that's funny."

"I am going to go to the shop and beg for my old job back."

"Well, you are the best mechanic in town. Everybody knows that." Pete was trying to sound encouraging.

"That's probably the only thing I have going in my favor."

Tony hit the small dinner bell in the window. "Food's up!"

"I don't know why he insists on ringing the damn bell. I'm standin' right here." Pete turned around, picked up the burger, and placed it in front of Mitchel. "Bon appetite."

Mitchel corrected him. "It's *bon appétit.*"

"Yes, sir. Mr. Fancy Pants."

"And I doubt there is anything *bon* about it," Mitchel mocked back.

Pete was reaching for Mitchel's mug when Mitch stopped him. "Thanks, man, but I'm good."

Pete leaned in and peered into Mitchel's eyes. "You all right, boy?"

"Yeah. Fine. I'm already on the cops' radar. I don't want to get pulled over and get a DUI. I can't afford it. Financially. Legally. And whatever. I need to behave until all this is over."

Pete nodded. "Makes sense. Finish your mystery meat. I've gotta go down to the basement and get a few bottles of gin. Keep an eye on things for me?"

Mitchel had a mouthful of burger. He gave Pete a thumbs-up.

Mitchel hoped he would be able to finish his burger in peace, without listening to Clay ramble on. He thought he was in the clear, but Clay spotted him and came lumbering across the alley.

"Yo, man. What's up?" Clay gave Mitchel such a slap, Mitchel thought he might choke on the food in his mouth.

Mitch finished chewing and swallowed. "Man, never slap someone when they have food in their mouth." But then Mitchel realized this was Clay he was talking to.

"Sorry, man," Clay cackled. "So, like what are you doing here?"

"Trying to eat my burger." Mitchel wiped his mouth with a napkin and pulled two more out of the dispenser.

"Cool. Want to shoot a round of pool?"

"Maybe." Mitch took the last bite of his burger and shoved the leftover fries in Clay's direction.

Clay immediately attacked the fries as if he hadn't eaten in weeks.

Mitch took a good, long, hard look at him. *I don't want to be that guy. The one who can't keep it together. The one who has no direction except down. No, I don't wanna be him.*

CHAPTER TWENTY-FOUR

Ellie noticed Frank and Jeanne's car pulling into their driveway and saw Colleen greet them. From what she knew, Frank and Jeanne were a solid couple. Retired, with a son, daughter-in-law, and grandson in Arizona. They traveled a lot and spent a good deal of time visiting the family in Tucson. Ellie knew that Frank had been in Special Ops in the military, so she felt well protected when he was around. She felt a pang of loneliness when she witnessed the big hugs Colleen got from the couple. Ellie could feel her desire for companionship growing. She didn't know if that was a good thing or a bad thing. Given the recent developments with Colleen and Mitchel, and a new family moving in, Ellie was yearning to have face-to-face human contact. In her previous life, her weekly planner was filled with art exhibits, concerts, plays, dinners, and fund-raisers. She knew she should be making better progress, but then decided not to be too hard on herself. At least, that's what her therapist told her. The two words that kept playing in her head were "baby steps." But she was getting restless and being torn in several directions, and she still had to figure out what had gotten her there in the first place. Some of it was obvious, at least to her. It was the stuff in the shadows that haunted her. If only she could figure it out.

Hearing about Rick and finding her old sneakers had triggered something in her memory. It had also triggered a migraine, but she was able to shake it off more easily than before. That had to be a sign she was getting better. The situation with Rick vexed her. She was determined to peel that onion, even if it was only one layer at a time.

She poured herself a glass of water and dived into her search engines. She didn't necessarily want to jump in headfirst, but she resigned herself to do a deep dive into Rick's whereabouts. The notion that he needed money for a start-up sounded like some of the bull-pucky he was known to throw around. It was the idea that he had to resort to asking an old friend for money that sent up a red flag. Surely, with all of his connections, he could find someone who had beaucoup bucks to toss him a few grand. Then it struck her. Maybe it was his way of trying to find her. That would be very bad for Ellie, which is why she had made up the story about a government contract and having to move about frequently. There should be no way that he could locate her. If he did, it could be disastrous. For both of them.

Ellie took a deep breath and looked at Buddy and Percy. "Wish me luck, guys!" She turned to her keyboards and began delving into the deep, dark corners of the World Wide Web.

After a few minutes, she was logged in to the New York State Department of Motor Vehicles website. It wasn't the site people used to renew their license, file paperwork, or pay fines. No, this one was where all the important data was kept, all the information about everyone who had a driver's license in the state. She wanted to find out if his license had been renewed or if he had filed a change of address. She shuddered when his face popped up on the screen. It was the same photo from when they had dated, and the address was the same. *Where is he?* She decided to call Kara and see if she could get Christian to find out. Ellie felt something flicker in the back of her mind.

Ellie pulled out the burner phone and dialed. Pretending Buddy and Percy could understand sign language, she put her finger to her lips to indicate that they shouldn't make a sound. She shook her head at her silliness. *As if,* she said to herself. But at that moment, she didn't care. She didn't care if she had to tell Kara another made-up story. She needed to speak to her. Now.

"Hey!" Kara answered on the third ring. "Everything all right?"

"Yes. Kinda. Sorta," Ellie sputtered.

"What's going on?"

"I need Christian to find out where Rick is." There was a moment of silence before Kara answered.

"Because?" she asked suspiciously.

"Because I think it will help me."

"Help you what?" Kara asked.

"Help me figure out a few things." Ellie was nervous but resolute.

"Like what?"

"Like what happened the night I ended up in the hospital," Ellie declared.

"Girlfriend, do you really want to go there?"

"I *need* to go there. I *have* to go there. I have to go to the place where all of this began."

"I know you don't mean that literally."

Kara paused. "Do you?"

"Maybe at some point. But no, not now. I have to start putting the pieces together; otherwise . . ." Ellie stopped. She was on a slippery slope. She could reveal what she thought she knew, but then she would have to reveal where she was.

"Otherwise what?" Kara's concern was obvious. "Are you sure you're OK?"

"Yes. And I want to get better. In order for me to get better, I need more information."

"Ellie, when you took this job, everyone thought it was good for you to get away and have time to regroup. But now I wonder if it was the best thing for you. You don't have a support group."

"I have a therapist I talk to."

"Really?" Kara was dubious. "And how often is that?"

"As often as I need."

"And how often is *that*?" Kara repeated herself.

"Kara. I need to know if you are going to help me or not." Ellie was getting adamant.

"OK. OK. Let's think about this." Kara paused. "Of course I am not going to agree to let Christian lend him the money."

"Rick asked for him to deposit it into a PayPal account, correct?" Ellie asked.

"Yes. That was the first red flag. Actually, I suppose, the phone call was the first. Rick hadn't been in touch for two years; and then, out of the blue, he calls asking for $5,000. Second red flag was asking for it to be deposited in a PayPal account. Third, the idea that he was involved in some kind of start-up was also odd."

"Exactly," Ellie agreed. "What if Christian tells him that in order to get him the money, it has to be in the form of a check. Then the question would be where should he mail the check?"

"Brilliant," Kara exclaimed. "But then again, you always were."

"Except for the time I was dating him," Ellie scoffed.

"And so what happens if Rick gives him an address? I don't want Christian to actually send him money."

"Let's take this one step at a time," Ellie mused. "He gets the address from Rick. He doesn't mail a check. Rick calls back, asking about it. That would indicate how desperate Rick is for the money. Plus, it would buy me some time."

"Time for what?" Kara asked.

"A little undercover work."

"Are you sure you want to do that?"

"No, but I am sure I need to do *something.*

This seems like a good place to start. Who knows? I might not care once I find out."

"I certainly hope you don't care," Kara added.

"I don't care about *him.* I care about me, and I need to start moving past this, this thing." Ellie was certain about that.

"OK, girlfriend. I will talk to Christian when he gets back later. The only thing is, we don't know how to contact Rick, so we're going to have to wait until he calls back."

"Did he indicate when that might be?"

"He said a few days. I guess it depends on how eager he is."

"Right you are." Ellie relaxed her shoulders. She had been unaware of how tightly wound up she was. "Hang on a minute." Ellie put the phone down and stretched her arms behind her back and moved her neck from side to side. She groaned and picked up the phone. "Sorry, I had to disconnect my shoulders from my ears."

"Your what?" Kara asked.

"You know. The tightness in the neck and shoulders when you're stressed? Well, now I feel much better."

"Oh, yes. That's the feeling I get when I have to go to a Junior League meeting."

Ellie laughed. "Have you ever thought of

quitting?"

"Nah. What would I have to complain about?" Kara chuckled.

Ellie looked over at Buddy. His tail was thumping. She knew she should end the call soon.

"OK. We have a plan," Ellie said. "A work in progress. Kind of like my life."

"You crack me up." Kara chortled. "Yes, a plan."

"I'm going to give you a phone number. Do not call me unless it's urgent. Ring twice, and I will call you back."

"Wow, you really are top secret, aren't you?"

"You have no idea. Write this down — 857-555-1968," Ellie responded. "Gotta go. Love you." Ellie ended the call.

Ellie had a surge of energy. It was a feeling of renewal.

It was at that moment she decided to invite Hector in for coffee. She scribbled a note:

Hector, I'd like you to join me for coffee. Let me know what's good for you.

She jumped up from her desk. "Come on, guys," she called to Buddy and Percy. Buddy needed no invitation. Percy yawned,

255

stretched, and slowly moved his way to the floor. Buddy was hot on Ellie's heels as Percy meandered down the steps.

Ellie put the note in her daily envelope to Hector and put it on the table next to the kitchen door, in the enclosed porch. She smiled at what she thought Hector's reaction would be.

Looking at the kitchen clock, she noticed that Jackson hadn't shown up yet. It was almost 4:00. She hoped she hadn't hurt his feelings again. She didn't know how she could have, but she hadn't known the first time either. Not until she noticed his absence. She decided to give Colleen a call. Maybe she would be the next person to invite into her house. *Easy girl. One visitor at a time.*

Ellie searched for the phone she had designated for Colleen and Jackson and remembered it was on her desk. She had put a "C & J" on theirs and a "K" for Kara's. She ran back upstairs and glanced through the windows that overlooked the front. She noticed Jackson skipping toward her house. It appeared he was coming from Jeanne and Frank's. Another pang of loneliness hit her. She would get through it. Baby steps.

The bell from the side gate rang. Instead

of just letting him in, she spoke into the intercom from her loft. "Hey, Jackson. I was getting worried." Ellie laughed lightly.

"Sorry, Miss Bowman. I went over to say hello to Mr. and Mrs. Chadwick. They just got back from Arizona. He brought me an Indian arrowhead. It's the real deal." He proudly held it up, assuming she could see it from somewhere. He didn't realize that there were cameras surrounding the place. She was just a voice coming out of a box.

"Very cool," Ellie answered.

"It's going to be my good-luck charm," Jackson said with certainty, and slipped it into his pocket.

"Excellent. Take good care of it," Ellie said, then buzzed him in.

Buddy was already anticipating playtime. As soon as he heard the ding from the gate, he scampered downstairs, leaving Ellie behind. "I am beginning to think you like Jackson better than you like me," she yelled after him. Ellie put the phone in her pocket and started toward the steps. Percy was at the bottom of the steps, meowing. "And you. You're so aloof sometimes." Percy stretched and rolled over and exposed his belly. That was the signal that he wanted to be rubbed. Ellie descended the stairs, talking to Percy all the while. "You guys are *so* spoiled." Percy let out a coo of approval as Ellie accommodated his request. "Come on. We need to figure out what we're having for dinner."

"Dinner" was a word Percy understood. He immediately sprang from his supine position and followed Ellie into the kitchen. Ellie had a good view of the yard. She didn't mind if Jackson could see her, although he was too distracted tossing the ball to notice her. As long as she didn't have to go past the threshold, she felt safe.

Ellie opened a can of food for Percy and put it on the counter. She snickered, knowing most people would be appalled that she fed her cat on the kitchen counter. Too bad. This was her house and her cat. She knew it would be another hour before Jackson and Buddy were finished running around the yard, so she decided to wait before she put out Buddy's food. No countertops for him. She chuckled, trying to imagine her big dog on the counter. Ellie looked out the window, watching the boy and the dog chase each other. She knew that Hector was always on top of his job of cleaning the yard. She didn't want Jackson going home with poop on his shoes or his pants. There were times when Jackson would roll around in the grass with the big pooch. Ellie was surprised that

Colleen didn't have a fit when Jackson would return home with grass stains and dirt all over him. But the kid was happy. That was all that mattered.

Ellie grabbed the remote for the TV, which was sitting in a corner of the countertop. She clicked on the local news. Nothing earth-shattering. At least not in her small area of the world. North Korea was still looking ominous. The UK was still struggling with the fallout from Brexit, and the world was recovering financially from the pandemic. It had been a difficult time for everyone, but things were starting to come into balance again. Maybe it was time for her to find it for herself.

Ellie checked the refrigerator to figure out what she was going to fix for herself. Time to make a grocery list. She grabbed the last package of chicken breasts and stared blankly. *How many things can you make with chicken?* She decided on chicken Milanese. She had made it many times, but it was always satisfying. Even the prep work was therapeutic. She mixed the breadcrumbs with parmesan cheese, oregano, parsley, basil, garlic powder, salt, and pepper. She cracked a couple of eggs and beat them in a bowl. Ellie poured extra virgin olive oil into the frying pan and heated it up. After she washed the chicken and patted it dry, she pounded it with a meat mallet. First, she dipped it in the eggs and coated the chicken with the flavored breadcrumbs and placed it in the hot oil. After several minutes, she turned the cutlets. While they were cooking, she pulled out a bag of mixed greens: arugula, radicchio, and endive. She then cut an orange and squeezed some juice into the large, stainless-steel salad bowl, then a little more olive oil.

She'd wait until the last minute to toss in the greens, which she would then place on top of the chicken cutlets.

Ellie was so engrossed in her meal preparations that she jumped when Jackson hit the bell to be let out. She walked over to the intercom. "Good night, Jackson!" she called and hit the gate lock button.

"Thanks, Ms. Bowman! Something sure smells good!"

Ellie laughed. "It's chicken Milanese."

"Chicken what?"

"It's kinda like Italian fried chicken." That was the best way to describe the taste. "With some salad on top."

"I like fried chicken. Salad, not so much." Jackson waved toward the window from which the fine aroma was coming. "Bye!"

Ellie hit the lock button after Jackson

exited, and Buddy came galloping through the laundry room and kitchen.

"Oh, now you want to be my friend?" Ellie fixed Buddy's bowl. He wagged his tail in agreement as she set it on the floor.

Ellie tossed the salad, removed the chicken from the pan, and topped it with the greens. Jackson was right. It sure smelled good.

Ellie pulled a stool from under the counter, plopped herself in her usual position, and continued to watch TV. Sometimes, the news was so dreadful that she would channel-surf, looking for something uplifting. She stumbled upon *The Andy Griffith Show* and remembered Hector's description of Hibbing. "It's like Mayberry." And that was fine with her.

CHAPTER TWENTY-FIVE

Colleen was relieved that Frank and Jeanne had returned. She felt safer with them next door. The big issue was going to be the new neighbors across the street. She was concerned about Randy Gaynor, the twelve-year-old delinquent. She thought again about asking Officer Bob Pedone for information. Instead, she figured she would simply mention it and see if he could offer any information or thoughts. The last thing she needed was for a new kid to be a bad influence on Jackson.

Mitchel's court date was coming up, and Colleen thought that would be a good excuse to call the policeman. She walked over to the bulletin board, picked up the phone, and nervously dialed the number.

"Pedone," he answered.

Colleen hesitated, then cleared her throat. "Hello. It's Colleen Haywood. How are you?"

"Well, hello, Colleen Haywood." Pedone wasn't sure if he should be informal and call her by her first name. "How are you? Everything all right?"

"Yes, fine, thank you." Colleen felt like a schoolgirl talking to this man.

"What can I do for you today? You haven't had to use that Taser, I hope."

Colleen could sense he was smiling. "Oh, no, nothing like that. Mitchel's court date is coming up, and I was checking to see if you were going to be there."

"Yes, since I was the arresting officer and filed the report," he explained.

"Oh, good. I thought that was the case, but I wanted to be sure." Colleen hesitated. "Do you think you could stop by some time for coffee? I want to run a few things past you." *There. I said it.*

"Anything serious?"

"I'm not sure yet."

"What do you mean?" he prodded.

"I'd rather discuss it in person, if that's OK with you." She winced, waiting for his response.

"Sure. No problem. When do you want to meet?"

"I'll be finished with school around three-thirty today. We have a meeting. I should be home by four, if that's not too late. Or early."

"Not a problem. Will Jackson be staying with you at school?" Pedone asked, recalling Colleen's telling him about Mitchel hanging around.

"No. My neighbor Frank will meet him and walk him home. He'll sit with him until he finishes his homework. Then Jackson will most likely go down the block to Ellie Bowman's."

"That's good. Is Mitchel still hanging around at the end of the block?"

"He wasn't there yesterday. Morning or afternoon. And I don't see his car right now."

"Maybe he's behaving himself," Pedone added.

"He and Jackson had a good visit on Saturday. I'm hoping that's a step in the right direction."

"There is something to be said for a good father/son relationship."

"I agree. Mitchel's dad died when he was only ten, so he never really had much of an opportunity to bond with him. Do you have any kids?" Colleen asked. "I'm sorry. It's none of my business."

"No problem. I have a son who's a freshman in college." It was his turn to clear his throat. "My wife and I — I should say my ex-wife and I — divorced when he was thirteen. But we were civil and made sure we did whatever was necessary to make sure Drew had a normal upbringing. As normal as you can, with divorced parents."

"I could probably use some tips in that field." Colleen was relieved to hear that the man wasn't married. Or had he remarried? "So you've been divorced five years?"

"Give or take. It was my job as a cop that got to her. She didn't like it if I was called away to a scene when I was supposed to be off duty."

"That can be tough."

"Well, it isn't like Hibbing is the crime capital of Missouri," he said, chuckling.

"True."

"I think she just used it as an excuse. We got married straight out of high school. Right after I graduated from the academy, we had Drew. I think that after she turned thirty, she felt like she had missed something in her life and started to get restless. I don't know. But enough about me."

"Oh, that's all right. We seem to have something in common."

"What's that?"

"Divorce," Colleen sputtered. She had made up her mind. It was time to cut

Mitchel loose. Or maybe herself.

"You're planning on filing?"

"Yes. As soon as the hearing is over. I don't want too many legal messes happening at the same time."

"Good thinkin'," Pedone said.

"I'd better get going and make sure Jackson is ready for school."

"You betcha. See you around four. Enjoy your day, Colleen." There, he said it. Her first name.

Colleen was all atwitter. She almost felt foolish. *Was this normal behavior? Does every woman fall for the man who she thinks saved her?* She shrugged, then smiled. At the moment, it didn't matter. She felt safe, and she was moving forward.

"Jackson? Ready?"

"Yes, Mom." Jackson came running out of his room. "Is it OK if I go to Ms. Bowman's after I finish my homework?"

"Are you sure you're not making a pest of yourself?" Colleen squatted down and looked him in the eye.

"Gee, I dunno, Mom. She was really nice yesterday."

Colleen looked at him curiously. "You spoke to her?"

"Through the box." Jackson was pulling on his backpack. "I showed her my ar-

266

rowhead."

"How did you do that?"

"What?"

"Show her your arrowhead?" Colleen's curiosity was peaked.

"I held it up in the air." Jackson thought nothing of it.

"OK. So you didn't go in the house?"

"No, Mom."

"And she didn't come outside?"

"Nope." Jackson checked his shoelaces. Tied. Double knots.

"What else did she say?"

"She said she was getting worried 'cause I was late. That's when I showed her my good-luck charm."

"Oh. OK." Colleen realized that nothing Jackson had said differed from every other experience, even though she was secretly hoping for some kind of breakthrough.

"But she was cooking some kind of fried chicken when I was leaving. I told her it smelled real good."

"So she was in the kitchen when you were there?"

"Yup."

"And you could see her?"

"Yup," Jackson repeated. "But I didn't get a real good look."

"Well, all righty! Let's get moving. You

remember that Frank is going to walk you home today, and he'll sit with you while you do your homework. Then you can go play with Buddy."

"Yippee!" Jackson put on his baseball cap and stomped out the door.

As the two of them headed toward school, Colleen noticed again that Mitchel's car was not lurking on the side of the road. On the one hand, that made her feel better, but on the other, she wondered if Mitchel had some nefarious plan up his sleeve. She shrugged off her concern. For the moment.

At the end of the school day, Frank greeted Jackson outside the front entrance to the school. "Hey, Mr. Chadwick!" Jackson waved to his friends. "See ya tomorrow!"

"Hey, Jackson!" Frank put his hand on Jackson's shoulder. "How was school to-day?"

"Oh, pretty much the same as yesterday, except Kevin brought a frog into class and it got out of its box. It was hopping all over the place. Some of the girls were scream-ing." Jackson was laughing as he described the scene.

"Did someone finally catch it?"

"Yeah. Kevin put the box over him, but then he couldn't figure out how to turn the box over without the frog getting out."

"So then what happened?"

"Mrs. Massa called the custodian. He came with a net and threw it over the box. It was hard to see because he was bent over. But when he stood up, the frog was back in the box, and the lid was on it."

"Well, that sounds like a bit of excitement, right?" Frank was amused.

"Then Mrs. Massa made Kevin put tape on the box so the frog wouldn't get out again."

"I assume there were holes in the box so the frog could breathe?"

"Oh, sure. He even had some grass stuff, but that got all over the floor. I guess the frog is gonna have to wait 'til it gets home before he can have a snack."

Frank smiled. The wonder of childhood.

The walk home took less than ten minutes. Once they got inside, Jackson took off his backpack and pulled out his homework assignment.

"What are you working on today?" Frank asked.

"We're studying the solar system."

"Wow. That's impressive."

"I guess. We have to draw a map."

"Do you get to look at your book while you're doing it?"

"Yeah. Mrs. Massa said we should try to draw the planets first, then close the book and try to remember the names."

"But you could peek if you wanted to?" Frank wanted to learn how Jackson would react to being honorable.

"I guess. But I won't. That wouldn't be fair." Jackson said this as if it were obvious. "Besides, we're going to get a quiz on it Friday. So if anybody cheats on their homework, they might not pass the test."

"Jackson, you are very astute."

"What is a stute?"

Frank chuckled. "The word is 'astute.' It means smart."

"Uh. OK. I guess we'll find out when I take the test on Friday!"

"Well, get busy then. I'll check your work after you're done."

"Okeydokey." Jackson sat at the kitchen table, took a blank sheet of paper, opened his science book to the map of the solar system, and began to make circles. He stopped once he got to Mars and realized he was not going to have room on his paper for the rest of the planets. He scrapped the first attempt and started again.

Frank leaned over and turned the paper sideways. "That oughta give you more room for Jupiter, Saturn, Uranus, and Pluto."

Jackson looked up at Frank and nodded.

"Here's a way to remember the names. M.V.E.M.J.S.U.N. M stands for Most. V stands for Valuable. E stands for Earth. M stands for My Name. J stands for Jackson. And the rest is easy. S.U.N."

"Wow! How did you do that?" Jackson's knee was bobbing.

"It's called a mnemonic."

"A what?"

Frank replied phonetically. "A neh monic."

"Do I have to remember that, too?" Jackson made a face.

Frank chuckled. "No. But give it a try."

Jackson looked down at the letters. "But what if I forget the letters?"

"You know all the names, right?"

"Well, yeah."

"OK. First thing you do is write down all the names. They don't have to be in order. Then you take the first letter of each name and underline it," Frank instructed. "Go ahead. Give it a try."

Jackson got very serious and spoke as he wrote: "Mars, Jupiter, Saturn, Earth, Venus, Neptune, Mercury, Uranus." He looked up at Frank. "What about Pluto?"

"Is it still a planet?" Frank asked.

"They call it a dwarf planet." Jackson was

proud that he knew that tidbit.

"Well, then, it should be easy to remember him last. Like a period at the end of a sentence," Frank said.

"What if I get Mars and Mercury mixed up?"

Frank hadn't thought about that. "How about this. Earth is spelled 'e, a, r, t, h." What comes after the E in Earth?

"A."

"Mercury starts with m, e. Mars starts with m, a. What comes after the E in earth?"

"An A."

"Correct. So the planet that comes after earth, has an a."

Jackson thought about all of this.

"Are you confused yet?" Frank half-teased him.

"Kinda."

"Give it a try."

Jackson thought really hard. He under-lined the first letter of each planet. M is for Most. And it comes before Earth — E— so it can't be Mars. Right?"

"Right."

"V is for valuable. So it has to be Venus. Then Earth. Then Mars. Jackson, Jupiter!" He squealed with delight. "Saturn, Uranus, Neptune! And a period for Pluto!"

"Excellent!"

"Wow. That was kinda hard. But I think I'll remember them!" Jackson looked up at Frank, and they gave each other a high five. "How come you were never a teacher?"

"I taught other things."

"In a classroom?"

"Sort of," Frank explained. "I worked with men in the military, and I had to teach them tactical things. You play video games, right?"

"Only when my mom lets me."

"Well, you know you have to develop skills to win, right?"

"Oh, sure."

"That's kind of the same thing. I taught soldiers how to win."

"Cool." Jackson took out a clean sheet of paper and drew his circles again. This time, he included the names of each planet inside the circles as he was going through the mnemonic Frank had just taught him. When he finished, he slid the paper over to Frank. "Did I get it right?"

"You did indeed! Good job!" They gave each other another high five.

"Is there anything else you need to work on today?"

"Nope. And ya know what, Mr. Chadwick? It didn't take as long as I thought it would."

"Glad to hear it. Now go change your

clothes, then you can head over to Buddy's."

"Yay!" Jackson bolted from his chair.

"Hold on a second. Put away your papers and pack up your bag so it's ready for you tomorrow."

"Yes, sir." Jackson spun around and did what he had been told.

"Good boy!" Frank patted him on the shoulder.

Jackson whipped down the hall and put on a pair of jeans and a sweatshirt. He grabbed his ball and glove, donned his cap, and marched toward the front door.

"Do you have a key?" Frank asked.

Jackson halted and thought a moment. "In my backpack."

"Maybe you should take it with you."

"Good idea, Mr. Chadwick. Jeepers, you are full of good ideas."

"I don't think my wife would agree with you." Frank laughed, and so did Jackson.

Both left the house, with Jackson locking the front door. Frank went to his house, and Jackson headed to Buddy's.

Right on schedule, Colleen returned home just before 4:00. She changed into a pair of linen pants and a clean blouse, checked her makeup, and ran a brush through her hair. She refreshed her perfume just a little. She didn't want to knock Officer Pedone over when he came into the house. On the other hand . . .

When the front doorbell rang, she got butterflies in her stomach. She was almost giddy. She smoothed the front of her pants and opened the door.

"Good afternoon!" She was beaming.

"Good afternoon to you." Officer Pedone removed his hat.

"Please come in." She swung the door open and stepped back to let him in. She had forgotten how tall he was. Probably because she had been sitting down most of the time when he first came. He was also in great shape. She could see the muscles pushing against the sleeve of his shirt. *Calm down, girl.* "Sit. Please." She motioned toward the dining-room table. "What kind of coffee do you prefer? Decaf? Caffeinated? Espresso? American?"

"Wow. This is like a Starbucks," Pedone joked. "Do you have something between espresso and American? Or did I come to the wrong coffee bar?"

"I have a Nespresso coffee maker. It uses capsules. I have a nice one that might be to your liking. Decaf or regular?"

Pedone checked his watch. "Better do decaf; otherwise, I might be up all night."

"Decaf it is. How do you take it?"

"You are quite the barista, eh?" Pedone teased.

"Yeah. Just in case I need to get a second job." *She* wasn't joking.

Pedone sensed she wasn't kidding. "Seriously?"

"Well, yes and no. But if Mitchel doesn't have a job and can't come up with child support, I just might have to."

"What's he doing to find gainful employment?"

"I have no idea. We haven't spoken since that night." Colleen was working on the coffee.

"How do you communicate about Jackson?"

"Through his mother, Vivian."

"And how is that going?" Pedone asked.

"Not too bad, considering."

"Considering what?"

"I don't want to speak ill of people, but let's just say that Vivian can be difficult at times." Colleen was not exaggerating. There were always arguments as to who was going where during the holidays, and Vivian had never been flexible. And in Colleen's mind, there was no reason for her not to be. It was just Vivian that Vivian had to worry about. It wasn't as if she hosted a dozen people. Greg and Elaine were always flexible, so they weren't the issue. After enough fights with Mitchel, Colleen acquiesced and spent her holidays resenting Vivian's stubbornness. "But I have to admit, she's been fine lately. No one can seem to guess what's gotten into her."

"What do you mean?" Pedone was curious.

"I don't want to gossip, but evidently when she took Jackson and Mitchel out last Saturday, she came back in a most upbeat mood. Everyone was in shock. It was as if she'd had some kind of epiphany."

"That doesn't sound too bad." Pedone nodded in her direction.

"True. I just hope it lasts." Colleen took the mug from the coffee maker. "Cream? Sugar?"

"Just a little cream, please. Thank you," Pedone said politely.

Colleen poured some into the mug, got a napkin and some cookies, and placed them on the table. "I baked them on Saturday. I think they might still be fresh. Or close."

"A barista and a baker? You sure you don't want to open your own café?" he teased her again.

"Not if I don't have to." She smiled and took a seat across from him.

"So, what did you want to talk about?"

Pedone finally got to the point.

"I have new neighbors moving in across the street." Colleen was fidgeting with her spoon. "They have two children. A son and daughter. The son is twelve, and the daughter is a little younger than Jackson."

"Well, that should be a good thing for him. Having other kids on the block, right?"

"Here's the thing." Colleen went straight to the heart of the matter. "The kid was in trouble. He stole a motorcycle or moped or something. They knocked it down to shoplifting and sent him to a facility where he would be scared straight."

"I'm familiar with the program. Surprisingly, if you get the kid at the right age, and he's essentially not a bad kid, that often works. After a year of probation, we rarely see them again." Pedone took a sip of his coffee. "This is good."

"Thanks," Colleen said, and continued, "Is there any way to know if he *is* a good kid who had a lapse in judgment? I know the records are sealed and all." Her voice drifted off.

"That's true." He looked up at her and realized she was concerned about it. "But that doesn't mean people can't remember what happened."

"I'm not following you." And she wasn't.

"Let's just say someone has a conversation with someone who is familiar with the incident. There is no law saying that you can't speak about it. You simply cannot have access to the legal documents; therefore, the information cannot be used against the person in any way, such as keeping the person from employment et cetera."

Colleen gave him a sideways look. "Interesting. That makes sense because the real-estate agent had no problem telling me."

"Exactly." Pedone helped himself to a cookie. He took a bite. "I can attest that these are still fresh. And delicious."

Colleen thought she might be blushing and got up to fix another cup of coffee. "Are you ready for a refill?" she asked over her shoulder.

"If you don't mind, that would be great. Thank you."

"Would it make you feel better if I ask around? See if anyone has any recollection? Obviously, I can't access his jacket."

"Jacket?"

"Police lingo for a file on someone who has a record."

"Aha." Colleen ran her wrists under cold water. "If you wouldn't mind, and if it doesn't get you into any trouble, I would appreciate it immensely."

"Let me see what I can ferret out for you. I know you've been through a lot and have a rocky road ahead of you. You don't need to be worrying about something else. You have his name?"

"Yes, it's Randy Gaynor. I don't know if it's Randolph or not."

"The name Randolph would be enough to put anyone in a bad mood," Pedone joked.

Colleen laughed at his joke. "Oh, I cannot thank you enough. You are so right. I'm trying to keep it together for Jackson's sake, and I almost unraveled the other day when the real-estate agent told me about the kid."

Pedone initially resisted the temptation to take her hand, and he was delighted when she touched his. "You have no idea how grateful I am."

"I haven't done anything yet," Pedone said, leaving his hand under hers.

"You have done more than you think." Colleen realized that she had kept her hand on top of his for a tad longer than she probably should have and pulled it away. "Really. The night of the incident, the Taser, and your kindness." She started to get choked up. "It has meant a lot to me." As hard as she tried, she could not stop the tears from running down her face.

Pedone picked up his napkin and handed it to her. As much as he wanted to wipe her tears away, he thought that might be just a little too personal.

"Thanks." She sniffled. Then she let out a big sigh and dabbed her face.

"Any time," Pedone said. He was getting a little uncomfortable. His first reaction would have been to take her in his arms and tell her everything would be OK, but he couldn't. It would be unprofessional, and how did he know if things really would be OK?

He finished his coffee and decided it was better that he leave before he made a fool of himself.

He checked his watch. It wasn't as if he needed to be anywhere, but he thought the gesture would be a good way for him to leave graciously. "I'd better get going. Thanks very much for the coffee and cookies. It was a treat compared to the swill they serve at the station."

"Thank you for coming by, and for, well, everything." Colleen resisted the temptation to kiss him on the cheek.

"I'll be in touch as soon as I hear anything." Pedone put his hat under his arm.

"Thanks again." Colleen opened the door for him to leave.

A few minutes later, her phone rang. It was Ellie. In unison, they both said, "Is everything all right?" And then they laughed. Ellie said, "You go first."

Colleen told Ellie she thought something might have happened to Jackson, and Ellie told Colleen she was worried about the patrol car in front of the Haywood house again.

"Everything is fine." Colleen was coming to grips. "I had some questions for Officer Pedone, and he was kind enough to come by so we could talk."

"Glad to hear it. There have been more visits by the police in the past two and a half weeks than in the whole time I've lived here," Ellie noted.

"It's just that I'm so popular with the men in blue." Colleen laughed lightly.

"Apparently so," Ellie stated.

"It's good to know someone has your back. You know what I mean?"

"Absolutely. I don't know what I would do without Hector."

"He's a great kid," Colleen said, acknowledging how much he did for Ellie.

"So all is OK on Birchwood Lane?" Ellie prodded.

"So far," Colleen answered, and changed the subject. She didn't want to let on that she might have a crush on the kind, attractive officer. "I hope Jackson isn't making a pest of himself."

"Jackson? Not at all. I look forward to his visits as much as Buddy does. I'm very happy my big pooch has someone who will play with him. For hours no less. It takes the guilt off me." Ellie was acutely aware how easy it was to talk to Colleen. And she liked the feeling.

"You can send him home anytime," Colleen reminded Ellie. "By the way, he mentioned something about Italian fried chicken."

Ellie laughed. "Last night, I was making dinner when he and Jackson were in the yard. I guess the aroma wafted outside."

"He said it 'smelled real good,' so I hope you'll give me the recipe, unless it's a family secret."

Ellie thought, *No, I'm the only family secret.* "It's not complicated. It's called chicken Milanese, but when I told him what it was called, he didn't seem to know what I was talking about. I mean, what kid knows what Milanese is, so I told him it was Italian fried chicken."

"Too funny. It must be better than the Colonel's, I'm sure."

"Without a doubt. I'll write the recipe

down and have Hector bring it over to you."

"Thanks, Ellie. That would make a nice surprise for Jackson."

"Yes, but when I told him I put salad on top, he didn't seem very impressed anymore." Ellie chuckled.

"I'll give it a go anyway. Thanks."

"No problem. I've gotta go. Someone is having a computer crisis."

"OK. Talk soon." Colleen disconnected the call. She was feeling a lot better about things. *Onward.*

CHAPTER TWENTY-SIX

Several days after Officer Pedone visited Colleen, a large moving van pulled onto the street. She hadn't heard back from him and was beginning to feel anxious. She thought of calling him again but didn't want to make a pest of herself. She had to leave for school, so she would not get to watch the new family move in. No point in belaboring the subject. Time to get herself and Jackson out the door.

Andy was sitting in the front sunroom of his house. It was the only place other than the kitchen that there was a chair that wasn't piled with papers. He sipped his instant coffee and watched the van unload furniture and boxes. He was curious as to their taste. Was it modern? Midcentury? Early American? That style was something he loathed. Rustic? Even that could give him the willies if it weren't done right.

First came a parade of boxes, followed by several beds. He was getting antsy waiting for the big reveal. He didn't want to miss going to Sissy's but could not resist spying on the new neighbors. *It wasn't exactly spying,* he told himself. It was a healthy curiosity about the people who would be living within a hundred or so feet from him. He had a right to know. He sat up and peered through the window. The sofa. Modular. *Meh. Maybe it was for the family room.* He continued watching the contents of the large van being moved into the house. A coffee table. Another *meh.* More of the same cookie-cutter, chain-store furniture collection. Then came the enormous television. Andy wondered if it would fit through the door. He hadn't had any personal experience with flat screens. True, he had visited people who had them but had never paid much attention. He had been using the same television for the past twenty-five years. With rabbit ears for an antenna, no less. It was no wonder he could only tune in three stations, but he didn't care. The news was the news, and there was little or nothing he could do about it. He was resigned to the adage that ignorance is bliss.

He waited and watched for another hour before deciding it was time to go. He would see the final décor at some point. He would give them a few days to settle in and go over and introduce himself. He knew they would still be unpacking boxes, but the furniture should be in place. He maneuvered his way to the front door and hobbled to the blue Lincoln Mark V he had brought back to the house after the last time he had visited his cars. He was glad he had swapped it out with the Cadillac. He carefully inched the car out of the driveway and slowly moved past the neighbors. He gave a wave as he passed the van and drove slowly to his destination.

Jeanne and Frank were as curious as everyone else on the block. Frank practically had to hold Jeanne back physically. "You don't want to seem like a nosy neighbor."

Jeanne looked at him and laughed. "Have you not met me? I *am* a nosy neighbor."

"Well, not right now." Frank grabbed her by the back of the waistband of her slacks.

She playfully slapped his hand away. "I'm only going to look out the window. Carefully."

Frank shook his head. He knew that when Jeanne got an idea into her head, it would take a crowbar to get it out.

But he, too, couldn't resist. He sneaked

up behind her, and they both had a look-see. Andy's car was passing in front of their house at the same time.

"He's such a sport," Frank commented. "Look at him. Well dressed and driving a classic car. I hope I can do that when I'm his age."

Jeanne chuckled. "I'm not sure about a light blue Lincoln, though."

"Maybe Andy will leave it to me."

"Oh, shush." She gave him a slap on the arm.

After staring out the window for a half hour, they realized there wasn't much to see.

"When should we go over there?" Jeanne asked.

"Hon, can you wait for the van to leave at least?"

"All right, but I am going to get started on making some baked ziti. I'll take it over to them later." Jeanne was being very sincere. Sure, she was curious, but she also wanted to make the neighbors feel at home. They were, after all, going to share the same street for a long time. Better to get on their good side right away.

"That's my girl. I'm sure they'll appreciate it, too." Frank gave her a pat on the fanny. "Don't forget to make some for me."

"I wouldn't dream of forgetting you." Jeanne blew him a kiss as she entered the kitchen. "Let me know if there are any signs of the kids." Jeanne knew that Frank would stand guard at the window until he was satisfied. It was in his protective nature to suss out every situation.

"Roger that," he replied.

Ellie was sitting on her perch in the loft, holding her binoculars. She watched Andy inch his way out of his driveway and navigate around the big van. Three strapping young men were rapidly moving boxes and furniture from the moving truck. She caught a glimpse of a woman talking to a person who appeared to be the supervisor. She was nodding and pointing to something on a clipboard he was holding. There didn't appear to be any issues, simply an exchange of information. Had there been an issue, Ellie would have clearly seen an expression of discontent on the woman's face. Her binoculars were *that* good. She could almost see the woman's nose hair. Ellie let out a guffaw at that thought. Ew.

So far, nothing appeared to distinguish them from any other middle-class, modern family. Modular furniture, big-screen TV. The dining-room table was a simple rectangle with light wood. She counted six cream-colored, chevron-patterned parsons chairs. Now that's adventurous, considering there were two kids in the house. Maybe they weren't allowed to sit on them. Maybe they never used the dining room. She could only guess. She waited to see if there was another table, perhaps for the kitchen. There was. It was a light-wood trestle table with a bench and four matching chairs. That was more like it.

After the first group of modular seating had been carried in, another modern sofa was pulled from the van. It was also cream-colored. Probably to go in another room, one the kids were not permitted to enter, she surmised. The woman disappeared into the house, most likely to supervise the placement. A sound from her computer told her that someone was likely in need of her help. She reluctantly set down the binoculars and looked at Buddy and Percy. "You guys keep an eye on things. Mommy's got to get to work." Percy yawned, and Buddy thumped his tail.

When Jackson and Colleen got home from school, the boy was excited to see the movers finishing up. He couldn't wait to meet the new neighbors. He had heard there was a boy four years older, and he hoped they could be friends. He knew some twelve-year-old kids kind of liked girls. While Jackson was still of the mind that they might have cooties, he understood it was a part of life. Maybe they could do some guy things, like go fishing or something. He knew he didn't want to share Buddy with him. That was his special time and his special place. Besides, he didn't think Ms. Bowman would want another kid running around her yard.

He unpacked his homework and went to the kitchen table to get it done. Maybe he would stop by and say hello on his way to see Buddy. "Hey, Mom?"

"Yes, honey."

"Do you think I could go over and say hi to the new neighbors on my way over to Buddy?"

Colleen got a shiver up her spine. She wasn't ready for that, especially since she hadn't heard from Officer Pedone.

"Let's give them a day to settle in, OK?"

"But if I walk past them, I want to say hi. Is that OK?"

Colleen couldn't think of a good reason why her son couldn't be cordial. She could only think of a bad one. Her maternal instinct kicked in, and she went for the phone. She made her way into her bedroom for privacy and dialed Pedone's number.

"Pedone," he answered on the second ring. Perhaps it was because he knew it was her from the caller ID, but he wasn't going to let on.

"Hi. Bob?" She asked as if she wasn't sure she should call him Bob, even though he had told her to.

"Hey, Colleen. I was just about to call you. Can you give me a minute and let me call you back? I want to take this outside."

"I'm sorry. I don't want to make a pest of myself. But . . ."

He interrupted her. "You're not being a pest. I just want some privacy. I'll call you in less than five minutes. Promise."

"OK. Thanks." Colleen hung up, feeling dejected. But before her imagination could turn the conversation into something she would regret, the phone rang again, causing her to jump." *Get a grip, girl.* She also realized that she had said that to herself a few times when it came to the handsome, unmarried policeman. Only this time it was because of her concern for her son.

"Hey." Pedone's voice was soothing and familiar.

"Hey," Colleen replied.

"I did a little recon and found out the boy was with some other older kids who had bullied him into jumping on a moped. This happened in another town."

"So it wasn't a motorcycle at all?" Colleen was still not sure if she should be relieved.

"No. It belonged to a pizza delivery guy who the little gang of hoodlums liked to taunt. So instead of getting themselves in trouble, they pushed the kid into taking it. He managed to get about a block away before the pizza guy caught up with him. The kid had no idea what he was doing, but luckily, he didn't hurt himself. And the bunch of ne'er-do-wells not only put the pizza guy in a tizzy, they laughed hysterically at Randy. The embarrassment was bad enough, but then the owner of the pizza shop wanted to press charges against all of them, but he couldn't, since Randy was the only one driving. If you could call it that. So they dropped the charges down to shoplifting, mostly to teach him a lesson. It will be expunged when he turns eighteen if he doesn't get into any other trouble. Which I doubt he will. The reason they moved here is to get him into a better school, away from those other kids."

Colleen sat down on a dining-room chair. "That is such a relief. Thank you so much."

"From what I gathered, they're a decent, hardworking family. The father's an accountant and the mother a librarian. So you have something in common. Books."

Colleen almost started to cry from the news.

"You still with me?" he asked into the void.

"Oh, yes. Yes. I'm trying to absorb this. I was so worried."

"I know you were. But you can relax now. Sometimes, there's a road to redemption."

"You are so right." Colleen took in a gulp of air. "How can I thank you?"

There was a moment of silence. She thought they might have been disconnected. "Hello?"

"Yes. I'm still here. Listen, this may be a little unconventional, but after all this is over, the trial and all, and once you get yourself settled, would you consider having dinner with me? I'll understand if you don't want to, after all you've been through. But it would be nice to have a dinner partner. Someone to talk to and share a meal."

Colleen was speechless. She couldn't remember the last time she and Mitchel had "shared a meal" in a nice, quiet atmosphere.

"Are *you* still there?" Pedone asked.

Colleen laughed softly. "Yes. Yes, I am, and I would be delighted to have dinner and enlightened conversation with you."

Pedone chuckled. "I can't guarantee

'enlightened,' but I'll try for entertaining. How does that sound?"

"Sounds good. It may be a while, but it will be something to look forward to." Colleen was beaming.

"Me too. Remember, if you need anything in the meantime, give me a call."

"Thanks *Officer* Pedone," she teased. "I mean Bob."

"Anytime, Colleen." They ended the call, with both of them feeling good about the future. Even if it was only dinner.

When she hung up, there was a spring in her step as she made her way into the kitchen, where Jackson was doing his homework. "Honey? I thought about what you said, and it would be nice if you went over to say hello and introduce yourself. We need to be good neighbors. Do you want me to go with you?"

"Sure. Then I'll go to Buddy's." Jackson was working on his homework — math problems — that day. "Hey, Mom? Did I tell you about how Mr. Chadwick helped me with the solar-system stuff? Which planets are where?"

"No. Tell me about it." Colleen pulled up a chair.

"He showed me a trick to remember things by using letters. It had a funny name

I can't remember."

"What was the trick?"

"First, I write the names. I have to remember them first, but I know them. Then I underline the first letter of each name. Then I remember by saying Most Valuable Earth. My name is Jackson. Then S.U.N. for Saturn, Uranus, and Neptune. And Pluto is P for the period at the end."

"That's terrific. And you remembered everything?"

"Yep. At first I was a little confused, but I figured it out." Jackson was wiggling his pencil.

"Well, you did a great job. And Mr. Chadwick, too!" She leaned over and gave him a hug from behind.

"Yep. He's pretty smart."

"Yes, he is," Colleen concurred.

"He told me that he was kind of a teacher."

"Oh?"

"Yeah. When he was in the military, he had to teach guys how to do stuff."

"I bet he was really good at it," Colleen said.

"Prob'ly." Jackson continued to work on his multiplication tables.

"How are you doing with your math?"

"OK, I guess. I don't know any tricks, so

can you check it for me?" Jackson looked over his shoulder at his mother.

"Of course. Anything in particular you're troubled about?"

"Nah. But it does seem hard. I gotta memorize a lot of junk."

"It's not junk, but you are correct. It's a lot of memorization."

Jackson repeated the word "Mem-o-riz-ation. That kinda sounds like a word Mr. Chadwick used yesterday when he told me about the letters and the trick."

"You mean mnemonics?" Colleen asked.

"Yeah! That was the word." Jackson's delight was evident.

Colleen knew that further explanation would only confuse him more. But she was happy he understood the concept and was grateful for Frank's assistance.

"You almost done?" she asked.

"Yep." He handed her his paper.

Colleen checked it for errors. He had gotten all the answers correct. "Great job."

"Mom? How come we have to memorize all this stuff when we could use a calculator?"

"Because we can't always depend on having access to machines, computers, or our phones," she explained carefully. "They say that knowledge is power, so the more you know on your own, the more powerful you become."

"Like a superhero?" Jackson was intrigued.

"In a way, yes." Colleen handed him his paper. "Now, go change your clothes."

Jackson packed up his backpack and headed to his room. A few minutes later, he returned with his usual jeans, sweatshirt, cap, ball, and glove. "Ready?"

"Give me one more second. I want to wrap one of the zucchini breads I made."

"Yuck. Zucchini." Jackson made a face.

"Bet you'll like this." She handed him a piece from another loaf. He took a bite and nodded.

"Yeah, but I don't like zucchini."

Colleen smiled. "Well, you're liking it now!"

Jackson held the piece in front of him. "This?" He looked at it suspiciously.

"Yes, honey. *That* is zucchini bread."

"I wish you hadn't told me." He took a sniff and made a face.

"Come on, Jackson. You have to admit you like it." Colleen smiled.

"I guess," Jackson reluctantly agreed. "Just don't tell me when you trick me."

"I wasn't tricking you, sweetheart. Just a lesson in good eating."

He shrugged and munched down the rest

of the fragrant slice.

He resisted asking for another. He was still miffed his mother had tricked him into eating a vegetable.

"Wash your hands."

"But I just did."

"Yes, but now they have grease from the zucchini bread all over them. And wipe your mouth, too, please."

A few minutes later, he appeared from the bathroom, holding up both hands for inspection.

Colleen laughed at her son's attempt at humor. She picked up her phone and called Jeanne.

"Hey, Jeanne. Jackson and I are about to greet the new neighbors. Want to be part of the welcoming committee?"

"Sure. I have a pan of ziti cooling on the stove. It should be ready to go. Meet you outside."

Colleen and Jackson left the house, Jeanne and Frank stepped out as the van was pulling away.

"Come on. Let's go meet the new neighbors."

Frank started the small parade of well-wishers across the street.

"Too bad Andy isn't back yet." Jeanne noticed that his car wasn't in his driveway.

"Maybe we should have waited for him," Colleen said.

"I'm sure he'll have plenty of opportunities to descend on these unsuspecting folks soon enough." Frank kept walking.

Just as they were crossing the street, the big baby-blue Lincoln crept its way down the block. They stopped midway and waved him down. Jackson ran over to the window.

"Hey, Mr. Robertson! We're gonna go meet the new neighbors. Wanna come?"

"Well, hello to you, Jackson. I would be delighted to meet the new neighbors, but I have to park my car first. Can you wait for me?"

Colleen, Frank, and Jeanne knew that could mean another fifteen minutes in limbo. They looked at each other. Frank chimed in first. "I'll go and walk him over. You two are bearing gifts. I only have my charm." He winked. Jeanne laughed out loud.

Frank approached Andy's window. "Go park, and we'll walk over together."

"Marvelous. Thank you." Andy rolled up the window and moved his car slowly in the direction of his driveway. It seemed like an eternity before he finally put it in gear and got out of the vehicle.

Frank slowly made his way over to Andy's

driveway and greeted him again. "Lovely day, isn't it?"

"It certainly is." Andy held onto the driver's door as he pulled himself from the front seat.

"Here, let me help you." Frank moved toward Andy.

"That's very kind of you, but it's quite all right. I have a routine." Andy spoke with eloquence and perfect diction. Frank wondered why Andy had chosen Hibbing to retire. He was a man of many talents, with a love for art and theater, and art and theater weren't exactly abundant in such a small town. Frank finally decided to ask why. It was something he had wondered about all these years.

The two men walked slowly to the sidewalk, then in the direction of the new neighbors. Frank began. "Andy, may I ask you a question?"

"Certainly. Ask away. Let's hope I can remember the answer." He was only half joking.

"After living in St. Louis and being surrounded by art, culture, and music, what made you decide to move to Hibbing, of all places?"

"Well, I was interested in antiques. I had thought about opening a shop in the city, but after doing a little research, I discovered that city people preferred to forage for antiques in the countryside. Sounds silly, but you know how some folks can be. Perhaps they think that if they don't actually *find* it, it isn't authentic." He paused walking for a moment, took a deep breath, and continued on their path. "One day, I decided to drive west to see what the rest of the state looked like. It was lovely, and there were a lot of homesteads that had gone up for sheriff's sales. I thought it might be a treasure trove for me to cull. I settled here because it's halfway between Kansas City and St. Louis, so I could have clientele from both cities. Remember what I said about people foraging for their own? Well, I am here to tell you that's nonsense."

"What do you mean?" Frank asked.

"They love to go 'antiquing,' provided someone does the work for them. But getting back to how I ended up here. As I was saying, I took a drive and discovered a good supply to start with. The next thing was to find a place to put it, so I bought a local newspaper, and there was a house for rent on the main highway. It was just the right size for a store but not big enough for me to live there as well. And I didn't want to be so close to work that it took over my entire life."

"That was a smart move. I marvel at people who work from home and can separate themselves after putting in an eight-hour day."

"Exactly. When I rented the shop, I asked the real-estate agent if there were any modest homes for sale, and she sent me here. And that's the whole story, kit and caboodle. The only thing I'm dealing with now is all the items that I didn't sell with the rest of my inventory. To be quite frank, Frank" — Andy chuckled — "I could be buried under all the things I have, and no one would find me for days."

Frank had a gruesome thought. What if that actually happened? He knew that no one on the block had ever stepped foot *in* Andy's house. Then he thought about Ellie Bowman. She never stepped *out* of her house. Quite a contrast. Five houses and five different stories. Frank felt that he and Jeanne were probably the most ordinary of the bunch, but he hadn't yet met the new neighbors. Perhaps they would get the prize for normalcy. Or maybe for being the most unusual. He thought that Andy and Ellie would be hard to beat. Then he thought of Mitchel, but it occurred to him that Mitchel's problem wasn't all that unusual. Alcoholism strikes millions of families. As they got closer to the front door, Frank's thoughts lightened up again.

The door was open, and Jeanne, Colleen, and Jackson were standing in the foyer, speaking to a petite brunette and a studious-looking gentleman. Two children were standing behind them.

"Here's my husband now. Frank, meet our new neighbors. This is Brenda." She indicated the small woman. Frank shook her hand. "Frank Chadwick."

The man chimed in, "Charlie Gaynor. Nice to meet you." The men shook hands.

Frank ushered Andy into the crowd. "This is Andy Robertson, your next-door neighbor."

"How do you do." Andy reached for a handshake.

Charlie pointed to his children. "Randy and Megan."

Randy walked over to Frank and shook his hand. "Nice to meet you, sir." Then he shook Andy's. "And you, sir."

Colleen was impressed with the kid's manners. Megan squeezed her way between her mother and father. "And I'm Megan!"

Frank leaned over and extended his hand to her, and she eagerly shook it.

Andy slightly leaned forward. "I can't bend down that far or I might fall over." He said it with a smile, causing Megan to giggle.

She raised her hand up to greet him. "Nice to meet you, Mr. Robertson." Then she turned to Frank. "You, too, Mr. Chadwick."

Colleen directed her attention to Megan. "I heard that you're in second grade?"

"Yes."

"Do you know which school you'll be attending?" Colleen asked. There was a public grammar school and a private school that went from kindergarten to the twelfth grade.

"Daniel Boone Elementary School," Megan proudly replied. "I'm in second grade."

"Then you'll be in my class," Colleen announced.

Megan's eyes grew wide. "You're going to be my teacher?"

"Yes. We only have one second grade, and I'm the teacher."

Colleen saw that Megan was in awe. No one ever lived near their teacher. Teachers had mysterious lives outside of school.

"Jackson and I usually walk together. You are welcome to join us." She looked up at Brenda.

"That would be very nice. Thank you.

We're going to need a little guidance as we settle in." Brenda looked around at the piles of boxes. They were everywhere. "I'm sorry we don't have a place to sit yet."

"That's quite all right," Colleen said.

"We're not going to stay," Jeanne jumped in. "We just wanted to stop by and introduce ourselves." She finally handed over the ziti. "I thought you might need dinner."

"And dessert." Colleen handed Charlie the zucchini bread.

Jackson looked at Randy and made a face. "It has vegetables in it." His comment caused a flurry of giggles and chuckles.

Charlie Gaynor scoured the room. "Andy, so you're next door, and Colleen and Jackson are across the street, next to Frank and Jeanne."

Everyone was anticipating the next question. "Who lives at the end of the street?"

"That's Ms. Bowman. She has a dog named Buddy," Jackson answered swiftly. "But she doesn't come outside."

"Oh?" Charlie asked.

"We're not sure what the reason is, but she is generous and kind," Colleen was quick to add.

"We won't keep you from your unpacking. As Jeanne said, we simply wanted to say hello. If there is anything you need, like where to get decent pizza, the best dry cleaner's, the good coffee spots, let us know." Frank, as was his wont, had taken charge.

Words of "thanks," "nice meeting you," "see you soon" went around the group.

Colleen turned as they were leaving. "Let me know when Megan starts school."

"Will do. Thanks again," Brenda answered.

The group dispersed, and Frank walked Andy back to his house. Jackson followed and continued on to Ellie's.

"They seem to be a nice family," Andy noted. "At least the children are polite."

"She's a librarian, and he's an accountant. I doubt they'll be having any heavy metal bands in the backyard," Frank joked.

"You'd be surprised about librarians." Andy chuckled.

Frank walked Andy to the entrance of the picket-fence gate. He was curious as to how much clutter was behind the door.

"Andy, if you ever need a hand with all your stuff, we'd be happy to help."

"Thank you very much. I have some people who are interested in the silver. As soon as I can get to it."

"That's what I mean. I'll gladly help you with that."

"I appreciate the offer and will certainly keep it in mind," Andy answered politely, knowing he would keep it in mind but never act on it. The thought of doing anything about the clutter was too overwhelming. "Thank you for escorting me. Enjoy the rest of the afternoon." He turned and shuffled toward the front door. Frank watched in amazement. He recalled his recent conversation with Jeanne. *Sure hope I'm as spry when I am ninety.*

CHAPTER TWENTY-SEVEN

Rick was pacing the floor. He was desperate for the $5,000 he had asked for. It was the only way he could find her. Pay someone. He called his friend Christian again. "Hey, man. How's it goin'?" He was trying to sound relaxed.

"Hey, Rick. Everything's good here. What's happening with you?" Christian knew full well that *something* was going on, but was not sure what it was exactly.

"Were you able to talk Kara into letting you lend me the money?"

"First of all, it's not about Kara 'letting' me. It's about what's best for the both of us. Kara and I are partners. You know, as in life partners?" Christian knew that Rick had no idea what a real partnership was like.

"Yeah, man. I get it." Rick was still pacing.

"I need more information, Rick." Christian was stern. "I, we, can't write out a check without knowing where the money is going and why."

"That's why I wanted you to send it via PayPal."

"I don't think you're hearing me. Check or cash. Either way, I need to know what the money is for."

"I said it was for a start-up, but I had to sign a nondisclosure agreement." Rick was very close to whining.

"If it's such a good investment, why don't you ask your family for the money?" That was more of a rhetorical question. He knew why.

"Oh, man, you know I can't ask any of them."

"Well, what about some of your other friends?" Christian knew full well that Rick didn't have any other friends.

"Look, I need to know if you're going to help me out or not." Now Rick was getting testy.

"I'm not going to send it to PayPal. That's out of the question. It has to be a check, so I can have a record of it in case you don't pay me back. And I need an IOU from you, indicating receipt of the loan and the terms under which you will repay it."

"Of course I'll pay you back. I'll even throw in interest. What do you want, ten percent?"

"If it's such a good investment, then how about giving me a cut?" Christian was testing to see how far Rick would go.

"Plus interest?" Rick asked.

"Why not? You'll be making lots of money, right?"

Rick was getting caught up in his own lie. He wasn't going to be investing in any sort of start-up. He needed the money to find her, but he wasn't about to tell Christian that. "Yeah. Yeah. OK. I'll tell you what. I'll go talk to the other investors and see if we can swing it." In truth, Rick had no idea how he would ever repay any money he got. Nor did he intend to. What he was talking about was, all things considered, stealing money from Christian and Kara.

"Let me talk to Kara again. But like I said, it has to be a check. So if she agrees, I'll send it to you by FedEx. Give me your info."

There was dead silence on the line. "Yo, Rick? You still with me?"

"Yeah. The thing is, I'm traveling a lot, and I don't know where I'm going to be over the next few weeks. That's why I wanted the PayPal thing."

"No can do, Rick. You think about it and call me back."

Rick hesitated. "Let me check my schedule. I'll figure out where I'll be at the end of the week and call you back."

"Sounds good. Later." Christian ended the call.

Kara was standing near him. "No?"

"Not exactly. He's desperate. He's going to try to figure out something. The thing is, even if he got a check from me, how would he cash it?"

"If he's in Vegas, that wouldn't be a problem. I'm sure some of the casinos would be happy to see him again," Kara offered.

"True. They'll think he's going to gamble with it."

Kara gave Christian a funny look. "We sound like criminals."

"No. If anyone is the criminal here, it's Rick. I'm sure that he has no intention of repaying the loan, even if he had the means to do so. If you want to outsmart a criminal, you have to think like them."

Christian made a good point.

"So what's next?" Kara asked.

"My guess is that he'll think of something similar to what you suggested. Depending on where he is, there are check-cashing places all over. I have no idea what the limits are, but Rick is pretty cunning."

"That's for sure," Kara agreed.

■ ■ ■ ■

Rick wasn't happy with the way the conversation had gone. He couldn't give Christian an address because he truly didn't know where he was going to be from one day to the next. He had worn out his welcome with some of his prior gambling buddies, and he was no longer on good terms with several of the casinos. He also knew that the person he wanted to hire would not take credit or a check. It had to be cash. Up front. Otherwise, it was no deal.

He snapped his fingers, remembering something. There was one more person he could try to woo into handing him some cash. Sheena, the previous girlfriend, before her. He knew she lived in LA and had had some bit parts in movies. Maybe she could spare a few bucks for an old flame. The relationship hadn't ended badly. They simply grew apart, so there were no hard feelings. At least not to his knowledge. It had been almost four years. He wondered how she would react. Would the start-up story work on her? Then it hit him. He would tell her that he knew she was working her way to stardom, and that if she had a little extra cash, it might be a good idea to invest in something. He'd give her the routine: "If you'd invested $1,000 in Amazon, you'd have $23,000 now, and if you'd invested $1,000 in Apple, you'd have $24,000." He'd continue with, "The company will go public in three years. Your investment will be worth over a hundred grand. You know show business is a rocky road. This way you'll have a cushion." Oh yeah. That was a great story. Maybe Sheena was still the little lamebrain she was when they had dated.

He puffed up his chest and scrolled through his contacts list. He never deleted anyone's number, just in case of situations like this one. He dialed her number. It went to voice mail. "Hi ya. You've reached Sheena." Giggles. "Well, not really." More giggles. "Hit me with your best shot. Bye for now." Rick gave the phone a disgusted look. Some people never change, but that could easily work in his favor.

"Hey, Sheena. It's your old pal, Ricky Barnes." He cringed at referring to himself as Ricky, but that's what she had called him. "I heard you're doing well out in La La Land. Thought I'd give a check-in and see how things are with you. I'll call back again. Ciao." Rick didn't want to leave a number, and his caller ID said OUT OF AREA. And he was. He had bought a burner phone with cash. That was the only kind of financial transaction he had made for the past two years. Cash. Ever since he had bolted. Some people thought he was backpacking in Guatemala; others thought he was doing a walkabout in Australia. Obviously, neither was true. But there was one thing he was certain of. Nobody really cared.

Even his own mother had thrown him under the bus after she wired him $10,000. She had forgiven him for bolting out of town without giving her any notice, but then months went by after she sent him the first $10,000. And he never contacted her, not until he needed more. She was livid at the audacity he showed to call and ask her to wire him cash again.

Initially, she was worried. Why had he left so abruptly? Why was he at an airport in Chicago? The second call was the last straw. She had babied him all his life. It had practically ruined her marriage after she insisted that her husband give him a job. When that went south, she pushed his father to find him another means of support. Richard Senior was done having his ungrateful, lazy son embarrass him. He was furious when he discovered she had wired him $10,000 without discussing it with him. But that was the point. She knew that if she had brought it up, he would have uttered a resounding "over my dead body." She loved Richard and knew he was right. Enough was enough. Tough love. Rick needed to figure it out on his own, and that would never happen if people kept bailing him out.

Rick scrolled through his contacts list again. There had to be somebody who was still speaking to him. Someone who had some spare cash. He thought about Christian's offer to send a check via FedEx. The question was where to have it sent without making it easy for anyone to find him. The airport routine had worked for his mother. People just assumed he was traveling. He could be going anywhere. But that meant he would have to pick it up at a FedEx location at an airport. He had to think. And think fast. The opportunity to get someone to find her was not going to last forever.

He thought about the casinos in Atlantic City. He could still probably get comped for a hotel there, but sending money to the Atlantic City airport would be too obvious. There is nothing else to do there but gamble. No, it had to be an airport that was in a large hub but was also close to a casino.

He pulled out his phone and hit the app for casinos. There were several in Black

Hawk, about forty minutes from Denver. Perfect. If his luck held, he could probably get a free room at the Ameristar. He had walked away from their tables with almost twelve grand. They might want him back to see if they could recoup. It was worth a try. If he got the room, he'd give Christian the address of the FedEx at the Denver airport.

Rick was feeling pretty positive about his chances of completing his search and locating her. Several things had to happen. First, he had to get himself to Denver. Second, he needed to get the cash. Third, he had to get the money to the person who would do the job. Fourth, he needed to secure a hotel room. He thought about it. A lot of "ifs," to be sure, but he had gotten himself out of bad situations several times before when he thought there was no way out. Yet he always landed on his feet. The last two years had been challenging, but he had managed. He had been casino-hopping all over the country. He didn't make a killing at any of them. Just enough for them to want him back, but not enough to call too much attention to himself. In spite of his winnings, he still didn't have an extra $5,000 for the job he needed done.

He checked the time. Should he call Christian or Sheena? Still too early. He

317

decided to go to the bar and kill some time.

Rick walked through the lobby of the small hotel and headed down the street to a local bar. He slapped a twenty on the counter. "Milagro Silver." It was a moderately priced tequila. He'd save up for the good stuff once he accomplished his plan. He just didn't know when or how long it would take.

Chapter Twenty-Eight

If it hadn't been for the change in the foliage, with all the new blossoms, it would have been hard to tell what day it was. Most of hers blurred from one to the next, except for Sundays, when she would make her weekly calls. Even Jackson's visits were regular, except for the previous Saturday, when he had spent the day with his father and grandmother. She suspected it would be like that every Saturday — for the time being, at least until the custody hearing. She had no idea what the outcome of that would be. If Mitchel stayed on his downward spiral, he surely wouldn't get joint custody. Colleen hadn't spoken to him directly, so she didn't know what kind of frame of mind he was in. Ellie felt for her. It's one thing to know when things are horrible. You can figure out a way to cope. She knew about that all too well. That's how she had gotten to where she was. But not knowing what is going to happen from one day to the next is terribly unsettling.

Her ruminating was interrupted by the ding-dong of the back gate opening. Ellie could see from the CCTV that it was Hector. First footsteps, then the back-porch door, then the doorbell.

Ellie stood straight and calmly approached the laundry room. From there, she swiftly opened the back door. It was like a Band-Aid. Rip it off fast.

"Hello, Hector." She gave him a warm smile. She hesitated about a hug, so she put out her hand.

"Hello." Hector had a shy look on his face. "I am honored to be invited into your home."

"It's a pleasure. Truly." Ellie stepped aside to let him pass. "Do come in."

"Is now a good time for coffee?" Hector shuffled his feet.

"Yes, of course."

"I suppose I should have left you a note this morning, but I was running late for school."

"It's fine, Hector. I am so glad we can sit and talk. Please come in." Ellie guided him over to the dining-room table overlooking the porch and the yard beyond.

He tried not to seem nosy, but he looked

around to see how she had decorated the room. Hector had worked with the electrician and helped get the place ready, but he had never been inside after Ellie moved in.

"You've done a beautiful job." Hector appreciated the minimalist look, which Ellie had warmed up with large plants, several throws on the sofa, and a few large, framed photos of trees and flowers. One photo was an enlarged pink peony, another an iris. Others were close-ups of different-shaped leaves. They were not exactly like the paintings of Georgia O'Keeffe, but the similarity was there. "I really like the photographs," Hector remarked.

"Thank you. Photography used to be a hobby of mine," Ellie replied.

"Wow." Hector was doubly impressed.

"We seem to have a few things in common, Hector. Please, sit down." She motioned to one of the high-backed, natural rattan chairs. "You and I are gamers, and we also like gardens, trees, plants, and flowers."

"That's true. I hadn't thought about it. When you asked me to put in a garden, I figured it was because you wanted a nice yard."

"I did, and thanks to you, I have one. You did a beautiful job. I enjoy looking at it."

Hector was a little nervous. Even though he had been Ellie's personal assistant for two years, he had never had a face-to-face encounter with her. Before she moved here, all communication was over the Internet. When he was helping her find a place to live and get it ready, they would occasionally speak on the phone. They had Skyped a few times, but their interactions were never in person. This was totally new. Hector was fidgeting. "Is there a problem?"

"No. Why do you ask?" Ellie was surprised at his question.

"You've never invited me inside before." Hector's tone was even.

"I know, and I apologize. It's long overdue." Ellie smiled at him.

"Is everything all right?" Hector was still unsure why, after all this time, he would be invited in for coffee.

"Yes, Hector, everything is fine." She was telling a small lie. Some things were fine. Others not so much, but she didn't need to get into any of that. She couldn't. "I've been doing a lot of soul-searching."

"Do you not want me to come by anymore?" Hector wanted her to get to the point. Was she going to fire him?

"Oh, Hector. That's not it at all. I appreciate everything you do for me." Ellie got up and walked over to the coffee maker. "Coffee?"

"Yes, thank you."

"Regular or decaf?"

"Regular, please." He hesitated. "Strong, if you have it."

"Coming right up." She fished in the coffee canister and pulled out several pods. "Hector, you may have noticed that it's been two years since I moved in, and in all that time, I have never left the house."

"Well, yes, but I didn't think it was any of my business. You'd give me instructions, and I was happy to do whatever you needed. And I especially appreciate the money. It's going to be a big help when I leave for school." Maybe that was the problem. It dawned on Ellie that he would be leaving for college in the fall. What would she do without him?

"I know. And everyone is quite proud of you, I'm sure." Ellie popped a pod into the Nespresso machine.

Silence filled the room. It occurred to Ellie that she was on a schedule to either resolve her dark, haunting issue or find a replacement for Hector. She didn't know which was more challenging.

She brought the two cups to the table, set them down, and fetched several slices of blueberry pound cake from the counter.

"Hector, the reason I invited you is because you have been my closest confidant since I moved here. Actually, before I moved here."

"You have done lots for me. I could never have sold that game without you. That will help with my tuition, and the money you pay me will pay for housing. I owe you big-time."

Ellie laughed softly. "I guess we're even then."

Hector finally started to relax. "This is good. Did you bake it?" Hector knew that blueberry pound cake hadn't been on any of her grocery lists.

"Yes, I did. Thank you," Ellie replied. "Sometimes I wake up in the middle of the night and have to do something to busy myself." She thought about the nightmare the other night. Recently, she had been waking up, but it wasn't necessarily owing to nightmares.

"I don't think I'd have the ambition to bake at three in the morning." Hector took another bite. "But I'm glad you did!"

Ellie chuckled. "Hector, I want you to know something."

He stopped suddenly and looked up at her, expecting to hear something dreadful.

"What is it?"

"Before I moved here, there was an incident that put me in the hospital. When I woke up, I couldn't remember what had happened, but there was something in my subconscious that was making me afraid."

"Afraid of what?" Hector realized his question was foolish. He smacked himself on the forehead. "Subconscious. Duh. Never mind."

Ellie laughed. "My therapist said we bury things we don't want to remember. The problem is that by burying it, I'm not able to face it and deal with it. That's why I don't leave the house. I'm fearful, but I don't know the root of that fear."

Ellie felt a huge burden being lifted by telling someone face-to-face how she was feeling. She then continued her story.

"After I got out of the hospital, I wanted to get as far away from where I was as I could. That's when I got in touch with you."

Hector was nodding.

"My family thinks I'm working for a government contractor and moving from country to country." Ellie paused.

"You mean they don't know where you are?" Hector was stunned.

"No."

"How come?"

"Because I don't remember anything, and I didn't know whom to trust."

"Not even your mother?" Hector was aghast at the thought of someone not trusting their own mother.

"It's not like that. Since I don't know what happened, I needed to find what some people would call a safe house. I had to put enough space between me and everyone I knew, just in case. I entered into a sort of witness protection program, so no one could know where I was." Ellie paused.

"In case of what?" Hector was trying to figure out where this was going.

"In case what happened to me might put someone else in danger."

"How would that be?"

"That's the point. If I can't remember, then I can't keep my family safe by warning them."

Hector was still confused. "Let me see if I understand. Something happened to you. You don't remember what, but it scared you somehow. You needed to get away from the situation to sort things out."

"Hector that's exactly what's going on."

"Have you figured out any of it yet?" Hector's curiosity was growing.

"Only that I still have occasional nightmares and migraines."

Hector nodded again, sorting through what Ellie had just told him.

"Do you have a therapist?" Hector stopped himself. "I'm sorry, that's none of my business."

"Hey, I brought up all this psychological mumbo-jumbo, so don't apologize," Ellie reassured him. She also wondered if the conversation was getting too intense for an eighteen-year-old. But Hector was no average teenager. "Yes, there is someone I speak to a couple of times a month."

"Has it helped?"

"You're sitting in my house, aren't you?" Ellie teased.

Hector looked around. "Yep. So is this all your stuff from where you came from?"

"No. I gave up my apartment and put my things in storage. I had to made it look like I was going away for a while, which is true, to a certain extent." She looked around the living space. "That's why it's a little sparse. I had some of my photos blown up to give it some color and hoped that looking at them might trigger my memory. But I had taken those a year before the incident, so they're not helping me recover my memory. Probably just as well. They actually give me comfort.

"Anyway, I've been thinking that just

because I can't or won't leave the house, that doesn't mean I can't have a friend over. I love Buddy and Percy, but they're not the best conversationalists. Though I do appreciate that they don't talk back. Well, in all honesty, sometimes Buddy does." Ellie smiled.

"I'm glad you think of me as a friend." Hector smiled back.

"So much so that you are the very first person I invited in."

Hector seemed surprised, but knew it had to be true, unless she was sneaking people in when he wasn't around. "Wow. I am honored." And he meant it.

"I couldn't think of anyone else better than you, Hector. You have been a lifesaver. Probably in more ways than one."

Hector started to blush. "Thank you. I enjoy working for you."

"And the garden?" Ellie looked out the window. "It's absolutely beautiful. I'm glad you suggested that seating area in the back. Last weekend, Jackson fell asleep on the swing with Buddy lying underneath. It was a sweet sight."

"Jackson is a very good kid. I'm glad he has Buddy to play with. I felt really bad when I heard about Mrs. Haywood and the trouble she had with Mr. Haywood."

"Yeah, that's kind of a mess right now, but I think things will smooth over in a while."

"Really?" Hector knew from some other kids at school that a divorce could be awful for everyone involved. Even people on the fringe.

"I think so. Just a feeling I have. Jackson had a good day with his father and grandmother. At least that wasn't traumatic."

"He had a nightmare that night, but his mother thinks it was because he was upset when his grandmother dropped Mitchel off at his brother's house."

Ellie cut another piece of pound cake for Hector.

"It's gotta be rough on a little kid."

"It's a lot to absorb and understand. When things like this happen, children tend to blame themselves. Why, I don't know. Maybe it's because they don't have a lot of different reference points." Ellie hoped she wasn't too far over Hector's head.

"Well, sure. It's Mama and Papa, and family. School. Not a big universe to draw from." Hector was rather astute.

"You are very impressive, my dear." Ellie wasn't lying this time. Those lies were saved for the big issues.

"It's like playing a video game. You have

so many players in a universe. The more players, the more you have to figure out how to deal with them."

"I like your analogy, Hector." Ellie took a sip of her coffee, which had gone cold. She drank it anyway.

"I know there are people who think that video games are a waste of time, but for me, it challenges my mind. You have to think and react fast."

"And that's why you're so good at it," Ellie reminded him.

"Yes, but you're better." Hector gave her a thumbs-up.

"I've had more practice."

The back gate buzzed. It was Jackson arriving for his daily visit. Ellie walked over to the intercom. "Hey, Jackson! How was your day?"

"Hey, Ms. Bowman. It was OK. My mom made me walk with the new girl this morning. She's all right, I guess. But she sure does talk a lot."

Ellie laughed. "Most girls do at that age, unless they're really shy."

"I don't think she's shy. She was talkin' up a storm both ways. To and from school."

"Maybe she was excited. This is all new to her."

"I guess." He shrugged. Ellie buzzed him

in. Jackson and Buddy ran to greet each other.

"I think that's the longest conversation I've ever had with him." Ellie watched from the window. "Hmm."

"What?"

"This is a big day for me. I invited you for coffee. I had a conversation with Jackson that exceeded two sentences. I'm making progress." She sat back down at the table and turned her chair so she could see outside and speak to Hector. "I love to watch the two of them play. Jackson has been great for Buddy."

"I'm sure Buddy has been good for Jackson, too." Hector checked the time on the microwave. "I better get going. I promised my mother I'd stop at the store for some Adobo. Thank you very much for inviting me. I feel honored."

"You're very special to me, Hector."

"And you are to me. And my family. They appreciate the trust you put in me." Hector resisted the temptation to give her a hug. "My father said it's helping to build character."

"And you're helping me to build confidence."

Hector stopped. "Seriously? You are awesome sauce!"

Ellie laughed out loud. "Thank you, Hector. Give my regards to your mother. Did you tell her you were coming here for coffee?"

Hector looked a little embarrassed. "Not yet. I wasn't sure if you were going to fire me, and I didn't want her to worry."

"Fire you?" Ellie guffawed. "As if."

"I didn't know." Hector shrugged.

"Well, now you can tell her. And also tell her I said she should be enormously proud of you." Ellie placed her hand on Hector's shoulder. There have been studies on how important hugs are, and how they trigger endorphins in the brain. Hugs also release dopamine and serotonin that boost one's mood and relieve symptoms of depression. She didn't think hugging Hector was appropriate, but a hand on the shoulder was good enough. Her mood had been elevated. Perhaps it was his company, or perhaps the major breakthrough she had had by inviting him in. Whichever it was, she knew she was on the right track. If only her momentum continued, her life might eventually achieve a normal different from that of the past two years.

CHAPTER TWENTY-NINE

It had been a full week since Mitchel had been on a bender. He had limited his drinking to two beers a day rather than two six-packs or a pint of whiskey, or both. He had also started wearing a nicotine patch to help him stop smoking. It occurred to him that heavy drinking and heavy smoking went hand in hand. The less he did of one, the less he would do of the other. Much to his surprise, it wasn't as hard as he thought it might be, or as hard as he kept telling himself it would be. No more excuses. He knew he had to get himself together if he ever wanted a lasting relationship with his son.

The day they had spent together was a real eye-opener for him. He couldn't recall the last time he had spent a few sober hours with Jackson, and Saturday felt good. He was still contemplating what had happened with his mother. He knew the change in her mood had helped considerably.

He winced when he thought about the exchange with Lucinda. Seeing her in daylight, and being sober to boot, was a real eye-opener for him. It was as if he were remembering someone else's life. In retrospect, it was embarrassing to recall their previous relationship. When she had sauntered over to their table, his first impulse was to drink two shots of anything eighty proof or more. But looking at his son's face, seeing the innocence in it, stopped him from stepping off the straight and narrow. He thought he had handled the situation well. Of course, the look on his mother's face was another story. If looks could kill, he and Lucinda would both be at the coroner's office. He gave a wry laugh at that scenario and shuddered. Thinking back to the time of his philandering, he couldn't blame Colleen for her hostility. He was rarely home, and when he was, he was invariably in a foul mood. He wasn't sure what the trigger was that had turned him into a worthless drunk, but he had decided that he was not going to be that guy anymore.

He thought about his own father. What little he could remember was that he was a mild-mannered, hardworking man. He would get up at the crack of dawn and tend the fields. Dinner was often the only time he saw his father, but it was usually a pleasant occasion unless his mother had an ax to grind, which happened frequently. Even so, his father would softly address her and remind her, "Not in front of the children." That, too, could set her off. He thought about it some more. Maybe the problem had been that she didn't feel appreciated or fulfilled. Having two sons didn't mean a person had a sense of self-worth. Anyone, well almost anyone, could bear a child. Three hundred million Americans were proof. Then there was the rest of the world. He then realized she was saddled with raising two boys, essentially on her own, as well as trying to keep the farm afloat. He unexpectedly viewed her in a different light. She was, after all, a human being,

He went over to the small set of weights in the corner of the basement and did a few sets. He was determined to continue on his mission to be a better person, for himself and his son.

Mitchel knew there was little hope for reconciliation with Colleen. He had done too much damage. But if he could rehabilitate himself, perhaps they could have a civilized relationship for Jackson's sake. Mitchel believed that if he could become a decent human being once again, he and Colleen could work together and raise their son. Even if it was in two different households.

Households. That was another hurdle. He needed a job for that to happen. After his talk with Pete at the bowling alley, Mitchel had decided to go to his former boss and plead for his job back. He knew he was an asset to the shop, provided he showed up.

After his workout, he jumped in the shower and began his grooming routine. He looked at himself in the mirror as he was shaving. "Who are you, man?" And then he laughed. He hadn't had deep thoughts about much in ages. He looked intensely into his own eyes. Nice to see they weren't bloodshot. Even the bags under his eyes, which were usually there, were starting to subside.

He put on another nicely ironed shirt, compliments of Elaine. He thought she was helping out because she wanted him out of the house. He couldn't blame her. He had been quite the jerk the first two weeks. Nonetheless, he was grateful. A clean, pressed shirt and a clean pair of jeans would convey a "new Mitch" to anyone who saw him. At least that was his hope.

He took the steps two at a time. When he

entered the kitchen, Elaine was standing with a coffeepot in her hand. "My, don't you look nice."

"Thanks to you." Mitchel gave a short bow in her direction. "Elaine, I know I've been a bit of an ass lately. Actually, for a while now, but I want to be a better man."

Elaine almost dropped the coffeepot. "You don't say?" She was being sincere, in spite of her shock.

"Yeah. The other day, when I was with Jackson and my mother, I realized how important it is to be a good father. A father who is present."

Elaine set the coffeepot down in fear she would truly drop it. "That's wonderful news, Mitchel."

"And my mother? Boy, was that a turn-around."

"I know," Elaine said.

"When I saw how happy Jackson was coloring on the place mats, and my mother being so nice, I thought how good it would be if we could try to be a happy family."

Elaine cleared her throat.

"Oh, I know that Colleen and I are over. I treated her like dirt, but that doesn't mean we can't be good parents."

Elaine walked over to Mitchel and felt his forehead. "You all right?"

Mitchel laughed. "I'm fine. I've been doing a lot of thinking."

"The reason I've been a lousy father is probably because my dad died when I was ten. I had no role model. Greg did his best to fill in, but he was only two years older than me. No one could expect him to take that kind of responsibility."

Elaine sat down before she fell down. "Mitchel, I don't think I've ever heard you talk like this before."

Mitchel grunted. "Probably because I never felt like this before. Or at least gave it any thought. I think because I was the youngest, everyone coddled me and tried to protect me. In some ways, I was spoiled rotten and allowed to get away with a lot of crap. Even Colleen gave me a lot of slack. But I guess what I really needed was some good old-fashioned discipline."

Elaine got up and returned to the coffee maker. "You want a cup?"

"Yes, please," Mitchel responded. "Looking back, I realize what a dumbass I've been to a lot of people. Colleen, Jackson, my boss, you, Greg. I'm lucky to have any of you even talking to me now."

Elaine poured him a mug. "Sounds like you've been doing a *lot* of thinking."

"Yes, ma'am. And I want you to know I

338

acknowledge all the stupid stuff I've done and want to thank you for putting up with me."

"We're family." Elaine patted him on the wrist.

"Well, some families disown jerks."

"We're not that kind of family, Mitch."

"I know that now, and I'm truly grateful."

"So what are your plans for today?" Elaine asked, sincerely interested.

"I'm going to the shop and beg for my job back."

"Really? What do you think Otto will say?"

"I have no idea. I'm just hopin' he'll say 'yes' and maybe take me back on probation."

"You always were the best mechanic there," Elaine said with encouragement.

"I'm hoping that counts for something."

"I'll pray it will." She smiled at Mitch. "Want any breakfast before your big interview?"

"If it's no trouble," Mitch answered sincerely.

"No trouble at all. Eggs? Over easy? Toast?"

"Sounds good to me."

Several minutes later, Elaine had the plate ready for Mitch. "Here you go." She paused. "You know, I only want what's best for you and Jackson. Colleen, too, but for now, it's about you and your son."

"Thanks, Elaine. That's what I'm focusing on." Mitch dunked a piece of toast in his eggs. "I think if I can do good by Jackson, Colleen will come around. I don't mean by taking me back, but by being a good parenting partner."

"That's a great attitude, Mitch."

He wiped the plate clean with his toast and finished his coffee. He rinsed the dishes and put them in the dishwasher. Another first for him since his stay at Greg and Elaine's had begun. She watched him move across the kitchen in amazement. *Maybe there's some hope.*

"Thanks for the breakfast and the talk." Mitch washed his hands and wiped them on a paper towel.

"You're welcome, Mitch. Glad we had time this morning." She got up as he was walking toward the door.

"Wish me luck!" He gave her a two-fingered salute. "Oh, and prayers are most welcome!" *Prayers.* Another word that rarely, if ever, appeared in his vocabulary. He hadn't protested when Colleen took Jackson to church as long as he didn't have to go with them. Maybe that might also change. *One step at a time, bro.* He smiled

340

to himself.

Mitch got in his truck and traveled to his former place of employment, silently asking the Lord to give him another chance.

He pulled up to the shop, recognizing most of the other cars. He checked his teeth in the mirror and took a swig of Listerine. But this time he spit it out in a cup. It wasn't as if he was trying to hide the smell of booze. He wanted to come off squeaky clean when he spoke to Otto.

When he opened the door, the bell rang in the back of the shop, signaling that a customer had arrived. Otto came out with a big smile, but it turned into a frown when he saw that it was Mitchel.

"What are you doing here?" Otto asked, more out of curiosity than anger.

"Hey, Otto. Can we talk a minute?" Mitch was close to fawning over him, but that kind of schmaltz wouldn't work on the hard-nosed Otto.

"What about?" Otto was wiping some grease off his hands with a towel.

"Let me start out by saying I know I was a real jerk."

"You won't get an argument from me." Otto leaned against the counter.

Mitchel snickered. "Listen, you know Col-

341

leen and I are going through an ugly time."

"So I've heard." Otto wasn't much for words.

"Otto, I know you gave me a lot of chances to keep my job when I was screwing up."

"I ain't gonna argue that either."

"Otto, I'm trying to get my act together. I've cut down on my drinking. I'm even trying to quit smoking." He rolled up his sleeve to show him the nicotine patch.

"I'm guessing you want your old job back." Otto eyed him closely.

Mitch looked down at his feet. "Yes. But before you say no, I want you to understand how much I need this. Not just for me, but for Jackson. I want to be able to pay good child support."

"You and Colleen gettin' a divorce?"

"Most likely. But I'm going to do my darn best to make it easy for Jackson. A broken home isn't good for anyone." Mitchel paused, trying to get a sense of what direction Otto was going. "I know you knew my pop, but I really didn't. I was only ten when he died, so I don't know much about being a father, and I don't want to blow it with Jackson. He's a really good kid and deserves some kind of stability."

Otto was nodding. Mitchel thought it was a good sign.

"Otto, I really need the job." Mitchel was on the verge of groveling.

"How'm I gonna trust you to show up?" Otto peered at him.

"I know it's a lot to ask, after all the bull I put you through, but I'd like to think I'm changing for the better. I know I did good work."

Otto interrupted and repeated the reminder. "When you showed up."

Mitch put his hands up. "I know. I know." He took a deep breath. "I'll tell you what. You take me back, and I'll work overtime for regular pay."

Otto scratched the stubble on his face. "How many hours overtime are you talkin'?"

Mitch was calculating in his head. "Ten? Twelve?"

"A week?"

"If necessary."

"For how long?"

"Six months?" Mitchel figured he had nothing to lose at this point.

Otto thought a minute, wiped his hands again, and put it out to shake Mitch's. "You better watch your butt. When can you start?"

A huge wave of relief came over Mitch. He thought he would cry. "Thanks, Otto. I promise, I will not disappoint you. I can start today. The only time off I'll need is for court, but I'll work late to get any of the jobs done."

Otto threw the towel at him. "Go suit up. Your old uniform is still in the back. I was going to burn it, but then I decided I didn't want a grease fire." Otto chuckled. He was glad to have his top mechanic back. He wouldn't let on, but he had lost a couple of good customers, and now he could tell them Mitch was back.

Mitch was walking on air. Obstacle one was out of the way.

His court date for the hearing was in two days, then the custody hearing in a week. At least he was gainfully employed. He felt the urge to call someone. He decided it was Elaine. She had been good to him in spite of his bad behavior, and she was a warm, welcome ear earlier that day. He dialed her number.

"Hello, Mitch?" She saw his name come up on the caller ID. "Everything all right?"

"Hey, Elaine. Everything is fine and dandy. Otto gave me my job back."

"That's great! When do you start?"

"I'm here now. I just wanted to say thanks. Thanks for your hospitality, breakfast, and those prayers." Mitchel's voice essentially sounded upbeat. "I'm sure you were prayin' for me to get out." He laughed.

Elaine knew it wasn't far from the truth, but she was happy for him and Jackson anyway.

Mitchel continued. "I'm going to have to figure out some kind of living situation for myself, so if you can bear with me for another couple of weeks, until the hearings are over, I would greatly appreciate it. And I'll give you guys some cash for letting me stay there."

"That's fine, Mitchel. We'll try to help out as much as possible."

"Thanks, Elaine. It's very much appreciated." Mitchel was still trying to avoid getting choked up. "I better get inside before Otto changes his mind."

"Good idea!" Elaine laughed. "Good luck! See you later."

"Bye." Mitch clicked off the phone and wiped the small tear at the corner of his eye.

CHAPTER THIRTY

Ellie was pleased at how easy it had been to have Hector in the house. She had felt no anxiety or panic once she let him in. Their conversation was congenial and friendly. Not that she would have expected anything less, but it was a new experience for both of them. She was feeling emotionally stronger and decided to call Zach to share her progress.

When she explained to the therapist that she had invited someone into her space and had coffee, he was thoroughly pleased at Ellie's progress. "Do you think you'll do it again?" Zach asked Ellie.

"Yes. I want to invite Colleen, Jackson's mom, over for tea. She must have invited me a dozen times, and I always felt I had to decline."

"How are the nightmares?"

"I've only had one lately."

"What do you think brought it on?"

Ellie sighed. "My friend Kara got in touch to tell me that Rick called her husband looking for a loan."

"What did he say?"

"According to Kara, Rick wanted $5,000 to invest in a start-up company. But get this, he wanted it sent via PayPal."

"That's an odd way to get capital for an investment," Zach noted.

"Exactly."

"When was the last time anyone heard from Rick?"

Ellie paused. "It was around the time I was in the hospital."

"And no one has heard from him until this recent phone call?"

"Not anyone I know of." Ellie wasn't aware of any contact.

"So, after two years, he calls your friend's husband to ask for a loan?" He waited, but it was clearly a rhetorical question. "Doesn't that strike you as odd?" That one was *not* rhetorical.

"Of course it does. I think that's why I had a nightmare."

"Do you think he's trying to locate you?" her therapist asked. The thought gave Ellie the chills.

"As far as I know, he hasn't contacted my mother, who would be the obvious choice if that's what he was doing. And from what Kara told me, he didn't ask about me."

"How does that make you feel?" The typical therapist question.

"Honestly, I haven't given it any thought until now." Ellie wasn't lying.

"So, your friend tells you that your former boyfriend called her husband, asking for money, and didn't check to see how you were?"

"That pretty much sums it up," Ellie said, matter-of-factly.

"And you're all right with that?"

"I suppose. But I did have a nightmare that night."

"Do you remember any of it?"

"The only part I remember is that I was falling down a dark hole. Then I woke up in a sweat."

"Do you think you're falling down a dark hole?"

Ellie snickered. "Am I not living in one?"

"That's up to you, Ellie. You made a lot of progress by inviting Hector into the house. You also let Jackson into your yard. Clearly, you're beginning to allow more people into your life."

"Yes. It's the rest of it I still can't sort out."

"Remember what I've said, 'Baby steps.' But this was a pretty good leap for you. Do you think you'll follow through with inviting Colleen?" Zach asked.

"Yes. We've had several conversations on the phone. She is easy to talk to, and I think she needs a friend."

"Oh? What makes you say that?"

"She is going through a messy divorce and child-custody dispute. The police were here a couple of weeks ago, and they arrested her husband for domestic violence."

"That does sound like a bad situation," the therapist acknowledged.

"Sometimes I'm glad I don't have to deal with that sort of thing."

"Which part?" he prodded.

"Having to compromise for another person, especially if that person has issues."

"Good point." Zach paused before he asked the next question. "Are you still feeling anxious?"

"Not as much as I used to. Getting to know Colleen, even if it's over the phone, and having Hector help me have made me feel much more secure."

"But Hector will be leaving for college in the fall. Have you thought about what you're going to do when he's gone?"

Ellie chuckled. "Baby steps. Remember?"

The therapist also laughed. "I think you're doing well, Ellie. Please keep me informed of your progress, or any issues you may have."

"Thanks, Doc. I certainly will. Take care."

"You do the same."

The call ended with Ellie feeling more lighthearted than she had in a long while. She knew she had made progress, and it felt good to be able to share that with someone. Someone who knew about the fears, even if she, herself, didn't know exactly what she was afraid of. After the call, Ellie wrote a note to Colleen:

Hi, Colleen,
It's been way overdue, but would you like to have tea or coffee with me sometime this week? Perhaps one afternoon when Jackson is playing with Buddy? You can see them in action. Let me know. Kind regards, Ellie

She clipped a note to it for Hector:

Please deliver to Colleen. Thanks.

Ellie finished up with the latest of her distressed online customers. She had three more hours on the clock. Finally, at midnight, she logged off and went to bed. It had been a draining evening. But in a good way.

Somewhere around 2:30 in the morning, she shot upright in her bed. She had had a nightmare similar to the previous one, with her spiraling down a dark whirlpool. But this time there was something different. She could see Rick's face at the top of the whirlpool. Her hand was reaching out for him to rescue her, but Rick just turned and walked away, leaving her to be swept into the abyss. There was something familiar and haunting about that image. She knew she couldn't call Kara at that hour, so she scribbled down the bits and pieces she could remember from the nightmare while it was still fresh in her mind. She was trembling and had a fuzzy sensation in her head. It was almost like the buzzing of a mosquito. Was it simply from the nightmare, or was the nightmare a clue to what had happened to her?

Ellie threw the covers back and got out of bed. Buddy gave her an odd look but remained in his nice warm spot. Percy did the same. "I guess I'm on my own, huh, guys."

Ellie made herself a cup of tea and went up to the loft. She powered up her PC and pulled up a search engine.

Ellie wondered why she'd not done anything like this before, dozens of times. In the end, she simply chalked it up to pure laziness. Laziness — and fear of what she might find. Well, that was then and this was now.

She found the website of the most likely newspaper in New York City to report on falls resulting in hospital stays and typed in the date the incident took place, hoping there would be something in its archives that would give her a clue. If there was nothing there, she would look at the archives of other newspapers.

She scrolled through the pages and stopped short at an article with the headline:

WOMAN FOUND IN BROWNSTONE STAIRWELL

She read the text of the article:

A woman in her early thirties was found unconscious and bleeding at the bottom of the front steps of a brownstone in Greenwich Village last night. A resident spotted the woman and immediately called 911. She was taken to a nearby hospital with traumatic brain injuries. The identity of the woman is not yet known. Police are asking anyone who has information to please contact 311.

She read the article several times. Could

that have been her? She closed her eyes, straining to remember. She and Rick often stopped for a bite to eat at a restaurant in the village. She searched the article again for an exact location of the brownstone, but no address was given. Perhaps she could get a copy of the police report. That was something she could do from her own computer. It was public information.

Ellie went to the police-blotter pages and scrolled through dozens of incident reports from that evening. There were arrests for drunk and disorderly, distribution of a controlled substance, loitering, harassment, shooting, purse snatching, breaking and entering, armed robbery . . . the list went on and on. Then she found what she was looking for among reports on a series of muggings. As she combed the report, a chill went up her spine.

12:45 A.M.
Location: 349 West 11th Street
Victim: White female/age 30+/−
Name: Missing identification

Description: Mugging — Subject was found at base of the front steps of a brownstone, unconscious. Head wound either by blunt object or due to fall. Purse

and contents not on scene.
EMS arrived and took subject to Lenox
Health. No witnesses.

It was right around the corner from the
Pasteria, a place where she and Rick used
to hang out.

She read and reread what little information there was. A strange buzz went through
her head again. She started to get dizzy. She
had to fight the sensation. She knew she
was getting closer to the truth. Why hadn't
anyone told her? She looked at the clock. It
was almost 4:00 A.M. She reached for the
phone designated for her mother and Kara.
Ellie could not possibly wait until dawn.
Two years had been long enough.

"Mother. Don't panic. I'm OK. But I had
to speak with you now."

Ellie's mother was groggy. "Oh dear, what
is it? What is going on at this time in the
morning? Or whatever time it is where you
are?"

"I had another nightmare. About the
incident. Rick was in it. He was standing
over me while I was falling into an abyss. I
reached out to him, and he let me fall."

There was silence on the other end.

"Mother?"

"I'm here, honey. It's just that no one has

heard from him since he skipped town."

"That's not entirely true," Ellie answered.

"What do you mean?"

"Rick called Christian and asked him for $5,000."

"After all this time? What on earth for?"

"He claims it's for some sort of start-up company. He wanted Chris to put the money in a PayPal account."

"Isn't that a bit odd?"

"Of course it's odd."

"What did Christian say?"

"He said he would discuss it with Kara. That's how I found out. Kara called me the other day. She told Christian that she would kick his butt if he did what Rick asked."

"Sounds like Kara." Her mother chuckled. "I don't suppose he asked about you?"

"Of course not. Why should he? He didn't seem to care when I was in the hospital." Ellie felt her stress growing.

"Do they know where he is?"

"He said he was traveling."

"Yes, like he traveled right out of here the morning you were admitted to the hospital."

"Mother, I think I have an idea of what happened that night." Ellie was resolute.

"I don't understand." Her mother had waited for over two years. Why now?

"Let me explain." Ellie took a deep breath.

"My nightmare. This was the second time I was being swallowed into a dark hole, but this time Rick was in it. When I woke up, I had a strange buzzing in my head."

"Honey, you know you have to be careful of those recurring migraines."

"Luckily, I've had very few over the past several months. I'm OK now."

"That's good news, dear," her mother cooed.

"Here's the thing. I went online and searched the newspapers for the date of the incident. I found a small article in the *Daily News* about a woman who was found unconscious at the bottom of the front steps of a brownstone."

More silence from the other end.

"Mother?"

"Yes, yes. I heard you."

"Then I went to the police blotter to try to get more information. Mother? Was that me?" Ellie cringed, waiting for a response.

Her mother took a deep gulp before answering. "Yes."

"And no one told me?" Ellie was getting agitated.

"You couldn't remember what happened. The doctors said you would in time and that we should not push you."

"Instead, you made me wonder for two

years?" Ellie was pacing now.

"It was a severe trauma, honey. No one wanted to do anything that would upset you." Her mother sounded tearful.

"Mom? Rick was there when I fell."

"What?" Her mother was stunned by her remark.

"That's why he disappeared," Ellie said blankly.

"But your purse. It was missing."

"We were having an argument on the street." Ellie felt like she was in a trance. "He was really angry and grabbed me by the shoulders. When I tried to push him away, I lost my footing and fell backward. He grabbed the strap of my purse, to keep me from falling, and it broke." Ellie was in a sweat. "He must have taken off with it to make what happened look like a mugging."

"But why didn't he stay to help you?" Ellie's mother was irate.

"Because he never takes responsibility for anything. He probably thought no one would believe that it was an accident."

"Do *you* think it was an accident?" her mother asked suspiciously. "Your memory isn't that good. Perhaps this is what you want to remember — an accident."

"Mother, I can't think of any reason why Rick would purposely push me down a flight of stairs."

"Because he's an obnoxious, selfish, nasty piece of work, that's why."

"But to what end? What would be in it for him? Rick never did anything that was not in his own interest." Ellie was perplexed.

"Maybe he didn't feel like waiting around for the police and having to answer questions. Why do you think he fled town?" Her mother was resolute.

"That is the sixty-four-thousand-dollar question." Then it occurred to Ellie that her mother might be right and that Rick would be looking for her to finish the job that had begun that night. "Gosh, do you think that's why he called Christian? To try to find me?" Ellie tried to control her panic. "But he didn't ask about me."

"No, but he asked for money. Maybe he's going to pay someone to find you." Her mom took a deep breath. "It's a good thing you're working on a government contract out of the country, so it will be difficult to locate you."

Ellie resisted the urge to tell her mother the truth. She wasn't out of the country. Then a horrible thought came to mind. If Rick was trying to find her, she needed to do something about it. About him. She didn't want to cause her mother any more concern. "Right." That's when she decided she would do a deep dive into finding Rick. Before *he* found *her.*

"Mom? I know you worry about me, but I cannot tell you how relieved I am that I can finally remember the gist of what happened that night and that I didn't have some sort of mental breakdown."

Although she thought she might have one momentarily.

"Libby, I am so happy to hear it."

Yes, her real name was Elizabeth Gannon. That much she did know and always had.

CHAPTER THIRTY-ONE

The morning of Mitchel's hearing had arrived. He went to court, dressed in a suit and well-groomed. He felt good. He knew that he had disappointed a lot of people in the past, but he was determined to continue on his path of redemption. He owed it to his son, Colleen, Greg, Elaine, and Otto, not to mention all the others he had insulted and failed along the way.

Colleen arrived with her mother. Vivian was with Greg. Colleen was surprised at the warm welcome she received from her soon-to-be-ex mother-in-law. Maybe what they said was true. Vivian had had some kind of epiphany. They sat on opposite sides of the courtroom; Mitchel sat at the defendant's table with his lawyer. Officer Pedone stood against the wall, in full uniform. He nodded to Colleen when she entered. It gave her goose bumps. In a good way.

Mitchel looked over in her direction and

smiled. It was a genuine smile.

Once the judge was seated, the clerk announced the charges.

"How do you plead?"

"Guilty, Your Honor." Some people gasped in horror, but many others weren't the least bit surprised.

Mitchel's lawyer had approached the prosecutor early on to offer a guilty plea and obtain the best deal for Mitchel that he could.

"If I may, Your Honor," Mitchel's lawyer asked the court.

"By all means," the judge replied.

"My client understands that by pleading guilty, he will not go to trial, saving everyone, including the fine taxpayers of the county, time and money."

"That's quite generous of him," the judge said, a bit sarcastically.

"Mr. Haywood has agreed to serve two years' probation and perform one thousand hours of community service. He is asking the court to recommend additional counseling, to be appointed by the court." The lawyer cleared his throat. "In the matter of the temporary restraining order, Your Honor, Mr. Haywood asks that it be lifted."

"And why should I do such a thing?" asked the judge.

"My client has been attending meetings for anger management and alcohol abuse. He is once again gainfully employed and wishes to have an ongoing relationship with his son."

"Mr. Haywood, is this what you are agreeing to?"

"Yes, Your Honor."

"Mrs. Haywood. Would you care to make a statement?"

Colleen stood. "Yes, Your Honor. I've known Mitchel for many years. And while the evening of the event was horrifying, it was nothing like the way he normally behaved. Yes, he was drunk, and that is no excuse, but I believe he is making a valiant effort to turn his life around. I, too, want him to have a relationship with his son, so I will not object to lifting the order."

Murmurs and whispers went around the courtroom. Colleen looked over at Officer Pedone, and he gave her a nod of approval. He understood the importance of a father-son relationship and how vital it is for divorced parents to have good rapport.

"Very well. The clerk will enter your plea, and I will accept the terms of your punishment and lift the temporary restraining order." He banged his gavel, and just like that, the hearing was over.

Colleen walked over to Mitchel. "I've heard good things, Mitch. Jackson will be very happy to see you more often."

"Thanks, Colleen. You know I'm very sorry for the way I treated you. You deserve better. I know there's no future for us as husband and wife, but I hope we can be partners in raising our son."

"So do I. We can work it out with our lawyers. Where are you planning on living?"

"Believe it or not, I'm moving back into my mother's house. She could use someone to help with chores. Besides, the house is big enough that we won't get in each other's way. Jackson can have his own room and decent meals when he's with me. You know I'm a crummy cook." Mitchel smiled.

Colleen smiled. "I'm glad things are turning around for you. And I know you're the one doing the work. Let's talk on the phone and come up with a plan. Personally, I would prefer to have him during the week so as not to disrupt his school schedule, and you can have him on weekends. Naturally, if anything comes up in the middle of the week, we can work things out. Does that sound good to you?"

"Sure thing. You know how much I hate doing homework." Mitchel chuckled.

"Sounds good. Take care." Colleen walked

over to her mother.

"What did he have to say for himself?" Judith sneered.

"Oh, Mother, you're getting your wish. We're getting a divorce," Colleen said, with the slightest bit of exasperation. "And we're working out custody."

"Really? Where is he going to take Jackson? Greg and Elaine's basement?" she scoffed.

"No. He's moving into Vivian's."

"That sounds like a horror show to me." Judith was appalled.

"I don't know about that. She's been rather mellow lately. Or so I've been told."

"Speak of the devil," Judith muttered under her breath.

"Hello, Colleen. Judith." Vivian smiled at both of them. "I'm happy to see that you and Mitchel can be civil with each other. He's working hard at redemption."

"I can tell. He said he was moving back into your house?"

"Yes. To be honest, I was on the verge of putting it on the market. It was getting to be too much for me. But Mitchel's being around will be a relief, and I do so want to keep the place in the family. It can use some TLC, and I'm sure Jackson won't mind dipping a brush in a can of paint." She chuckled.

"As long as you and Mitch do the laundry." Colleen laughed. "Have a good day, Vivian."

"You both do the same." Vivian caught up with Mitchel in the hall.

"What's come over her?" Judith referred to Vivian's mood.

"I told you, she seems to be on her own path of rehabilitation. Frankly, I don't know, and I don't care, as long as she stays that way," Colleen said.

"I'm sure everyone around her does."

"Mom, I'll be right back. I want to speak to Officer Pedone." Colleen walked in his direction.

"Thank you for coming today. It was comforting to see you."

"I'm glad it worked out for everyone," Pedone said.

Colleen looked up at him. "About that dinner."

Pedone thought she was going to change her mind.

"Would Saturday night be too soon?"

"Not at all. What time?" His serious face turned into a big grin.

"Six?" Colleen knew Jackson would be with his father for an overnight, so she didn't have to think about asking Jeanne and Frank to babysit. Not that they would mind, but she hoped that this was the first date of many, and she wanted to save up her favors.

"Perfect. I'll pick you up in an unmarked car." He laughed.

Vivian and Mitchel spoke for a few minutes, then Vivian went on her way. Mitchel headed to the shop, where a new, clean uniform awaited.

Vivian got in her car and checked the gas level. *Enough to get her there and back.* She put the car in drive and proceeded to the outlet shops. Cranking up the radio, she started singing along with Linda Ronstadt, as she belted out "When Will I Be Loved."

Vivian found the shop where she had nicked the scarf for half of what it was worth. She confidently sauntered in and pulled another floral scarf from the rack. The price tag said $38.00.

She walked up to the counter and plunked down $40.00. As the cashier was putting the scarf in a bag, Vivian pulled out another twenty and slipped it on the counter where the clerk wouldn't see it right away. The clerk handed her the bag without noticing the extra money sitting there. Vivian walked out of the store with a spring in her step.

Mitchel isn't the only one who can experience redemption. She smiled to herself. If the math added up, the store was ahead of the game, and Vivian was happier for it.

While everyone was at the hearing, Ellie was typing away on her computer. She was able to pull up traffic cams of the neighborhood where the incident had occurred and was examining the videos. She halted when she spotted someone looking exactly like Rick dashing across Seventh Avenue. The time stamp was 12:35 A.M. She looked at the police report again — 12:45. Ten minutes. She had lain on the cold cement stairs bleeding nearly to death for at least ten minutes. She could have died. She almost died. She was now completely convinced that her vague recollection was true. The only question was, had Rick pushed her? But even if he hadn't, leaving her crumpled and bleeding at the bottom of the steps instead of calling 911 should be criminal. So, if she had the opportunity, she would assume it was assault and report it as such.

She picked up her burner phone and called Kara.

"Wow. Two calls in one week?" Kara laughed as she answered the phone. "They let you out of the box?"

"Very funny," she scoffed. "Are you sitting down?"

"Should I be?" Kara asked.

"Yes. Please."

"What's up?"

"I remember some of what happened that night." She took a very deep inhale. "I fell down a set of steps outside a brownstone in the Village."

Kara caught her breath. "You remember that? You fell?"

"That's the only thing that's a little hazy. I've had two nightmares since Rick got in touch with Christian."

"Darn it. I shouldn't have told you," Kara said, concern evident in her voice.

"No. It's a good thing you did. It triggered my memory. The first nightmare was me falling backward into a dark hole. The second one included Rick. He was standing over me, watching me fall. I reached out for him, and he did not keep me from falling."

"Holy smoke." Kara was stunned.

"When I woke up from the nightmare, I did a deep dive into some archives, one being a newspaper's. When I saw the article, I thought it might be me they were writing about because it said, 'Identity of the woman not yet known.' "

Kara interrupted. "That's because they

thought it was a mugging and it was an ongoing investigation."

"Maybe, but the police report didn't have my name either. It said the victim was taken to Lenox Health. That's where I was when I woke up."

"When the police questioned you, you couldn't remember anything, so they had no leads."

"Yeah, well, I also went through the traffic-cam footage from that night."

"You can *do* that?" Kara wasn't sure if she was impressed or shocked.

"Yes, but I'm not supposed to. And right now I don't care if I hacked into their system. I needed to find out for myself."

"I didn't realize they kept that footage for such a long time." Kara was intrigued.

"It's digital, so it doesn't require a lot of storage space, the way it did when they used videotapes. They've found that keeping archives for seven years has helped solve some cold cases."

"You sound like you work for *CSI* or something." Kara was amazed. "But why would Rick steal your purse?"

"I'm pretty sure he grabbed the strap as I was falling backward."

"So, he didn't push you on purpose?" Kara asked.

"I can't really be sure. But he definitely left me there. And I could have died — would have if someone hadn't found me and called nine-one-one. So he might as well have pushed me. Obviously, he could not have cared less if I lived or died. What does that tell you?"

"It tells me that he's scum," Kara answered, without hesitation.

"Kara, I need to find out where he is, just in case he's looking to finish the job, or even prevent me from filing charges against him."

"Do you think Rick has the guts to do something like that?" Kara asked.

"Maybe not himself, but he could hire someone to do it for him."

Kara gasped. "Oh my God. Do you think that's what the money is for?"

"Possibly. I need Christian to send it to him. Once I know where he is, I might be able to find him on my own."

"You mean in person?" Kara was aghast.

"Nope. I'll find him the way most cyber-sleuths find people. I have a lot of connections, and I'm pretty good at it myself." She took another deep breath.

"Next time Rick calls, have Christian send a check to the FedEx location of Rick's choice. Rick will most likely be somewhere near a casino."

"Wow. That's exactly what Chris and I said!"

"Some people are quite predictable. He'll ask the casino to cash the check for him, but before it can clear, you guys stop payment on it. That ought to get the casino in a snit. If he bolts, I'm sure the casino will send their goons to get him — unless I don't find him first."

"Once you locate him, what will you do?" Kara asked.

"Call the NYPD and speak to the captain of the precinct where it happened. I'll let him know it's a cold case, but I finally remember details of that night. I'll tell him that Rick tried to kill me. I hope that will be enough for them to get a warrant for his arrest and possibly extradite him when he's found."

"You sure sound like a detective, Libby," Kara remarked.

"About that."

"About what?" Kara asked.

"I've been using an alias since I moved."

"Wait. Explain. What do you mean when you moved?" Kara's curiosity was on the rise.

"Listen, there is a lot I cannot tell you right now, so you're just going to have to trust that I'm safe where I am."

"But what if he's looking for you?"

"I don't think he'll find my alias. I was careful about creating a new identity. A driver's license was all I really needed. Faking one of those was easy.

"So, do we have a plan? Christian will send him the check. As soon as he gets the address of the FedEx location, you e-mail it to me. Got it?"

"Got it. Be careful, Libby. Love you!" Kara hung up and immediately called Christian and told him that when Rick called, he should send him the money. She said she didn't want to explain over the phone but would discuss it when he got home.

Like clockwork, Rick called Christian later that afternoon for one more round of begging.

"Kara and I discussed this, Rick. I'm going to need a couple of things from you. The IOU I mentioned earlier and a letter of intent to pay me twenty percent of your profits. This way, you can leave your other partners out of it."

Rick was stupefied. "Seriously, man?"

"Yes, if you think it's a good investment, what's twenty percent of your earnings to you? It's a win-win for both of us."

Rick continued the lie. "You got it. How

soon can you send it?"

"I'll overnight it by the end of the day, so it should arrive in the morning. Just tell me where to send it. And I need a phone number for the label. They require that."

Rick thought fast and gave Christian a bogus phone number and told him to send it to the FedEx office at the Denver airport. Rick figured he could get there around the same time as the envelope.

"I can't thank you enough." Rick was ecstatic.

"Let's hope everything goes the way you want. Good luck."

Christian called Kara and told her the plan was in motion. Kara e-mailed Libby on her personal computer.

Denver Airport FedEx. Should arrive to-morrow.

Libby e-mailed her back.

Tks. Talk soon.

Rick figured his timeline. He'd arrive in Denver around 8:00 in the morning. It would take under an hour to get to Black Hawk. He put in a call to the concierge, letting him know he was planning to check into the hotel-casino and would there be any comps available? Rick was told he could have a room for three nights.

Perfect. That would give him time to get in touch with his connection. Finding Libby was finally within reach.

Libby, known to her neighbors as Ellie for the past two years, resumed pounding on the keys of her computer. She scoured the Denver area, looking for casinos. Black Hawk had several. She'd call each of them, asking if Richard Barnes was registered or expected. After the third attempt, she spoke to a perky young woman at Ameristar. "Hi, thank you for calling Ameristar. This is Angelica; how may I help you?"

"Hello, Angelica. I'm hoping you can help me. My boyfriend is supposed to be arriving sometime today, and I wanted to surprise him with a bottle of champagne."

"That's so sweet. What's his name?"

"Richard Barnes."

"Let me see. Yes, his reservation is for today, but he hasn't checked in yet. Did you have anything particular in mind?"

"Can I put you on hold for a moment? I have another call coming through." Then Libby hung up. She had learned where he would be, and hoped that he would stay for a couple of days.

A wave of relief washed over her. She contacted the captain of the precinct where the incident had occurred and explained that she now remembered what had happened and that she knew the whereabouts of her assailant, Richard Barnes. He took down her information but could not promise anything. "Things like this take time."

Libby was afraid that would be his response, but now it was on record. Meanwhile, she had to make sure Rick would not be able to ambush her. She checked and rechecked all her security systems, Taser, baseball bat, and pepper spray. She was counting on Buddy to restrain him should Rick get past the fortress she had erected.

She checked the time. It was almost 3:30. Jackson and Colleen would be arriving soon. She was anxious to find out how the hearing had gone.

At exactly 3:30, the buzzer at the side gate rang. "Come around front," she said through the intercom.

Jackson led the way as they walked through the front gate. Colleen was carrying a loaf of her famous zucchini bread. She heard the bolts and locks clicking and got a little jumpy.

Libby swung the front door open. "Please

come in. It's so nice to finally meet you in person." She shook Colleen's hand, then Jackson's. Buddy was woofing and wagging his tail. "Why don't you boys go out back? I know Buddy has been waiting. He'll show you the way." Buddy headed for the laundry-room door, and Jackson was about to follow him through the doggie door. Both women burst out laughing. "You can open the door, Jackson," Libby informed him. "The porch door, too." Jackson blushed. He was excited to be in the mysterious lady's house.

"Your house is pretty cool," he said as he was shutting the porch door.

"Please, come and sit." Libby motioned to the dining-room table that overlooked the yard.

"You have a lovely place. And the garden is beautiful," Colleen said with awe. Her mind was going a mile a minute. *What should she say next? Should she ask her any questions?* "It was so nice of you to invite me over. I feel honored." Colleen's face flushed.

Libby chuckled. "Honored to be invited to the 'crazy lady's' house?" She used air quotes for "crazy lady."

"You're not a crazy lady." Colleen leaned

in a bit. "Are you?" Both women gave out a guffaw.

"I certainly don't think so, but there may be others who would disagree." Libby was very comfortable with the situation and was considering telling Colleen her story. She felt it was some kind of insurance in case something happened to her, or if she were in distress.

"Do you prefer tea or coffee?"

"Tea. Herbal, if you have it."

"I do. Chamomile? Red zinger? Lemon zinger? I think I have every zinger flavor."

"Red zinger, please. Thank you," Colleen replied. "I brought you a zucchini bread. Jackson says 'yuck' because of the zucchini, but he loves the bread. He thinks I'm kidding when I say that there are vegetables in it."

Libby put the kettle on and took two dessert plates from the cabinet, along with two mugs. "Honey?"

"Yes, please."

They made small talk about the garden as they watched Jackson toss the ball to Buddy and Buddy return it. Then they started to run around the perimeter of the yard.

Colleen sipped her tea. "So that's what they do all afternoon?"

"Yes. It's exhausting to watch." Libby

smiled. She took a deep breath.

"Colleen, there's something I must confide in you."

Colleen was taken aback. "What is it?"

Libby took a moment. "Where do I begin? OK. Here goes. My name is not Ellie Bowman. It's Libby Gannon."

"Oh?" Colleen tried to act nonchalant.

"I came here after a terrible accident. Although now we don't know if it was truly an accident." Ellie proceeded to tell her the story and how she was found at the bottom of a set of steps that led to the front door of a brownstone in Greenwich Village. She went on to describe being in the hospital and not having any recollection of what had happened except for feeling anxiety and fear. Because she could not remember the incident, she was terrified to remain in New York and had moved to Hibbing under an assumed name.

Colleen's mouth was agape. "Oh my word. So you've been sequestered here because of the accident, and you had amnesia?"

"At first, the therapist said it was due to the concussion and that many people who have traumatic experiences suppress the memory. I had hoped I would remember something sooner than now."

"What do you mean?" Colleen was unclear as to Ellie's, Libby's, timeline.

"My boyfriend at the time left the city abruptly. Never visited me or called my family."

"Now that is what I would call scummy," Colleen said.

"No one had heard from him for two years until last week."

Libby took a sip of her tea.

"He called my best friend's husband, asking for $5,000."

"That is rather audacious, wouldn't you say?" Colleen was disgusted.

"I could think of a lot of words, but I'll keep it clean." Libby chuckled.

"Did they send him the money?"

"Christian is going to send it overnight to Denver."

"But why?"

"Because it was the only way we could find out what city or town he was sliming his way through."

"How will that do anything?"

"First off, I will know where he is, for at least a couple of days. I already found out where he'll be staying. At the Ameristar in Black Hawk."

"How did you find out?"

"Deduction, my friend." Libby continued

to explain how she had narrowed it down to an area where there was a casino, which was most likely where he would go. She then went on to tell her about calling the casinos to ask if he had checked in because she wanted to surprise him with champagne. If the concierge told her he didn't have a reservation, she moved on to the next casino until she found the one where he planned to stay.

"What are you going to do now?" Colleen was beyond intrigued.

"I notified the NYPD, for whom it was a cold case, and told them that I had my memory back, was assaulted by my boy-friend, and knew his whereabouts, at least for the next couple of days."

"What did they say?"

"It would take time." Libby sighed.

"Are you going to be all right?"

"Besides the security system, I have a Taser, a baseball bat, and pepper spray, so I should be. And I'm counting on Buddy to keep him at bay. But I also keep the pepper spray handy. I have a canister in every room. What, me paranoid?" Libby laughed.

"I don't blame you. No wonder you've never left the house. If you need anything, let me know. Officer Pedone has been won-derful."

Libby could sense a bit of a crush from the tone of Colleen's voice.

"I noticed he's stopped by a few times."

Colleen couldn't hide her excitement. "He's taking me to dinner on Saturday."

"How nice for you." Libby was genuinely pleased and relieved that someone close by knew her deep, dark secret.

It was getting close to five, and the women noticed Andy driving his blue Lincoln toward his house and gently pulling it into the driveway. He got out of the car slowly.

"God bless him," Colleen said. "He's quite a trouper."

But before Libby could respond, Andy took a tumble.

"Oh my gosh!" Colleen cried out. "I'll go see if he's OK. You call nine-one-one."

"Got it." Libby punched the three numbers into the phone.

She gave the dispatcher the address and was told an ambulance would be there in five minutes.

Libby watched Colleen try to help Andy off the ground, but he was too tall and wobbly. Libby opened the door, and called out, "How is he?"

"A few scrapes, but he may have sprained his arm."

"An ambulance is on the way," Libby

shouted across the yard.

Andy started to protest. "I'm fine. Really." But Colleen was having none of it.

"Andy, you need to be checked out. And don't give me any arguments."

A few minutes later, the screaming sound of an EMS vehicle was heard turning onto Birchwood Lane.

Jackson and Buddy came running to the front. Jeanne and Frank were on the front lawn, and the new neighbors peered out the window.

Frank jogged over as they were strapping Andy onto the stretcher. "I'll go with him," he said, and hopped into the back.

When they got to the hospital, Andy insisted he was fine, but they wouldn't release him until they did some X-rays to be sure he hadn't broken anything. They admitted him and informed him that he had to stay overnight, if not longer, depending on his contusions. He vehemently protested, but the doctor told him that, considering his age, they did not want to take any chances.

Knowing Andy lived alone, they assigned a social worker to help him with the paperwork. When she informed him that they wanted to do a safety check of his home, he turned paler than when he had arrived.

"No. I don't want anyone going into my house." Andy was vehement.

The social worker said that it was for his own safety. Andy almost started to cry.

Frank stepped in and addressed the social worker. "Can you give us a moment?"

Once the social worker left the room, Frank turned to Andy. "Talk to me."

Andy was trembling as tears ran down his cheeks. "They can't go in there. If they do, they'll never let me back in."

"Why not?" Frank was gentle with the frail man.

"It's piled high with . . . with so much that you can't really walk around. You can't even turn around. Please, Frank, don't let them in."

Frank had an idea. "This is what we're going to do. You will stay here for three days. Make something up."

"But I don't want to stay here." Andy was close to having a tantrum.

"Andy, if they go to your house, they almost certainly won't let you back in there. Listen to me. We are going to get a storage space and clear out your house. We'll do an inventory, and when you're up for it, you can go there and look through what you have. We'll get your house all cleaned up, and you'll still have all your stuff. It'll just be in a different place."

"How will you be able to do that?" Andy was shaking.

"Leave it to an ex-military guy to scramble. Deal?" Frank put out his hand.

"Deal." Andy winced.

"Sorry. Did I hurt you?"

"Not really. I'm practicing for the nurse. You did say three days, right?" Quickly, Andy was on board, and his spirits lifted.

Jeanne had driven behind the ambulance and met up with Frank in the lobby. "Is he all right?"

"More or less, but we have a major challenge."

"What kind of challenge?" Jeanne asked.

"We have to clean out his house in the next two days."

"How on earth are we going to do that?" Jeanne was dubious.

"We rally the neighbors. I'm sure the Gaynors have a lot of empty boxes. I'll get a couple of guys from the shooting range; you call to get a U-Haul truck and the storage place where he keeps his cars. See if they have space. This way, all of his stuff will be in one place. Colleen can get in touch with a cleaning service. By the time he gets home and social services visits, they won't have any reason to keep him from living there."

Jeanne was speechless but managed a "Whoa."

"Yes, my dear. Whoa is correct."

On the way home, Frank used his Bluetooth to call a few of his friends. Three of them were on board to get to work the next day, provided Jeanne could get the truck and the storage space. By the time they got back to their house, they had the day lined up. Frank went to the Gaynors' house to see if they could contribute the moving boxes. The Gaynors were more than happy to let them have them, saving them a trip to the recycling center.

Jeanne called Colleen's cell phone and explained the situation. Colleen's head was reeling. The day had started with the hearing, then Libby's news, and now this. Was it a full moon?

Colleen called the janitor from the school and explained that they needed to clean a house the day after tomorrow. "Scrubbed ceiling to floor." She admitted that she had no other information, but they should be prepared for the worst. Who knew what they would find?

Colleen explained to Libby what was going on. "What can I do to help out?" Libby asked, feeling helpless.

"Nothing right now, except figure out

where that creepy ex-boyfriend is and stay safe."

"I'll do my best." Libby signed off, determined to track that creep down. How she was going to do it she wasn't sure, but she wanted to be able to know his every move until someone in authority could nail him.

CHAPTER THIRTY-TWO

The following morning, Frank went to the U-Haul location and picked up the large box truck. He hoped it was big enough. If not, they'd have to make several trips. By 9:00, his buddies from the shooting range had arrived with tape and rope. No one had any idea what they were walking into.

Andy had let Frank take his keys from his jacket the day before. Frank stood at the front door and held his breath as he unlatched the key. "Jeez Louise." The enormity of the undertaking was overwhelming.

He turned to his friends. "Guys, I don't know where to start." Removing the magazines, newspapers, and junk mail seemed to be the logical first step. Frank began giving the men assignments. "Hank, you take the magazines and tie them up. Lou, you bag the junk mail. Joe, you handle the newspapers. Once we get them out of the way, we'll be able to see what else we need to do."

The men worked feverishly to clear out the mountains of paper, handing Frank the bundles for him to load onto the truck. It took about three hours before they could see the furniture.

Hank was the first to speak. "I'll head over to the storage place and drop this stuff off."

"Good idea. I'll tackle the kitchen to see if there's anything salvageable in there. I'll toss anything that looks like it could be a fire hazard or in disrepair. We can replace whatever small appliances he has. Frank went into the kitchen to find a hot plate with frayed wires. "Off you go." He tossed it into a box marked TRASH. He wasn't sure if throwing out old rusty appliances would upset Andy, but his ability to return to his home was uppermost. A coffeepot with a broken handle was next. He checked the stove to see if any of the burners worked. All were fine. Frank thought Andy probably used the hot plate because it was easier. But he didn't have time to ruminate over what possessed people to do the things they do. An hour later, the countertops were clear of any dangerous items.

Hank returned shortly, and they began removing the dozens of bolts of fabric that sat on top of the two antique sofas. Once the furniture was clear, they had a better sense of what to leave and what to store. The master bedroom was piled high with hatboxes collected over the ages. Frank didn't know if he should leave some or take all of them to storage. He'd better consult Jeanne about this, he decided, and rang her phone.

"Hey, hon, I have an aesthetic question for you. Can you come down here and help me out?"

"Sure thing. I'll be right there."

Libby watched from the loft as the piles of papers and bolts of fabric were removed from Andy's. It was astonishing to see how much he had saved. It was also a little disconcerting and somewhat sad. She turned and went back to deal with her own situation. Kara called to let her know that the FedEx envelope had arrived and been picked up by Rick. He was probably on his way to the casino. In a few hours, he would have the cash. Was it blood money?

Rick was elated when he arrived at Denver International Airport and found an envelope waiting for him. He hopped back into his car and drove to the casino, praying they would cash the check for him.

When he pulled up, the valet greeted him. "Welcome, Mr. Barnes." Rick felt like a celebrity. It was something he always enjoyed, feeling so incredibly important. The concierge was equally effusive. Rick leaned in to whisper in his ear.

"I have a check I need to cash. Who should I speak to?"

The concierge picked up the phone on the desk and dialed one of the floor managers. "Mr. Barnes wishes to cash a check." He nodded and hung up. "Please go to one of the cashier windows and ask for Mr. Lafferty. He'll take care of it for you. Enjoy your stay."

"I certainly will," Rick said, even though he knew it wasn't going to be a very long stay. He walked over to the cashier, endorsed the check over to the casino, and headed to the front desk to check in.

"Good afternoon, Mr. Barnes. Nice to see you. Your room is ready and, of course, compliments of the house."

Things were going exactly as he had planned. When he got to his room, he used his burner phone to call the man who was going to do the job for him. "Yes, I have all of it."

"OK. Wire it to me." The voice on the phone gave him instructions.

"How long will it take?" Rick asked.

"A day or two. Probably by Friday."

"Great. Thanks." Rick hung up, knowing his mission would finally be accomplished.

CHAPTER THIRTY-THREE

Frank and his crew had removed what one might consider debris and arranged the furniture so it would be conducive to human habitation. Jeanne had decided they should leave a couple of hatboxes for style and décor.

Next was the big cleanup. The janitor from Colleen's school sent a heavy-duty crew to Andy's house. Hazmat suits were the only thing missing. Colleen had to teach school, so Jeanne and Brenda supervised the work.

Again, Libby watched from the window. She called the hotel to see if Rick had checked in. "One moment, please, while I put you through." Libby immediately hung up. At least she knew he was there. If she could only get the Black Hawk police to track him, but how? She phoned the captain in New York. "I know you said it would take time, but I know his exact location now."

The captain was very patient. "We can't

execute an arrest warrant and get extradition so quickly."

"I understand." She hung up and racked her brain for what to do next. Suddenly, she remembered another gamer in the Denver area.

She pinged his e-mail:

You busy?

He typed back:

Nah. What's up?

How would you like to do a job for me?

What kind of job?

Tailing someone.

You mean like a private eye or something?

Yeah, kinda.

For how long?

Two days, maybe three. I'll make it worth your while. 200 bucks a day plus expenses.

I'm in! Send details.

Libby sent him the casino information and the make and model of Rick's car. At least the one she remembered. She didn't imagine he would have given up his BMW roadster. She mentioned that Rick had hired and paid someone $5,000 to find her. Then she dug out an old photo of her, Rick, Kara, and Christian. She cropped the photo so only Rick's face showed, scanned it in, and e-mailed it to her new partner. After she hit SEND, a sense of relief filled her.

Two days went by, and her new sleuthing pal reported no movement, but very early Saturday morning, he spotted Rick leaving the casino and heading east toward Denver. He followed the sports car for several hours until it made a pit stop in Colby, Kansas.

Libby thought that if Rick were heading to New York, he would take a more northern route. The hair on the back of her neck stood up. She felt he was coming for her. She texted her accomplice.

Stay on him.

Will do.

Five hours later, he sent her another text.

Kansas City.

Her heart was in her throat. He wasn't far away. She decided to call Colleen and tell her what she feared.

Earlier that morning, she saw Frank and Jeanne bring Andy home. He stopped short at the front door. Like Frank a few days before, he didn't know what he was walking into.

"Come on, Andy. You've made it this far," Jeanne urged him.

The minute he stepped foot in his house, he began to cry.

"Andy, we did the best we could. Everything is in the storage unit next to where you keep your cars. We only wanted to make it comfortable and safe for you," Jeanne continued.

Frank chimed in. "And you have a new coffeepot and a new toaster, and the refrigerator has a few staples for you."

Andy was trembling. Neither Frank nor Jeanne knew what else to say, but then Andy spoke. "You are the kindest people I have ever known. This . . . this is more than I could ever have hoped for." He looked around the room and spotted one of his favorite pieces, a cherry buffet cabinet. "My gosh. I haven't seen that in years!" He continued to take in all the wonderful items he had collected over the years. "I must say, I have very good taste." He smiled. Jeanne and Frank laughed.

"I don't know how to thank you." Andy moved toward the bedroom. "I have a Hepplewhite dresser! Whaddya know!" He was more than pleased.

"This is absolutely wonderful. Thank you again." He pulled out a handkerchief and dabbed his eyes. "I want to sponsor some sort of celebration to thank everyone."

"That's not necessary," Frank said.

"I don't care what you say, Frank. I'm going to do it anyway. So there." End of discussion.

"We'll let you get settled," Jeanne said. "Let us know if you need anything."

"I can't think of a thing," Andy replied.

Colleen watched from her window as Frank and Jeanne left Andy's house. She was happy they had gotten the industrial-strength cleaning service. But once they were done shampooing the rugs and putting the furniture in place, it was a lovely and impressive collection of antiques.

Colleen felt a sense of satisfaction that they were able to pull off this herculean feat. As she was getting ready for her date with Officer Pedone, her phone rang.

"Hi, it's Ellie. I mean Libby."

"Everything all right?"

"I don't think so."

"What is it?" Colleen asked. She hoped it

wasn't serious, not only for Libby's sake, but also because she had been looking forward to dinner with Bob.

"I think Rick is on his way here."

"What are you talking about?"

"Rick. I had someone tail him from Black Hawk to Kansas City. If he's on his way, he'll be here soon."

"OK. Don't panic. Bob will be here shortly. We'll stop by when he gets here, if that's all right."

"Colleen, I'm sorry to be bothering you with this, but you're the only one who knows."

"Don't worry. As soon as he gets here, we'll be there."

"Thank you." Libby was pacing the floor. A half hour later, the front gate signaled that someone was approaching the door.

She pulled out the pepper spray and had one finger poised above the alarm that went directly to the police station. She looked at the CCTV and saw that it was Colleen and Bob.

Libby let them in. "Tell Bob what you told me."

The three of them sat down, and Libby related the entire story. Bob always had a small notepad with him, so he took copious notes. When she was finished, he called into the station and spoke to the desk sergeant. "Hey, Pedone here. I need a BOLO on a blue BMW roadster, New York plates. Driver's name is Richard Barnes. Wanted in an assault case in New York City." He paused. "Thanks."

Pedone turned to Libby. "We put out a 'Be On the Lookout' for him. If anyone spots him, they'll pull him over."

"Then what?"

"We'll take him in for questioning. We can hold him for up to twenty-four hours. After that, we'll have to figure something out. Maybe you can file a report with us, even if it's not our jurisdiction. That could extend his stay at the Crowbar Hotel."

"The what?" Libby looked confused.

"That's what we call jail." Pedone chuckled. Libby followed suit.

"I know you have plans for tonight. I think I'll be OK knowing there are other people looking for him."

"I'll have them send a patrol car around every half hour."

"Thanks so much." Libby gave Colleen a big hug, and the hug felt good.

She watched them walk to Pedone's civilian car. He opened the door for Colleen. "Chivalry is not dead," she said to Buddy and Percy. But before they could pull away, the sound of a sports car could be heard. She looked toward the end of her street and saw the blue BMW make a quick turn onto Birchwood Lane. The car slowed down to a crawl until it stopped in front of her house.

He got out and headed for the front door. Libby pushed all the alarm buttons.

"Libby! Libby! I need to talk to you. Turn off the damn alarm and come out here!" The man was screaming in order to be heard over the screeching sounds of the alarms.

Andy hobbled out of his house and watched as a strange man was yelling. Rick turned around and walked toward his car. Libby didn't know what he was going to do next, but then the engine of the Lincoln started up and, instead of driving at his usual crawl, Andy stomped on the gas and hit Rick square in the middle, knocking him down. He tried to get up and run, but Pedone grabbed him by the collar of his shirt.

He threw Rick against Andy's car and zip-tied his wrists behind his back. "Sorry, pal, but there's just no way out."

Libby turned off the alarms and finally had the courage to walk outside. Colleen ran over to her. "Are you all right?"

"Better now."

"Libby. Libby. I came looking for you

because I wanted to apologize."

"For what? Trying to kill me?"

"No. For being such an ass. I should never have left you that night. I panicked."

"Tell it to the judge," Libby spat at him.

Andy got out of his car as the rest of the neighbors were congregating. "Who's Libby?"

"I'm Libby. Libby Gannon. And I am standing outside for the first time in two years!"

Whistles, hoots, and applause came from the crowd.

"Welcome to the neighborhood, Libby Gannon," Andy shouted.

Epilogue

Whether Rick was sincere about the apology was immaterial. He was being sent back to New York City to face assault charges. The downside was that Libby had to return to New York to file those charges. She had no problem doing that. It would give her a chance to visit her mother and Kara. But she planned on returning to Hibbing.

The casino also filed charges for the bad check. Rick would be up to his eyeballs in legal proceedings.

Andy was enjoying his daily trips to the storage unit and making lists of inventories. He discovered several fishing rods, which he turned over to Frank, Jackson, Mitchel, Randy, and Charlie, making them promise to bring him a large bass or two.

He also decided to give one of his cars to Hector in return for landscaping his yard.

Mitchel stayed sober and started remodeling his mother's house, with Jackson as his helper.

Colleen continued to see Officer Bob Pedone.

When Libby returned from New York, she threw a grand party in her yard for the neighbors. She had made a home in the small hamlet of Hibbing. A home where she could finally come and go as she pleased. Even when you think there is no way out, if you try hard enough, you can usually find a way.

ABOUT THE AUTHOR

Fern Michaels is the *USA Today* and *New York Times* bestselling author of the Sisterhood, Men of the Sisterhood, the Godmothers series, and dozens of other novels and novellas. There are over ninety-five million copies of her books in print. Fern Michaels has built and funded several large day-care centers in her hometown, and is a passionate animal lover who has outfitted police dogs across the country with special bulletproof vests. She shares her home in South Carolina with her four dogs and a resident ghost named Mary Margaret. Visit her website at FernMichaels.com.